More praise for

In Other Rooms, Other Wonders

"Intimate portraits that raise some of the biggest questions in Pakistan today. . . . Offers a richly observed landscape that is written with the tenderness and familiarity of an old friend."   —*New York Times*

"A compelling collection of linked short stories [from] the steady hand of an exquisitely original writer."   —*San Francisco Chronicle*

"Reveals a writer who seems to combine the intimate rural rootedness and gentle humour of RK Narayan with the literary sophistication and stylishness of Jhumpa Lahiri. Perhaps the strongest resemblance, however, is to late 19th-century Russia. . . . Like Turgenev, Mueenuddin creates a world peopled by wholly believable, ordinary rural folk, generously sketched with a wonderful freshness and lightness. . . . *In Other Rooms, Other Wonders* is quite unlike anything recently published on the Indian side of the border, and throws the gauntlet down to a new generation of Indian writers. For the first time in this part of Asia, there is serious competition out there."

—William Dalrymple, *Financial Times*

"His prose, never flashy, neither sentimentalizes the poor nor demonizes the rich, but noses out the humanity of each. It is probably a mistake to lavish too much praise on a first book, but given the power and beauty and deeply affecting quality of *In Other Rooms, Other Wonders*, I can't stop myself from wondering if Pakistan has found its Chekhov."   —*Miami Sun-Sentinel*

"From the wistful title to the final pages, Mueenuddin transports you to a faraway land. . . . His crisp, vivid voice glides effortlessly into his various characters' heads, from the feudal landlord to the wealthy man's butler to the yearning woman his butler takes as a mistress."

—*Entertainment Weekly*

"Mueenuddin's storytelling propels readers through his troubled vistas of humanity and also provides them with glimmers of hope. His delicate prose conjures up an enlightening portrait of Pakistan and unravels the longing, cruelty and compromise that accompany life in Pakistan."   —*Times Literary Supplement*

"*In Other Rooms, Other Wonders* may be fiction—we have the author's word for it—but it is of such an authentic stamp that it is history as well, more so by the day, and deserves to be read as such."   —*The Times*

"Daniyal Mueenuddin . . . manages to make tangible the persistence of the ancient in the face of the modern. [His] prose unfolds to reveal a gorgeous set of layered realities, touched with love and dark foreboding."   —*O, The Oprah Magazine*

"A remarkable debut . . . a poignant picture of Punjabi life from top to bottom."   —*The Economist*

"Dust, lust, the sweet smell of jasmine, the stench of corruption, class struggle—modern Pakistan's beauty commingles with its brutality in Mueenuddin's fine debut collection. . . . In these linked tales Mueenuddin illuminates the intense colors of his homeland, and of human nature itself."   —*People*

"Each of the stories opens a door onto a life you had never expected, shines a light for a while and quietly closes the door again. . . . Mueenuddin writes with the freshness of an exile and the intimacy of an insider about Pakistani culture, both in rural Dunyapur in the Punjab, where most of the stories are set, and around the wealthy dining tables of Karachi and New York and Paris. There are tremendous stories here and if they are not autobiographical, then they are all clearly grounded in lived experience."   —*The Observer*

"It's always fun to read about the rich. To tell stories about the poor, the desperately poor, without making us feel we are turning the pages dutifully takes talent. . . . [Mueenuddin] has the gift of being both unflinching and gentle. He doesn't shove the harshness at you. He doesn't need to—it's woven into the texture of these delicate, sad, profoundly pleasurable tales."   —Bloomberg

"Much as Isaac Bashevis Singer re-created the lost Jewish shtetl in many of his short stories, Mr. Mueenuddin unveils a nuanced world where social status and expectations are understood without being stated, and where poverty and the desire to advance frame each critical choice."   —*Wall Street Journal*

"These stories are so engrossing that there is a wrench when one ends and the next must begin."   —*Sunday Times*

"The writing here has a clarifying beauty. . . . This is a marvellous collection."   —*Daily Telegraph*

"Marks the arrival of a highly sophisticated literary talent."
—*The Guardian*

"Mueenuddin's atmospheric prose aptly captures South Asian nuances, not just in dialect and cultural habits, but also in modes of thinking and relating. That is reason to pick up this collection from a writer destined to win greater laurels."   —*St. Petersburg Times*

"Daniyal Mueenuddin's masterful debut collection, *In Other Rooms, Other Wonders*, reveals a modern Pakistan that is as beautiful as it is brutal. . . . [His] work evokes 19th-century Russian masters like Turgenev and Gogol, along with the Southern Gothic tradition of Faulkner and Truman Capote. . . . Mueenuddin is a prodigiously talented writer, capable of imagining the inner lives of Punjabi aristocrats and their servants with equal sympathy, precision and power."
—The Daily Beast

"[Mueenuddin] has the gifts of insight into human behavior of Alice

Munro, the gift for detail we find in Updike and William Trevor, and the ability to make sentences and paragraphs that pack the punch of something out of James Salter and Richard Ford. . . . He has given us a country like our own, but different enough in landscape, religion, hopes, dreams, flaws, and fears, so that we can easily contrast—if we dare—our own troubles and triumphs against theirs."

—Alan Cheuse, NPR, *All Things Considered*

"Mueenuddin excels at . . . prizing out the complicated power structures that lie between master and servant, parent and child, husbands, wives, lovers. . . . A compelling storyteller."   —*The Independent*

"Mueenuddin is a deft and confident writer; his characters and their conflicts are rendered with nuance and authenticity. . . . Reading these stories is like watching a brilliant method actor at work: every character feels lifelike and flawed as they struggle to make their way in a landscape sharply governed by class. And yet, because Mueenuddin is such a gifted storyteller, he's able to describe the chaos of these lives with lyricism and beauty."   —The Rumpus

"The simplicity of these stories is . . . supremely artful. . . . Mueenuddin has sophisticated language and a powerful range of cultural references at his disposal, and a rare sensibility."   —*The Spectator*

"Mueenuddin's achievement . . . is to hold open two perspectives at once: on the one hand, the long history that produces the individual profile and the individual plight; on the other, the sensation of the present, experienced on the skin and in the emotions."

—*London Review of Books*

"Mueenuddin's story collection is a remarkably confident debut. Although the eight stories are broadly linked by a common Pakistani community, the narratives are diverse in both content and approach."

—*Booklist*

In Other Rooms, Other Wonders

Daniyal Mueenuddin

W. W. NORTON & COMPANY

New York London

Copyright © 2009 by Daniyal Mueenuddin

All rights reserved
Printed in the United States of America
First published as a Norton paperback 2009

For information about permission to reproduce selections from this book,
write to Permissions, W. W. Norton & Company, Inc.,
500 Fifth Avenue, New York, NY 10110

For information about special discounts for bulk purchases, please contact
W. W. Norton Special Sales at specialsales@wwnorton.com or 800-233-4830

Manufacturing by Courier Westford
Book design by Chris Welch
Production manager: Anna Oler

Library of Congress Cataloging-in-Publication Data

Mueenuddin, Daniyal.
In other rooms, other wonders : connected stories / Daniyal Mueenuddin.—1st ed.
p. cm.
ISBN 978-0-393-06800-9
1. Social classes—Pakistan—Fiction. 2. Pakistan—Social conditions—Fiction. I. Title.
PR9540.9.M84I52 2009
823'.92—dc22
2008040632

ISBN 978-0-393-33720-4 pbk.

W. W. Norton & Company, Inc.
500 Fifth Avenue, New York, N.Y. 10110
www.wwnorton.com

W. W. Norton & Company Ltd.
Castle House, 75/76 Wells Street, London W1T 3QT

1 2 3 4 5 6 7 8 9 0

for my mother

یہ ر قتل دک اے - جڑ
زن زمین زر

Three things for which we kill—
Land, women and gold.
            —*Punjabi proverb*

Contents

In Other Rooms, Other Wonders

Nawabdin Electrician

He flourished on a signature capability, a technique for cheating the electric company by slowing down the revolutions of electric meters, so cunningly done that his customers could specify to the hundred-rupee note the desired monthly savings. In this Pakistani desert, behind Multan, where the tube wells ran day and night, Nawab's discovery eclipsed the philosopher's stone. Some thought he used magnets, others said heavy oil or porcelain chips or a substance he found in beehives. Skeptics reported that he had a deal with the meter men. In any case, this trick guaranteed his employment, both off and on the farm of his patron, K. K. Harouni.

The farm lay strung along a narrow and pitted farm-to-market road, built in the 1970s when Harouni still had influence in the Lahore bureaucracy. Buff or saline-white desert dragged out between fields of sugarcane and cotton, mango orchards and clover and wheat, soaked daily by the tube wells that Nawabdin Electrician tended. Beginning the rounds on his itinerant mornings, summoned to a broken pump, Nawab and his bicycle bumped along, whippy antennas and plastic flowers swaying. His tools, notably a three-pound ball-and-peen hammer, clanked in a greasy leather bag that hung from the handlebars. The farmhands and the responsible manager waited in the cool of the banyans, planted years ago to shade each of the tube wells. "No tea, no tea," he insisted, waving away the steaming cup.

Hammer dangling like a savage's axe, Nawab entered the oily room housing the pump and electric motor. Silence. He settled on his haunches. The men crowded the door, till he shouted that he must have light. He approached the offending object warily but with his temper rising, circled it, pushed it about a bit, began to take liberties with it, settled in with it, drank tea next to it, and finally began disassembling it. With his screwdriver, blunt and long, lever enough to pry up flagstones, he cracked the shields hiding the machine's penetralia. A screw popped and flew into the shadows. He took the ball-and-peen and delivered a cunning blow. The intervention failed. Pondering, he ordered one of the farmworkers to find a really thick piece of leather and to collect sticky mango sap from a nearby tree. So it went, all day, into the afternoon, Nawab trying one thing and then another, heating the pipes, cooling them, joining wires together, circumventing switches and fuses. And yet somehow, in fulfillment of his genius for crude improvisation, the pumps continued to run.

UNFORTUNATELY OR FORTUNATELY, Nawab had married early in life a sweet woman, whom he adored, but of unsurpassed fertility; and she proceeded to bear him children spaced, if not less than nine months apart, then not that much more. And all daughters, one after another after another, until finally came the looked-for son, leaving Nawab with a complete set of twelve girls, ranging from infant to age eleven, and then one odd piece. If he had been governor of the Punjab, their dowries would have beggared him. For an electrician and mechanic, no matter how light-fingered, there seemed no question of marrying them all off. No moneylender in his right mind would, at any rate of interest whatsoever, advance a sufficient sum to buy the necessary items: for each daughter, beds, a dresser, trunks, electric fans, dishes, six suits of clothes for the groom, six for the bride, perhaps a television, and on and on and on.

Another man might have thrown up his hands—but not Nawabdin. The daughters acted as a spur to his genius, and he looked with satisfaction in the mirror each morning at the face of a warrior going out to do battle. Nawab of course knew that he must proliferate his sources of revenue—the salary he received from K. K. Harouni for tending the tube wells would not even begin to suffice. He set up a little one-room flour mill, run off a condemned electric motor—condemned by him. He tried his hand at fish-farming in a little pond at the edge of one of his master's fields. He bought broken radios, fixed them, and resold them. He did not demur even when asked to fix watches, though that enterprise did spectacularly badly, and in fact earned him more kicks than kudos, for no watch he took apart ever kept time again.

K. K. Harouni rarely went to his farms, but lived mostly in Lahore. Whenever the old man visited, Nawab would place himself night and day at the door leading from the servants' sitting area into the walled grove of ancient banyan trees where the old farmhouse stood. Grizzled, his peculiar aviator glasses bent and smudged, Nawab tended the household machinery, the air conditioners, water heaters, refrigerators, and water pumps, like an engineer tending the boilers on a foundering steamer in an Atlantic gale. By his superhuman efforts he almost managed to maintain K. K. Harouni in the same mechanical cocoon, cooled and bathed and lighted and fed, that the landowner enjoyed in Lahore.

Harouni of course became familiar with this ubiquitous man, who not only accompanied him on his tours of inspection, but morning and night could be found standing on the master bed rewiring the light fixture or in the bathroom poking at the water heater. Finally, one evening at teatime, gauging the psychological moment, Nawab asked if he might say a word. The landowner, who was cheerfully filing his nails in front of a crackling rosewood fire, told him to go ahead.

"Sir, as you know, your lands stretch from here to the Indus, and on these lands are fully seventeen tube wells, and to tend these seventeen tube wells there is but one man, me, your servant. In your service I have earned these gray hairs"—here he bowed his head to show the gray—"and now I cannot fulfill my duties as I should. Enough, sir, enough. I beg you, forgive me my weakness. Better a darkened house and proud hunger within than disgrace in the light of day. Release me, I ask you, I beg you."

The old man, well accustomed to these sorts of speeches, though not usually this florid, filed away at his nails and waited for the breeze to stop.

"What's the matter, Nawabdin?"

"Matter, sir? O what could be the matter in your service. I've eaten your salt for all my years. But sir, on the bicycle now, with my old legs, and with the many injuries I've received when heavy machinery fell on me—I cannot any longer bicycle about like a bridegroom from farm to farm, as I could when I first had the good fortune to enter your employment. I beg you, sir, let me go."

"And what's the solution?" asked Harouni, seeing that they had come to the crux. He didn't particularly care one way or the other, except that it touched on his comfort—a matter of great interest to him.

"Well, sir, if I had a motorcycle, then I could somehow limp along, at least until I train up some younger man."

The crops that year had been good, Harouni felt expansive in front of the fire, and so, much to the disgust of the farm managers, Nawab received a brand-new motorcycle, a Honda 70. He even managed to extract an allowance for gasoline.

THE MOTORCYCLE INCREASED his status, gave him weight, so that people began calling him "Uncle," and asking his opinion on world affairs, about which he knew absolutely nothing. He could now range further, doing a much wider business. Best of all, now he could spend every night with his wife, who had begged to live not on the farm but near her family in Firoza, where also they could educate at least the two eldest daughters. A long straight road ran from the canal headworks near Firoza all the way to the Indus, through the heart of the K. K. Harouni lands. The road ran on the bed of an old highway, built when these lands lay within a princely state. Some hundred and fifty years ago one of the princes had ridden that way, going to a wedding or a funeral in this remote district, felt hot, and ordered that rosewood trees be planted to shade the passersby. He forgot that he had given the order within a few hours, and in a few dozen years he in turn was forgotten, but these trees still stood, enormous now, some of them dead and looming without bark, white and leafless. Nawab would fly down this road on his new machine, with bags and cloths hanging from every knob and brace, so that the bike, when he hit a bump, seemed to be flapping numerous small vestigial wings; and with his grinning face, as he rolled up to whichever tube well needed servicing, with his ears almost blown off, he shone with the speed of his arrival.

Nawab's day, viewed from the air, would have appeared as aimless as that of a butterfly—to the senior manager's house in the morning, where he diligently paid his respects, then sent to one or another of the tube wells, kicking up dust on the unpaved field roads, into the town of Firoza, zooming beneath the rosewoods, a bullet of sound, moseying around town, sneaking away to one of his private inter-ests, to cement a deal to distribute ripening early-season honeydews from his cousin's vegetable plot, or to count before hatching his half share in a flock of chickens, then back to Dunyapur, and out again. The maps of these days, superimposed, would have made a tangle; but every morning he emerged from the same place, just as the sun came up, and every evening he returned there, tired now, darkened, switching off the bike, rolling it over the wooden lintel of the door leading into the courtyard, the engine ticking as it cooled. Nawab each evening put the bike on its kickstand, and waited for his girls to come, all of them, around him, jumping on him. His face often at this moment had the same expression, an expression of childish innocent joy, which contrasted strangely and even sadly with the heaviness of his face and its lines and stubble. He would raise his nose and sniff the air, to see if he could find out what his wife had cooked for dinner; and then he went in to her, finding her always in the same posture, making him tea, fanning the fire in the little hearth.

"HELLO, MY LOVE, my chicken piece," he said tenderly one evening, walking into the dark hut that served as a kitchen, the mud walls black with soot. "What's in the pot for me?" He opened the cauldron, which had been displaced by the kettle onto the beaten-earth floor, and began to search around in it with a wooden spoon.

"Out! Out!" she said, taking the spoon and, dipping it into the curry, giving him a taste. He opened his mouth obediently, like a boy receiving medicine. The wife, despite bearing thirteen children, had a lithe strong body, her vertebrae visible beneath her tight tunic. Her long mannish face still glowed from beneath the skin, giving her a ripe ochre coloring. Even now that her hair had become thin and graying, she wore it in a single long pigtail down to her waist, like a young woman in the village. Although this style didn't suit her, Nawab saw in her still the girl he married twenty years before. He stood in the door, watching his daughters playing hopscotch, and when his wife went past, he stuck out his butt, so that she rubbed against it as she squeezed through.

Nawab ate first, then the girls, and finally his wife. He sat out in the little courtyard, burping and smoking a cigarette, looking up at the crescent moon just coming onto the horizon. I wonder what the moon is made of? he thought, without exerting himself. He remembered listening on the radio when the Americans said they had walked on it. His thoughts wandered off into all sorts of tangents. The dwellers around him in the little hamlet had also finished their dinner, and the smoke from the cow-dung fires hung over the darkening roofs, a harsh spicy smell, like rough tobacco. Nawab's house had all sorts of ingenious contrivances, running water in all three rooms, a duct that brought cool air into the rooms at night, and even a black-and-white television, which his wife covered with a flowered doily that she had herself embroidered. Nawab had constructed a gear mechanism, so that the antenna on the roof could be turned from inside the house to improve reception. The children sat inside watching it, with the volume blaring. His wife came out and sat primly at his feet on the *charpoy*, a bed made of rope.

"I've got something in my pocket—would you like to know what?" He looked at her with a pouting sort of smile.

"I know this game," she said, reaching up and straightening his glasses on his face. "Why are your glasses always crooked? I think one ear's higher than the other."

"Come on, if you find it you can have it."

Looking to see that the children all had become absorbed in the television, she kneeled next to him and began patting his pockets. "Lower . . . Lower . . ." he said. In the pocket of the greasy vest that he wore under his *kurta* she found a wrapped-up newspaper holding chunks of raw brown sugar.

"I've got lots more," he said. "Look at that. None of this junk you buy in the bazaar. The Dashtis gave me five kilos for repairing their sugarcane press. I'll sell it tomorrow. Come on, make us some *parathas*. For all of us? Pretty please?"

"I put out the fire."

"So light it. Or rather, you just sit here, I'll light it."

"You can never light it, I'll end up doing it anyway," she said, getting up.

The smaller children, smelling the *ghee* cooking on the griddle, crowded around, watching the brown sugar melt, and finally even the older girls came in, though they haughtily stood to one side.

Nawab, squatting and huffing on the fire, gestured to them. "Come on you princesses, none of your tricks. I know you want some."

They began eating, pouring the brown crystallized syrup onto pieces of fried bread, and after a while Nawab went to his motorcycle and pulled from the panniers another hunk of the sugar, challenging the girls to see who would eat most.

ONE EVENING A few weeks after his family's little festival of sugar, Nawab was sitting with the watchman who kept the stores at Dunyapur. A banyan planted over the threshing floor only thirty years ago had grown a canopy of forty or fifty feet, and all the men who worked in the stores tended it carefully, watering it with cans. The old watchman sat under this tree, and Nawab and others of the younger generations would sit with him at dusk, teasing him, trying to make his violent temper flare up, and joking around with each other. They would listen to the old man's stories, of the time when only dirt tracks led through these riverine tracts and the tribes stole cattle for sport, and often killed each other while doing it, to add piquancy.

Though spring weather had come, the watchman still burned a fire in a tin pan, to warm his feet and to give a center to the little group that gathered there. The electricity had failed, as it often did, and the full moon climbing the horizon lit the scene indirectly, reflecting off the whitewashed walls, throwing dim shadows around the machinery strewn about, plows and planters, drags, harrows.

"Come on, old man," said Nawab to the watchman, "I'll tie you up and lock you in the stores to make it look like a robbery, and then I'll top off my tank at the gas barrel."

"Nothing in it for me," said the watchman. "Go on, I think I hear your wife calling you."

"I understand, sire, you wish to be alone."

Nawab jumped up and shook the watchman's hand, making a little bow, touching his knee in deference, a running joke; lost on the watchman these last ten years.

"Be careful, boy," said the watchman, standing up and leaning on his bamboo staff, clad in steel at the tip.

Nawab kicked over his motorcycle with a flourish, and in one smooth motion flicked on the lights and shot out the threshing floor gates, onto the quarter-mile drive that led from the heart of the farm. He felt cold and liked it, knowing that at home the room would be baking, the two-bar heater running day and night all winter on pilfered electricity. Turning onto the black main road, he sped up, outrunning the weak headlight, as if he were racing forward in the globe of a moving lantern. Nightjars perching on the road as they hunted moths ricocheted into the dark, almost under his wheel. Nawab locked his arms, fighting the bike as he flew over potholes, enjoying the pace, standing on the pegs, and in low-lying fields where the sugarcane had been heavily watered, mist rose and cool air enveloped him. At the canal he slowed, hearing the water rushing over the locks.

A man stepped from behind one of the pillars, waving a flashlight down at the ground, motioning Nawab to stop.

"Brother," said the man, over the puttering engine, "give me a ride into town. I've got business, and I'm late."

Strange business at this time of night, thought Nawab, the taillight of the motorcycle casting a reddish glow around them on the ground. They were far from any dwellings. A mile away, the little village of Dashtian crouched beside the road—before that nothing. He looked into the man's face.

"Where are you from?" The man looked straight back at him, his face pinched and therefore overstated, but unflinching.

"From Kashmor. Please, you're the first person to come by for over an hour. I've walked all day."

Kashmor, thought Nawab. From the poor country across the river. Each year those tribes came to pick the mangoes at Dunyapur and other nearby farms, working for almost nothing, let go as soon as the harvest thinned. The men would give a feast, a thin feast, at the end of the season, a hundred or more going shares to buy a buffalo. Nawab had been several times, and been treated as if he were honoring them, sitting with them and eating the salty rice flecked with bits of meat.

He grinned at the man, gesturing with his chin to the seat behind him. "All right then, get in back."

Balancing against the dead weight behind him, which made driving along the rutted canal path difficult, Nawab pushed on, under the rosewood trees.

HALF A MILE down the road, he shouted into Nawab's ear, "Stop!"

"What's wrong?" Nawab couldn't hear over the rushing wind.

The man jabbed something hard into his ribs.

"I've got a gun, I'll shoot you."

Panicked, Nawab skidded to a stop and jumped to one side, pushing the motorcycle away from him, so that it tipped over, knocking the robber to the ground. The carburetor float hung open and the engine raced for a minute, the wheel jerking, till the float chamber drained, and then it sputtered and died.

"What are you doing?" babbled Nawab.

"I'll shoot you if you don't get away," said the robber, on one knee, the gun pointed.

They stood obscured in the sudden woolly dark, next to the fallen motorcycle, which leaked raw-smelling gasoline into the dust underfoot. Water running through the reeds in the canal next to them made soft gulping sounds as it swirled along. When his eyes adjusted Nawab saw the man sucking at a cut on his palm, the gun in his other hand.

When the man went to pick up the bike, Nawab came and touched him on the shoulder.

"I told you, I'll shoot you."

Nawab put his hands together in supplication. "I beg you, I've got little girls, thirteen children. I promise, thirteen. I tried to help you. I'll drive you to Firoza, and I won't tell anyone. Don't take the bike, it's my daily bread. I'm a man like you, poor as you."

"Shut up."

Without thinking, Nawab lunged for the gun, but missed.

Dropping the motorcycle, the man stepped back and shot him in the groin.

Nawab fell to the ground, holding the place where it hurt with both hands, entirely surprised, shocked, as if the man had slapped him for no reason.

The man dragged the bike away from the fallen body, stood it up, and straddled it, trying to start it. It had flooded, and not owning a motorcycle, he didn't know what to do. He held the throttle wide open, which made it worse. At the sound of the shot the dogs in Dashtian had begun to bark, the sound fitful in the breeze.

Nawab, lying on the ground, at first thought the man had killed him. The pale moonlit sky tilted back and forth, seen through the branches of a rosewood tree, like a bowl of swaying water. He had fallen with one leg bent under him, and now he straightened it. His hand came away sticky when he felt the wound. "O God, O mother, O God," he moaned, not very loudly, in a singsong voice. He looked at the man with his back turned, vulnerable, kicking wildly at the starter, not six feet away. Nawab couldn't let him get away with this. The bike belonged to him.

He stood up again and stumbled toward the motorcycle, tackled the thief, fell on him, pushing him to the ground. The man rolled over, kicked Nawab, and stood up.

Holding the gun away at arm's length, he fired five more times, one two three four five, with Nawab looking up into his face, unbelieving, seeing the repeated flame in the revolver's mouth. The man had never used weapons, had only fired this unlicensed revolver one time, to try it out when he bought it from a bootlegger. He couldn't bear to point at the body or head, but shot at the groin and legs. The last two bullets missed wildly, throwing up dirt in the road. Again the robber stood the motorcycle up, pushed it twenty feet, panting, and then tried to start it. From Dashtian a torch jogged quickly down the road. Dropping the bike, the man ran into a little stand of reeds by the side of a watercourse.

Nawab lay in the road, not wanting to move. When he first got shot it didn't hurt so much as sting, but now the pain grew worse. The blood felt warm in his pants.

It seemed very peaceful. In the distance, the dogs kept barking, and all around the cicadas called, so many of them that they made a single gentle blended sound. In a mango orchard across the canal some crows began cawing, and he wondered why they were calling at night. Maybe a snake up in the tree, in the nest. Fresh fish from the spring floods of the Indus had just come onto the market, and he kept remembering that he had wanted to buy some for dinner, perhaps the next night. As the pain grew worse he thought of that, the smell of frying fish.

Two men from the village came running up, panting.

"O God, they've killed him. Who is it?"

The other man kneeled down next to the body. "It's Nawab, the electrician, from Dunyapur."

"I'm not dead," said Nawab insistently, without raising his head. "The bastard's right there in those reeds."

One of the men had a single-barreled shotgun. Stepping forward, aiming into the center of the clump, he fired, reloaded, and fired again. Nothing moved among the green leafy stalks, which were head-high and surmounted with feathers of seed.

"He's gone," said the one who sat by Nawab, holding his arm.

The man with the shotgun again loaded and walked carefully forward, holding the gun to his shoulder. Something moved, and he fired. The robber fell forward into the open ground. He called, "Mother, help me," and got up on his knees, holding his hands to his waist. The gunman walked up to him, hit him once in the middle of the back with the butt of the gun, and then threw down the gun and dragged him roughly by his collar onto the road. Raising the bloody shirt, he saw that the robber had taken half a dozen buckshot pellets in the stomach, black angry holes seeping blood in the light of the torch. The robber kept spitting, without any force.

The other villager, who had been watching, started the motorcycle by pushing it down the road with the gear engaged, until the engine came to life. Shouting that he would get some transport, he raced off, and Nawab minded that the man in his hurry shifted without using the clutch.

"Do you want a cigarette, Uncle?" the villager said to Nawab, offering the pack.

Nawab rolled his head back and forth. "Fuck, look at me."

The lights of a pickup materialized at the headworks and bounced wildly down the road. The driver and the other two lifted Nawab and the robber into the back and took them to Firoza, to a little private clinic there, run by a mere pharmacist, who nevertheless kept a huge clientele because of his abrupt and sure manner and his success at healing with the same few medicines the prevalent diseases.

THE CLINIC SMELLED of disinfectant and of bodily fluids, a heavy sweetish odor. Four beds stood in a room, dimly lit by a fluorescent tube. As they carried him in, Nawab, alert to the point of strain, observed the blood on some rumpled sheets, a rusty blot. The pharmacist, who lived above his clinic, had come down wearing a loincloth and undershirt. He seemed perfectly calm and even cross at having been disturbed.

"Put them on those two beds."

"*As-salaam uleikum*, Doctor Sahib," said Nawab, who felt as if he were speaking to someone very far away. The pharmacist seemed an immensely grave and important man, and Nawab spoke to him formally.

"What happened, Nawab?"

"He tried to snatch my motorbike, but I didn't let him."

The pharmacist pulled off Nawab's *shalvar*, got a rag, and washed away the blood, then poked around quite roughly, while Nawab held the sides of the bed and willed himself not to scream. "You'll live," he said. "You're a lucky man. The bullets all went low."

"Did it hit . . ."

The pharmacist dabbed with the rag. "Not even that, thank God."

The robber must have been hit in the lung, for he kept breathing up blood.

"You won't need to bother taking this one to the police," said the pharmacist. "He's a dead man."

"Please," begged the robber, trying to raise himself up. "Have mercy, save me. I'm a human being also."

The pharmacist went into the office next door and wrote out the names of drugs on a pad, sending the two villagers to a dispenser in the next street.

"Tell him it's Nawabdin the electrician. Tell him I'll make sure he gets the money."

NAWAB FOR THE first time looked over at the robber. There was blood on his pillow, and he kept snuffling, as if he needed to blow his nose. His thin and very long neck hung crookedly on his shoulder, as if out of joint. He was older than Nawab had thought before, not a boy, dark-skinned, with sunken eyes and protruding yellow smoker's teeth, which showed whenever he twitched for breath.

"I did you wrong," said the robber weakly. "I know that. You don't know my life, just as I don't know yours. Even I don't know what brought me here. Maybe you're a poor man, but I'm much poorer than you. My mother is old and blind, in the slums outside Multan. Make them fix me, ask them to and they'll do it." He began to cry, not wiping the tears, which drew lines on his dark face.

"Go to hell," said Nawab, turning away. "Men like you are good at confessions. My children would have begged in the streets."

The robber lay heaving, moving his fingers by his sides. The pharmacist seemed to have gone away somewhere, leaving them alone.

"They just said that I'm dying. Forgive me for what I did. I was brought up with kicks and slaps and never enough to eat. I've never had anything of my own, no land, no house, no wife, no money, never, nothing. I slept for years on the railway station platform in Multan. My mother's blessing on you. Give me your blessing, don't let me die unforgiven." He began snuffling and coughing even more, and then started hiccupping.

Now the disinfectant smelled strong and good to Nawab. The floor seemed to shine. The world around him expanded.

"Never. I won't forgive you. You had your life, I had mine. At every step of the road I went the right way and you the wrong. Look at you now, with bubbles of blood stuck in the corner of your mouth. Do you think this isn't a judgment? My wife and children would have begged in the street, and you would have sold my motorbike to pay for six unlucky hands of cards and a few bottles of poison home brew. If you weren't lying here now, you would already be in one of the gambling camps along the river."

The man said, "Please, please, please," more softly each time, and then he stared up at the ceiling. "It's not true," he whispered. After a few minutes he convulsed and died. The pharmacist, who had come in by then and was cleaning Nawab's wounds, did nothing to help him.

Yet Nawab's mind caught at this, looking at the man's words and his death, like a bird hopping around some bright object, meaning to peck at it. And then he didn't. He thought of the motorcycle, saved, and the glory of saving it. He was growing. Six shots, six coins thrown down, six chances, and not one of them killed him, not Nawabdin Electrician.

Saleema

Saleema was born in the Jhulan clan, blackmailers and bootleg-gers, Muslim refugees at Partition from the country northwest of Delhi. They were lucky, the new border lay only thirty or forty miles distant, and from thieving expeditions they knew how to travel unobserved along canals and tracks. Skirting the edge of the Cholistan Desert, crossing into Pakistan, on the fourth night they came to a Hindu village abandoned by all but a few old women. They drove them away and occupied the houses, finding pots and pans, buckets, even guard dogs, which grew accustomed to them.

During Saleema's childhood twenty years later the village was gradually being absorbed into the slums cast off by an adjacent pro-vincial town called Kotla Sardar. Her father became a heroin addict, and died of it, her mother slept around for money and favors, and she herself at fourteen became the plaything of a small landowner's son. Then a suitor appeared, strutting the village on leave from his job in the city, and plucked her off to Lahore. He looked so slim and city-bright, and soon proved to be not only weak but depraved. These experiences had not cracked her hard skin, but made her sensual, unscrupulous—and romantic.

One morning she lay on the bed of the cramped servants' quarters in Lahore where she and her husband lived. He was gone for the day, aimless and sloping around the streets, unwanted at the edge of the crowd in a tea stall. Though he knew right away that she slept with Hassan the cook, in this house where she served as a maid, the first time he opened his mouth she made to slap him and pushed him out of the room; and next day as usual he hungrily took the few rupees she gave—to buy twists of rocket pills, his amphetamine addiction.

She picked at the chipped polish on her long slim toe, feeling sorry for herself. Her oval face, taller than broad, with deep-set eyes, had a grace contrasting with her bright easy temperament. At twenty-four this hard life had not yet marked her, and when she smiled her dimples made her seem even younger, just a girl; she still had some of the girl's gravity. It was true, the cook Hassan had gotten everything from her, as always she'd given it too soon. She had been a maidservant in three houses so far, since her husband lost his job as peon in an office, and in every one she had opened her legs for the cook. She'd been here at Gulfishan, the Lahore mansion of the landlord K. K. Harouni, only a month, and already she'd slept with Hassan. The cooks tempted her, lording it over the kitchen, where she liked to sit, with the smell of broth and green vegetables cooking and sauce. And she had duties in the kitchen, she made the *chapattis*, so thin and light that they almost floated up to the ceiling. She had that in her hands. Mr. Harouni had called her into the dining room at lunch one day and said he'd never in seventy years eaten better ones, while she blushed and looked at her bare feet. And then, the delicacies that Hassan gave her—the best parts, things that should have gone to the table, foreign things, pistachio ice cream and slices of sweet pies, baked tomatoes stuffed with cheese, potato cutlets. Things that she asked for, village food, curry with marrow bones and carrot *halva*.

The entire household, from the sahib on down, had been eating to suit her appetite.

"Ask for it, my duckling," said Hassan in the mornings, when she drank her tea sitting beside him, hunched together in the kitchen. "I need to fatten you up, I like them plump."

"Don't talk that way, I come from a respectable family."

"Well, whatever kind of family, what should I stuff that rounded little belly with today?"

And he wobbled off to market on his bicycle with a big woven basket strapped on the back, riding so slowly that he could almost have walked there faster, pedaling with his knees pointed out.

BUT THAT HAD ended soon enough. Why are cooks always vicious? She knew that at lunchtime today she would go silently into the kitchen and begin making the *chapattis*, that Hassan would be standing at the stove, banging lids, ignoring her. She hadn't done anything, she had told the slut sweepress who was always hanging around the kitchen to fuck off somewhere else, and he exploded. Hassan ruled the hot filthy kitchen. He made food both for the master's table and for all the servants, more than a dozen of them. For days on end the servants' food would be inedible—keeping with Hassan's policy of collective punishment. Once, when the accounts manager had quite mildly commented on Hassan's reckless padding of the bills, they had eaten nothing but watery lentils for more than a week, until the manager backed down. "Well, I've got to cut corners *somewhere*," Hassan kept saying, shaking his grizzled head. Anyway, Saleema knew that he was through with her, would sweeten up and try to fuck her now and then, out of cruelty as much as anything else, to show he could— but the easy days were over, now she had no one to protect her. In this household a man who had served ten years counted as a new servant. Hassan had been there over fifty, Rafik, the master's valet, the same. Even the nameless junior gardener had been there four or five. With less than a month's service Saleema counted for nothing. Nor did she have patronage. She had been hired on approval, to serve the master's eldest daughter, Begum Kamila, who lived in New York, and who that spring had come to stay with her father. Haughty and proud, Kamila allowed no intimacies.

SALEEMA NEXT ANGLED for one of the drivers—forlorn hope!—a large man with a drooping mustache who didn't ever speak to her. The two drivers shared quarters, a room next to the cool dark garage where two aging Mercedes stood, rarely driven, because the old man rarely went out. Day and night the drivers kept up a revolving card game, with the blades from a nearby slum, the fast set. She would linger past the door of the room where they sprawled on a raft of beds. At night they sometimes drank beer, hiding the bottles on the floor.

As she walked past their room a second time on a breezy spring morning, one of the men in the room whistled.

"Go to hell," she said.

That made it worse.

"Give us some of that black mango. It's a new variety!"

"No, it's smooth like ice cream, I swear to God my tongue is melting."

"You can wipe your dipstick after checking the oil!"

One of them pretended to be defending her. "How dare you say that!"

She went into the latrine, holding back her tears. She didn't even have a place to herself for that, she shared the same toilet as the men. The dark room stank, there were cockroaches in the corners. She closed the wooden door of the stall behind her, pushed her face and arms against the flaking whitewashed wall, and began softly to cry.

"What is it, girl?"

Someone must have been in the shower, next to the toilet. Usually she called before entering.

"Who the hell is that?"

"Stay in there, my clothes are on the wall. I'm just finished."

She recognized the voice of Rafik, the valet.

"You can go to hell too. I'm done with you fuckheads."

"That's all right, quiet down, I'm just leaving." His thin arm reached to take the clothes hanging from a nail pounded into the wall behind the door. She heard him dress and go out, pulling the door shut gently.

SHE SQUATTED IN the dark, pulling down her *shalvar* and trying to pee. Nothing came. His voice had been gentle. Three bars of light filtered across the air above her head, alive with motes of dust, and this filled her with hope. The summer would be here in a month, the cold winter had passed. She loved the heat, thick night air, and the smell of water and dust, the cool shower spraying her breasts, water splashing on the furry walls in the dank room; and her body, coming out into the evening, drying her hair, head sideways, ear to her shoulder, combing its hanging length.

Rafik sat in the servants' courtyard on one of the dirty white metal chairs, smoking a hookah, not looking at her as she sat down on a low wooden stool, almost at his knees.

He cupped the mouthpiece of the hookah with blunt weathered hands, a heavy agate ring on his index finger. She had never before looked closely at Rafik. He wore clean plain clothes, a woolen mountain vest—spoke with the curling phlegmy accent of the Salt Range, despite having served in Lahore for fifty years. Black shoes cracked where the toes bent, polished. He said the five daily prayers, the only servant who did. A week earlier he had dyed his hair red with henna, to keep him cool as summer came. Hair parted in the middle, looking almost martial but without any swagger; a small brush of mustache, thick ears of an aging man. He must be sixty, came into service as a boy, fifty years ago. He spent more time with the master than anyone else, woke the old man and put him to bed, brought him tea, massaged his feet, dressed him, brought him a single whiskey at night. All of Old Lahore knew Rafik, the barons, the landlords and magnates and politicians, the old dragons, the hostesses of forty years ago.

She let herself cry a few more tears—she could cry whenever she wanted, she thought of herself, alone, her husband on drugs, that dried-up stick who picked her out of the village, when she thought he was saving her. She was still a girl, not just then, but now too. She cried harder, wiping her eyes with the corner of her *dupatta*.

Rafik's mouth worked, distorting his patient resigned face. He took a long pull on the hookah, the tobacco thick in the air.

They were alone, they could hear Hassan in the kitchen making lunch, pounding something. The drivers sat in their quarters playing cards, the gardeners tended their plants, the sweepers were in the house washing the toilets or the floors, or sweeping the leaves from the long tree-shaded drive at the front of the house.

"I know what you all think," she began. "You think I'm a slut, you think I poison my husband. Because of him I'm alone, and you all do with me as you like. I'm trying to live here too, you know. I'm not a fool. I also come from somewhere." Her words poured out clearly, evenly, angrily, entirely unplanned.

He didn't say anything, smoked, his heavy-lidded eyes half shut.

After a moment she got up to leave.

"Stay a minute, girl. I'll bring you tea."

He shifted to get up, putting aside the bamboo stem of the hookah.

"All right, Uncle. But let me bring it." His offering this meant so much to her.

Going boldly into the kitchen, she ladled tea into two chipped cups—the servants' crockery—from a kettle that simmered on a back burner morning till night. Hassan ignored her.

She brought the cups and handed one to Rafik, hoping as she sat down on a bench that someone would come and see them together.

Touching the hot tea to her lips, she peered at him.

He poured tea into the saucer and blew the clotted cream away, then sipped. "It's good, isn't it?" he said.

She wanted to stop it, because it seemed too soon after her tears, but a smile came over her, rising up. She beamed, her girlish yet knowing face lit and transformed.

"What are you laughing at?"

"Nothing. You look like my uncle, except he was huge and fat and you're thin. He always blew on his tea and then he sipped it and looked sort of gloomy and important, like you do."

"Gloomy?" He said it in the funniest way, startled.

I can get him, she thought, and it sent a shiver of happiness through her.

"I'm just joking with you. You're completely different from my uncle. Is that better?"

He smiled, not as a grown-up does, but like a child, smiling with his eyes and mouth and the wrinkles bitten into his face, cheerfully. She noticed this, and thought, He smiles all over, the same way I do.

"You're making fun of me. Well go ahead, I'm an old man. It's time for me to be a fool."

She thought of disagreeing with him, saying he would never be a fool—but stopped herself. Instead she said, "Well, whatever time it is, I don't think foolishness wears a watch."

"You're full of riddles, little girl."

"Little girl." Finishing her tea, she took both her cup and his into the kitchen and washed them carefully. Going out again and walking past him, she said, "Thank you, I feel better for talking to you, Uncle."

In her room, she sat on the bed cross-legged, closed her eyes, leaned back against the wall, and thought, *After all, why not? Why shouldn't I?*

SALEEMA AVOIDED RAFIK during the next few days, watching him, but not presuming on the intimacy of their one conversation. She had never been discreet, so that although she did this almost unconsciously, it suggested to her new possibilities of relation, defined not by constraint—which she understood—but by delicacy. Then fate stepped in to reward her. Every year, at the time of the wheat harvest, K. K. Harouni went for a week to his farm at Dunyapur, on the banks of the Indus. His daughter Begum Kamila that year accompanied him, and therefore Saleema went too.

Early on the morning of the departure the two cars stood in the front of the house, one under the portico, for the sahib and Kamila, and the other for the servants. The drivers polished the cars while they waited, leaning over to clean the windshields, experts. Saleema had tied her clothes in a bag. She had bought a new pair of sandals the day before, and now the red plastic straps were cutting into her feet. When the master came out, leaning on Rafik's arm, those who were sitting on their haunches stood up sharply. He got into the car, called Shah Sahib the accounts manager over, spoke to him briefly through the lowered window, and then the car pulled away, passed under the alley of ancient flame-of-the-forest trees, and turned out the gate. Everyone relaxed, Shah Sahib lit a cigarette, looked without interest over the scene, and returned to his office.

"Come on, come on, get it done," Samundar Khan driver said to the gardeners, who were loading provisions into the trunk of the second car.

Hassan sat in the front, wearing a lambskin cap that brushed the roof, Rafik and Saleema in the back, a basket of food on the seat between them. She had never before ridden in a private car. Sitting with her hands on her knees, she looked out the window at the old shops along the Mall, Tollington Market, where Hassan went on his bicycle to buy chickens and meat, then the mausoleum of Datta Sahib.

I suppose people looking in must wonder who I am, she thought.

As they came across the Ravi River bridge she asked if she could open her window, not so much because she wanted to, as to register her presence. Hassan and Samundar Khan were arguing about whether the fish in the river had been getting bigger or smaller in the last few years.

"O for God's sake," said Hassan, "what do you know about it. I'm a cook, and I've been cooking fish longer than you've been breathing. Listen to me, once upon a time the fish used to be half as big as this car."

"For you old guys everything used to be bigger."

With Hassan, this could go on for hours. Saleema asked again, "Can I open the window please?"

They were stuck in traffic going through the toll.

"Go ahead," Samundar Khan said. "The air's free."

She couldn't find the handle. Rafik leaned over and touched the button, and the window glided down. He pointed out at the river. The rising sun threw a broad stripe of orange on the chocolate brown water. Bicycles and donkey carts and gaudy Bedford trucks streamed in and out of the city over the bridge. He gestured with his eyes at Samundar Khan and Hassan debating nonsense in the front. "Wisdom against youth," he whispered.

SALEEMA DROVE BACK into her childhood, through towns the same as those around her home a hundred miles to the east, rows of ugly concrete buildings, crowded bazaars, slums, ponds of sewage water choked with edible water lilies, then open country, groves of blossoming orange trees, the ripe mustard yellow with flowers; but she rode in an immaculate car instead of a bus crashing along thick with the odor of the crowd. She had painted her nails the night before; her hand rested on the sill of the window, the spring air brushing her fingers. She felt pretty. They drove through mango orchards, fields of harvest wheat. Rafik sat telling a rosary of worn plastic beads, mouthing the ninety-nine names of Allah, his eyes dull, allowing the landscape to pass through him.

They turned onto a single-lane road, which led first through barren salt flats, then irrigated fields, and finally into an orchard of old mango trees.

"All this belongs to Mian Sahib," said Rafik.

They drove up a packed dirt road bordered with jasmine, along the brick wall that enclosed the house, running for several acres, and then into a cul-de-sac planted with rosewood trees. Ten or twelve men sat on benches and stools—the managers and other rising men who wanted to be noticed by the landowner. Rafik stepped out of the car and embraced them one by one. Several of them looked over at Saleema and said, "*Salaam*, Bibi jee."

After they had tea Rafik said to her, "Come on, I'll show you where Begum Kamila's room is."

They went through an ornate wooden door, set in the wall, and into a lush garden that stretched away and became lost among banyans and rosewood trees and open lawns.

She paused, shading her eyes with her hand, taking in the green sward.

"There's more than you can see. If you like, I'll show you later."

Walking through a grassy courtyard, Rafik came to a door, removed his shoes, and knocked.

"Come in," called Begum Kamila. She was sitting in an armchair reading a book. "So you've come, have you?"

She must once have been a very beautiful woman. She wore saris in bright colors and colored her long hair jet black, and on her third finger she wore an immense emerald set in gold, which Saleema once found lying next to the bathtub, and held in her palm for a long time, feeling the heft of the stone, guessing what it must be worth.

"Shall I light the fire, Begum Sahiba?" asked Rafik.

"Go ahead, it'll take away the damp. I suppose Daddy's about to call for lunch."

Rafik kneeled in front of the fire, twisting sheets of newspaper into sticks.

Kamila's bags had been placed on a long desk by the window, which overlooked another garden. Lines had been chalked in the grass for tennis and a net strung. Saleema took the toiletries into the bathroom and laid them out. Unlike the house in Lahore, where the doors were smudged with fingerprints and the paint flaked off the walls in strips, these rooms had been newly painted. The rugs were bright and clean, the brick floors had been washed, vases of flowers, badly arranged, had been placed all around, marigolds and roses.

Going out again into the dark chilly bedroom, Saleema found Rafik still kneeling at the hearth, the flames orange on his orange face.

"Is Bibi gone?"

"They announced lunch."

"May I sit down?"

He moved over.

"It's amazing. My village would fit in a corner of this garden, and we were thirty families. And it's so clean and comfortable, out here in the middle of nowhere."

"Harouni Sahib is a lord, and we're poor people. And then, these are the games that the managers play. The better the house and gardens look, the more comfortable he is, the less Mian Sahib notices the tricks they all get up to on the farms. I don't know what they're storing it up for, stealing fertilizer and the water and cheating in the books. In the old days no one dared. Mian Sahib made these people—the fathers ate his salt, and now the sons have forgotten and are eating everything else."

The fire cracked, the dry mango wood catching hungrily.

She threw a little twig into the fire. "At least their bellies are full."

IN THE MORNING she washed Begum Kamila's clothes, sitting by a faucet outside in the back garden, beside the unused tennis court. Foam on her arms, water splashing onto her bodice from the big orange bucket, she looked up at the trees blowing in the wind, the birds. She was alone. The swaybacked tennis net and the odd chalked lines made the lawn seem expectant, prepared. Last night she had taken a bowl of food quickly into her own room. She heard the men outside around a fire telling stories about the old tough managers and light-fingered servants, now dead, or about happenings on the farm, cattle thefts, dowries. Hassan and Rafik and even the drivers, who had after all been in service fifteen or twenty years, had old friends here.

Churning the clothes in the bucket, squeezing them out, she felt happier perhaps than she ever had been. The April sun had bite, even in the morning, reflecting off the whitewashed walls enclosing this back garden. The earth cooled the soles of her bare feet. Her thoughts ducked in and out of holes, like mice. I'll avoid him, she thought, settling on this as a way forward, knowing that she would be seeing Rafik at lunch if not before. Her love affairs had been so plainly mercantile transactions that she hadn't learned to be coquettish. But the little hopeful girl in her awoke now. Spreading the clothes to dry on a long hedge that bordered the tennis court, bright red and white and yellow patches against the healthy green, she sat there alone in the sun until lunchtime, undisturbed except once, by a gardener, who walked past with a can, stooping to water the potted plants arranged next to the building.

AT LUNCH SHE made the *chapattis*—no one in the village could do that properly. Hassan came into the big hot kitchen, which had a row of coal-burning hearths set at waist level in one wall, and lifted the covers off the saucepans and casseroles prepared by the farm cook— enough for several dozen people.

"Hey, boy," he said to the gangly farm cook, "I've never heard of chickens with six legs. I suppose you're one of those guys—if you cooked a fly you'd keep the breast for yourself. At least you could waft it past your lord and master once."

He pinched Saleema under her arm as she stood flattening the *chapattis* between her hands.

"Here's where the real meat is."

He laughed without mirth, a drawn-out wheeze.

The young cook didn't know what to say. He hadn't slipped anything away yet, though he certainly planned to.

Rafik stood beside another servant, who was spooning the food into serving dishes. The room had high ceilings, and a long wooden table in the middle. In the old times food for scores of people had been cooked here, when the master came on weeks-long hunting trips, with large parties and beaters and guides. Fans that had been broken for years hung down on long pipes, like in a railway station hall.

Saleema had become rigid when Hassan pinched her, raising her shoulders but keeping her eyes on the skillet.

Resting a hand on Hassan's shoulder, Rafik said, "Uncle, why do you bother this poor girl? What has she done to you?"

"You should ask, what *hasn't* she done to me." Then, after a moment, "The hell with it, she's a virgin ever since she rowed across the river, how's that? Don't 'Uncle' me, when you're my own uncle."

He threw down his apron, and left the kitchen, saying to the village cook, "Watch out for Kamila Bibi, young man. Mian Sahib doesn't care what he eats."

As he walked past Saleema, carrying a tray of food to the living room, Rafik made a funny stiff face and then winked.

THAT EVENING THE weather changed. This wasn't the season for rain, but just before dark the wind from the north had begun to blow across the plain, bending the branches of the rosewood trees like a closed hand running up the trunk to strip off the leaves, throwing in front of it a scattering of crows, which flew sloping and tumbling like scraps of black cotton. The rain spattered and made pocks in the dust, cold as rain is before hail. Then it fell heavily. Rafik had taken the drinks into the living room at seven, as he did every day. The food sat warming over coals, there was nothing further to be done till the bell for dinner rang at eight-thirty. The others were in the verandah of the servants' sitting area. Saleema leaned against the long table, while across from her Rafik sat on a stool. The dim bulbs with tin shades hanging from the ceiling threw a yellow light which left the corners of the room dark. Neither of them could think of anything to say, and Saleema kept wiping her eyes and her face with her *dupatta* as if she were hot.

When the rain became hard she said, "Come on, let's go see it come down."

They walked awkwardly through the empty dining room, which smelled of dust and damp brick, then through an arcade to the back verandah. A single banyan tree stood in the middle of the back lawn, the rain cascading down through its handsbreadth leaves. Saleema leaned against a pillar, Rafik stood next to her, his hands behind his back.

"God forgive us, there's going to be a lot of damage to the straw that hasn't been covered," he said.

"This will even knock down the wheat that hasn't been cut. Look at how hard it's coming down."

She looked over at him, his serious wrinkled face, his stubble. Despite the rain, moths circled around the lamps hanging from the ceiling. She kept bumping her hip against the pillar. *Come on, come on*, she thought.

Finally, he said, "Well at least they haven't started planting the cotton yet."

She turned, with her back to the pillar. "Rafik, we're both from the village, we know all this."

He looked over at her quickly. His face seemed hard. She had startled him. Then he did come over.

She put her arms around him. "You're thin," she said, as if she were pleading, "you should eat more," exhaling. The water splashed in the gutter spouts. He also pulled her into his body and held her, melted into her, she was almost exactly as tall as him, his thin body and hers muscular and young. He kissed her neck, not like a man kissing a woman, but inexpertly, as if he were kissing a baby. She kept her eyes open, face on his shoulder.

The electricity went, with a sort of crack, night extinguishing the house and the rain-swept garden.

"Let's go, little girl," he whispered in her ear. "They'll be calling for me." In the darkness, with the other servants hurrying to bring lamps and candles, no one noticed when Saleema and Rafik returned to the kitchen.

But the next morning, when the servants were eating their *parathas* and tea, he came over and sat down next to her, saying nothing, sipping the tea and chewing noisily because of his false teeth, his mouth rotating. So everyone knew. After that he ate his meals next to her, and when they had no duties went off into the empty back garden and sat talking. But they didn't make love, or even do more than hold hands.

At the end of the week Harouni and his retinue drove back to Lahore, Rafik, Saleema, and the rest.

THE SERVANTS HAD a game that they played, with Rafik surprisingly enough not just acquiescent but the ringleader. Up in Rafik's native mountains marijuana grew everywhere, along the sides of the roads, and thickest along the banks of open sewers running through the rocky pine woods below the villages, the blooming plants at the end of summer competing in sweetness and stench with the odor of sewage. Hash smoke clouded the late-night air in the little village tea stall when he was a young man. Now, every spring Rafik planted a handful of seeds behind some trees in a corner of the Lahore garden, and in the fall he dried the plants and ground up the leaves. He played tricks on the others, making a paste called *bhang* and slipping it into the food of one or another servant. Sometimes they would taste it and stop eating, but often not.

A few weeks after the visit to the Harouni farm at Dunyapur, Rafik began secretly compounding a batch of his potion in his quarters, with the help of Saleema. Kamila Bibi had gone back to New York, but Saleema had been kept on, through Rafik's intervention. The accounts manager Shah Sahib had been planning to tell the master that the girl was "corrupt" and a "bad character"—saying these words in English—and toss her out. But now he held his tongue, not wanting to cross Rafik. And Rafik spoke for her one evening as the old man went to sleep, with Rafik massaging his legs.

"I beg your pardon, sir, about the maid Saleema who has been serving Begum Kamila. She's a poor girl and her husband is sick and she's useful in the kitchen. She makes the *chapattis*. If you can give her a place it would be a blessing."

The old man did not merely lack interest in the affairs of the servants—he was not conscious that they had lives outside his purview.

"That's fine."

NOW SALEEMA WATCHED in Rafik's quarters as he boiled the dried leaves in water over an electric ring.

"Hey, girl, close the door, don't let anyone see."

She sat down on the edge of the bed, swinging her bare feet, kicking off her sandals, which fell by the door. Rafik squatted, stirring the leaves with a wooden spoon and peering into the cauldron. They still hadn't made love, though now he would lie with her in the afternoon during the servants' naptime, his hand on her breasts. He made no attempt to hide their relations, and all the servants thought they must be sleeping together. She would fold him into her body, and stroke his thinning hennaed hair while he slept.

"This is a strange kind of cooking for an old man."

"You're the strange one, following this old man around like a little sheep. Most shepherds are young boys."

"Please don't say that." She never in her life had spoken in these gentle tones.

He looked up at her, eyes smiling, pointing with the spoon. "Be careful or I'll give you a taste of this!"

"No thanks."

"No, I'm serious. When Mian Sahib goes to 'Pindi I want everyone to take some. I'll have it too."

"Are you kidding?"

"It'll be fun. And we'll be together. You can trust me."

• • •

TWO DAYS LATER K. K. Harouni flew to Rawalpindi, to attend a meeting of the board of governors of the State Bank—one of the few positions he still held, a sinecure—the real policy was decided elsewhere, Harouni and other eminences unknowingly acting to camouflage self-serving deals and manipulations.

Shah Sahib, who had accompanied his master to the airport, stood next to Samundar Khan in the parking lot, leaning against the hood of the car, wearing a gray suit with excessively broad lapels.

A jet taxied out and came hurtling down the runway, then climbed smoothly through haze, toward Rawalpindi to the west, locking its wheels up.

"Let's go," said Shah Sahib.

As they drove out the airport gate, Samundar Khan said, "May I take you home?"

Shah Sahib glanced over at him. "I need to pick up some things for my wife. *Then* you can take me home."

"WELL, SHAH SAHIB'S out of the way," Samundar Khan said, walking into the kitchen.

Hassan stood at the stove over an enormous pot of boiling oil, cooking the *samosas*, which Rafik and Saleema were assembling at a table, filling them with meat and *bhang*. Rafik had told the servants that he would be passing around *samosas* to celebrate good news from home, but everyone saw through this. The drivers and their gang were fully on board, and had sent Samundar Khan to make sure they got a heaping plate. The old gardener had left, but the younger one had sidled into the drivers' quarters and wanted to join in. The oldest of the sweepers, a thin balding man with a meek, servile expression, sat out in the courtyard hoping that he would be included. Whenever he could afford it he would buy himself a stick of hash to smoke at home after the day's work.

All the *bhang* had been used up. A pile of *samosas* steamed in a plate.

"Okay, now it's us," said Rafik.

Hassan turned his back and raised the lid on a saucepan. "Not me."

But he ended up having some.

Saleema and Rafik sat in his room eating *samosas*. At first she had refused, but he pressed her.

"Now what?" she said.

"Sit here and tell me a story. Tell me about when you were a girl."

Neither of them had spoken much of their pasts or their homes. She knew that he had a wife and children, two sons, and shied away from anything bringing it to mind.

"What shall I say? I was brought up with slaps and harsh words. We had nothing, we were poor. My father sold vegetables from a cart, but when he began smoking heroin he sold everything, the cart, his bicycle, the radio, even the dishes in the kitchen. Once a man—a boy—gave me a little watch—he brought it from Multan—and my father pushed me to the ground and took it from my wrist."

"Poor girl, little girl, how could he do it?" He rolled her over onto the bed and kissed her neck, under her chin. Stopping for a moment, he stood and locked the door.

She didn't tell him the worst, much worse things. Her father came into her room at night and felt under her clothes.

For the first time, Rafik touched between her legs. She opened the drawstring of her *shalvar,* then took off her shirt sitting up on the bed. Her small breasts stood out, her ribs.

He turned off the lights, but she said, "No, I want to see you."

"This old body? Leave it, there's nothing to see."

"For me you're not old."

The *bhang* had begun to affect her, she felt the dimensions of the room, the light, the calendar on the wall that showed a picture of the Kaaba, the black cloth covering the stone and crowds circling around it. How strange, she had never before seen the roof, made of bricks and metal rods, the little high window to let in air. She felt aroused, yet wanted to get up, to go somewhere. She took off his clothes, peeling off his tan socks. Their skin touched. Standing up and going to the corner, she bent down on purpose to pick up her shirt, letting him see her. She saw reflected in his eyes the beauty of her young body. They made love, he came almost immediately, then lay on her.

"Stay inside of me," she said.

Her thoughts were racing, from idea to idea. Oh would he marry her, and she knew he wouldn't. She had been taken by so many men; could have given herself to him so much more pure.

"Now turn off the lights," she said.

"No, let's go out in a minute. Let's go in the garden and look at the flowers."

In the garden he even held her hand. "Don't be afraid," he said. "If you have strange thoughts, remember it's the *bhang*. Be happy."

"Well, it's warm," she said. The sun beat down, the dust on the roses seemed heavy, under a banyan tree the grass didn't grow. She kicked off her shoes, felt the cool earth.

"Lie down here," she said, "next to me, hold me."

And though they might have been seen, he did.

ALL THE AFTERNOON they walked around together, even in the house, looking at the paintings, the furniture. Rafik wanted to sit with the drivers, but she said no, she wanted to be with him alone. Hassan banged around the kitchen, he had eaten too many of the *samosas*.

That evening she said to Rafik, "I'll be back in half an hour."

She went to her own room. Her husband lay on the bed, on his pills, twitching his fingers.

"Look," she said, standing over him. "You're a mess. You've been a mess for two years. Now I'll never sleep in your bed again."

He began to cry, his emaciated face, his long yellow teeth. This she hadn't expected. He sobbed, real tears. She sat down on the broken chair in the corner, looking at the shelf on which she kept her few things, a metal jar of eyeliner, a tin box thrown out by Kamila that once held chocolates.

"Will I still get my money?"

Then she stood up again. "Yes, but if you ever say one funny word, that's it."

She took some clothes, and when she hung them from a nail in Rafik's room he said nothing. She held him all night, his face in her breasts.

Only once, waking, she thought, That was our marriage feast, drugged *samosas*, and she felt sad and worn and frightened.

NOW SHE SLEPT each night in Rafik's bed, leaving her husband to his addiction. Fall and winter came, the leaves fell, at night they slept under a heavy quilt that the managers at the farm sent to Rafik as a present. She slept naked, which still after five months disturbed him. Rafik woke before dawn, to say his prayers, then went into the kitchen and had tea with Hassan. The sahib woke early, and Rafik had duties until mid-morning. When he came to wake her, she would pretend still to be asleep, face hidden in the quilt—she always slept with her head covered. He would bring a cup of tea and some toast.

"Come in with me," she would say, moving over in the bed, leaving a warm spot, and sometimes he would. Her long hair hung down, and she would brush it, while he told her about the guests who had come for bridge, or about some feud in the kitchen. He read the Urdu paper *New Times*, sitting in the morning sun, wearing ancient horn-rimmed glasses with thick lenses. She bought him a warm woolen hat and carefully washed and mended his clothes. She wanted everyone to see how well she cared for him. She said, "You wear me on your back, and I wear you on my face." Her face had softened.

She missed one period, then a second, but said nothing to Rafik.

They had finished making love one afternoon, and were talking, her head on his shoulder.

He was stroking her belly.

"I might as well tell you. See how I'm bigger? I'm pregnant."

He pushed her head away and sat up. "That's bad."

"If that's how you feel, I'll go to my village and get rid of it."

"I'm married. I have a son your age."

She got out of bed, dressed, and went out, turning for a moment at the door. "I'll never forget what you said when I told you."

Where to go? She walked out the gate, in the direction of Lawrence Gardens, a few blocks away. Looking up into the cradle of branches in an enormous flame-of-the-forest tree, she thought, God, I'm nothing, look at how small I am next to this tree. It must be hundreds of years old. But I won't give up the baby. I'd rather have the baby than Rafik.

That night she had nowhere else to sleep, and so went into Rafik's quarters—she couldn't bear to be with her husband, who used more and more of the rocket pills and stayed up all night smoking cigarettes.

"Forgive me," Rafik said.

"I'm going to have it, you can keep me here or throw me out. In any case, I'll have it in my village, there are no women here to help me."

The next day he went to the bazaar in the morning, and when she came to his room for the afternoon nap he gave her a tiny suit, blue knitted trousers, a blue shirt, mittens, and a hat with a pompom, printed with little white rabbits.

So he accepted her condition and would run his hands over her growing belly, speaking to the life within. When it moved, she would put his hand there to show him. None of the other servants said anything openly, though they had expected it; and of course she could claim it was her husband's child. Hassan once jokingly congratulated her, but she responded so gently that he too became silent.

Rafik obtained a month's leave for her.

Before she left for the village he gave her a lot of money, ten thousand rupees, which he had saved up over the years, even after sending maintenance to his family.

"I can't take this."

"For me, for our baby—in case you need a doctor."

SHE ARRIVED AT her village at dusk, taking a rickshaw from the bus station. The open field next to the village had become a collecting pool for the sewage from the city, the water black.

"Look, Saleema's come," the neighbors said, as she walked through the narrow lane to her mother's house, carrying two plastic bags full of food, meat and sugar, tea, carrots, potatoes. The walled compound didn't have a door, just a dirty burlap cloth made of two gunnysacks sewn together. Children ran behind her and peeked in.

Her mother sat on a *charpoy*, peeling potatoes, her long thin hair braided and red with henna.

She didn't even get up, she kept peeling the potatoes.

"I'm back."

"Are you in trouble? You're pregnant."

"No," she lied.

"I bought a goat with the money you sent."

"I can see." The goat, tied to a stake, nibbled at a handful of grass.

The single room was almost completely bare, not even a radio.

Saleema made a curry, sitting by the little hearth, over a fire of twigs.

As they ate, sitting on the bed, Saleema asked, "Where's my brother?"

"Bholu doesn't come here much. I don't give him money."

"Where do you get money besides what I send?"

"It isn't easy anymore, that I can tell you. You'll find out someday what it's like to be old. I sweep the Chaudrey's house, I sell milk from the goat."

The next day she told her mother about Rafik and the baby.

"Did your husband throw you out?"

"I forgot about him long ago."

She wanted to explain that she had become a respectable woman, but knew that her mother would never understand.

Her mother found out about the money and wheedled day and night. Saleema kept the money in a pouch that she wore under her shirt. Late one night, she woke to find her mother stealthily untying the pouch with thin practiced hands.

When Saleema sat up, her mother at first said, "I thought I saw a scorpion." Then, "You owe me, you gravid bitch, coming here puffed up after your whoring. This isn't a hotel."

"It's not my money. And I've been buying all the food."

"It sure seems like your money."

The mother lay in her bed, coughing.

The old midwife from the village, with filthy hands and a greedy heart, brought the baby into the world, a tiny little boy.

RAFIK IMMEDIATELY BONDED with his son. He had been in Lahore when his other children, conceived during ten-day leaves, were born and grew up. He named the child Allah Baksh, God-gifted one.

Saleema sat leaning against the wall of the quarters while Rafik played with the little baby, which held his finger in its tiny hand. He clapped and made a crooning sound, till the baby laughed, showing its red toothless gums.

"His teeth are like yours. Plus you two think alike." She saw that Rafik really did think like the baby, he would sit all afternoon playing with it, engaged with it and seeing the world through its eyes, till it tired. When she opened her blouse to feed the baby, Rafik would look away, embarrassed, lighting his hookah as a distraction, while it smacked and sucked, its tiny throat moving.

Happy months passed, then a year, Saleema became more rounded, she was at the peak of her strange long-faced beauty. Her breasts were heavy with milk.

Rafik sat cross-legged on the lawn one morning, holding the baby. He heard the screen door leading from Harouni's room open, and the master came out. Rafik quickly stood up.

"*Salaam*, sir."

"Hello Rafik." He was in a good mood. "Is this Saleema's baby?"

The master touched the baby with the flat of his hand. The baby, which had been sleeping, smacked its lips. Rafik always dressed him too warmly, a knitted suit with feet, a floppy hat.

"I must say, he's the spitting image of you," Harouni said, teasingly.

Rafik's face broke involuntarily into a broad smile. "What can I say, Hazoor, life takes strange turns. These are all Your Honor's blessings."

Harouni shouted with laughter. "There are some blessings that you shouldn't attribute to me!"

The old retainer's gentle face colored.

•   •   •

A LETTER ARRIVED from Rafik's wife. He kept it in his pocket all day, and that night showed it to Saleema. She literally began trembling, sat down on the bed with her head bowed.

"Will you read it to me?"

"All right." The village *maulvi* had taught Rafik to read as a boy, so that he could recite the Koran.

He took his battered glasses from a case in his front pocket and began.

As-Salaam Uleikum.

I am writing to you because you have not been home in so many months more than eighteen months and your sons and also I miss you and speak of you at night. The old buffalo died but the younger one had two calves both female so we will have plenty of milk though for a short while we have none. Khalid asks to come to Lahore and find a job there you can find a job for him perhaps with God's help. Your brother's shop was robbed but they found no money and now he wants to buy two marlas of land so he will not have cash which is better. The land is on the other side of Afzal's piece. Everything else is well. Please dear husband come home when Mian Sahib can spare you. We all send our respects.

As he read the *salaam*, Rafik had breathed, "*Va leikum assalaam.*"

She had signed the letter, written by a neighbor, with an X.

"Look," said Rafik, "she wept on the paper."

"Or watered it. What will you do?"

"I'll have to go."

She turned her face to the wall and held herself rigid when he touched her.

"Have I done you some wrong?"

"No," she said, "I've done you wrong."

"My wife is sixty years old, little girl. She and I have been together for almost fifty. She stood by me, she bore me two sons, she kept my house, my honor has always been perfectly safe in her hands."

"Honor." Saleema began to cry. "That's bad. You're tiring of me and this situation. Imagine how it feels for me."

He tried to reassure her, but she could tell that the letter had shaken him, as a man of principle. The baby and her love had made him gentler and more philosophical, taking a long view of life as he began to grow old—but the same gentleness would bend him toward his duty, which always would be to his wife and grown sons. He would punish himself and thus her for not loving his wife and for loving Saleema so much and so carnally.

She made him give her a phone number before he left, of a shop near his house, and every evening she wanted to use it, the paper burned in her pocket; but she never dared, what would she say, who would she say was calling? When he returned to Lahore he had changed. He had told his wife about little Allah Baksh.

A FEW DAYS later, Rafik's son and his wife came to stay in the Lahore house. Saleema was dusting the living room and happened to see them arrive, through a window looking out onto the drive in front. She heard the harsh puttering of a rickshaw, and then an old woman emerged, led by a young man with glistening hair and a strong manner. She knew immediately who this must be, her destruction come in this feeble guise. Panic overcame her, mixed with jealousy and a strange pride that came of knowing they had traveled with her in their minds, planning against her. She watched as they walked up the drive and through the passage to the servants' area. Suddenly remembering her son, who was with Rafik, she raced through the house to the back. But she arrived too late, the old woman had come to the quarters and found Rafik playing with the baby. Saleema walked past the open door, pretending to be on some errand, expecting to hear shouting and tears. The old woman sitting on the bed looked up at Saleema with rheumy eyes that expressed neither reproach nor disliking but simply a flat dismissal. She knew who this young girl must be.

Rafik brought the child to Saleema's quarters, where she had retreated.

"At least this one belongs to me," she whispered.

The grown son, when he met Saleema later that afternoon in the servants' sitting area, said to her, "*Salaam*, Auntie."

I'm younger than you, you country fool, she thought spitefully. She would much rather have been attacked, for then she could react.

That night she sat in the kitchen till midnight, the sleeping baby in her arms, watching the cockroaches scurry across the dirty floor. Finally going to her own room, she roughly pushed her husband over on the bed. He had become so thin that his face looked like a broken steel lantern, a gash of mouth and skin stretched over wires.

"Don't smoke," she ordered. "And don't touch me, stay against the wall."

"I lost all that long ago." He knew why she had come back to his bed.

Lying and staring at the ceiling, nursing the baby when it woke, she felt her love for Rafik tearing at her breast, making her a stranger to herself, breaking her. Now she slept again next to this man who disgusted her, while her love must be sleeping beside his ancient wife, who had known him in his youth, who knew all about him. How she loved the baby, its tiny feet and hands, its contented smacking noises and warmth beside her.

The next day she hid in her room with the doors closed. When Rafik knocked she said, "Please, I beg you. You'll only hurt me. Tell them I'm sick, and leave me alone."

"*Are* you sick?" he asked, concerned.

"What do you think?"

She heard his measured footsteps walking away.

She thought, If just once he would act rashly or even quickly, suddenly, without thinking. But he wouldn't. She remembered how slowly he had surrendered to her.

THREE DAYS PASSED. She and Rafik barely spoke, and when they passed each other she saw from his broken and haunted look that he missed her as she missed him. Yet also she saw how resolutely he had turned from her. Just once, when they were alone in the kitchen, at night, he reached over and touched her hand.

"You know, don't you . . ." he said.

The well inside her stirred, all the sorrows of her life, the sweet thick fluid in that darkness, which always lay at the bottom of her thoughts, from which she pulled up the cool liquid and drank.

"I know." And they knew that she forgave him.

Still she hoped. The wife sat in Rafik's room all day, the door open, cross-legged on the bed, eyes not responding to passersby, heavy and settled—Saleema couldn't help walking past on her way to the latrine.

ONE MORNING VERY early she heard the master's bell ring, and then people rushing around. She rose and went to the kitchen.

Hassan told her as soon she walked in, "The old man's sick, they're taking him to the hospital."

The other servants milled around the kitchen, no one spoke. The household rested on Harouni's shoulders, their livelihoods. Late that night he died. The daughters had come, Kamila from New York, her sister Sarwat from Karachi. Even Rehana, the estranged middle daughter, who lived in Paris and hadn't returned to Pakistan in years, flew back. A pall fell over the house. Already the bond among the servants weakened.

Hassan disappeared to his quarters, his face fallen in.

The house was full of mourners, the governor came, ambassadors, retired generals. There was nothing to do, no food would be served.

Rafik sought her out. He came to her room, where she sat on the bed, contemplating the emptiness of her future. Even the child had become silent. When Rafik came in she stood up, and he leaned against her and sobbed.

She couldn't understand what he said, except that he repeated how he had fastened the old man's shirt the last evening in the hospital; but he kept saying *butters* instead of *buttons*. He couldn't finish the sentence, he repeated the first words over and over. Finally he became quiet, face streaked.

THAT WAS THE last time ever that she held him. After a week Sarwat called all the servants into the living room. She sat wearing a sari, her face collapsed and eyes ringed, arms hung with gold bracelets.

"I'm going to explain what happens to you. Rafik and Hassan I've spoken to, as well as the old drivers. The ones who've been in service more than ten years will get fifty thousand rupees. The rest of you will get two thousand for each year of service. If you need recommendations I'll supply them. You served my father well, I thank you. This house will be sold, but until it is you'll receive your salaries and can stay in your quarters." She stood up, on the brink of tears, dignified. "Thank you, goodbye."

Crushed, they all left. They had expected this, but somehow hoped the house would be kept. It must be worth a tremendous amount, with its gardens and location in the heart of Old British Lahore, where the great houses were gradually being demolished, to make way for ugly flats and townhouses. That all was passing, houses where carriages once had been kept, flags lowered at sunset to the lawns of British commissioners. Gone, and they the servants would never find another berth like this one, the gravity of the house, the gentleness of the master, the vast damp rooms, the slow lugubrious pace, the order within disorder.

SHE FOUND HASSAN in the kitchen, muted for once.

"What'll become of me?" she asked. After all, something must come of his intimacy with her. She had slept with him, held him. The stark fact of her body shown to him, given to him, must be worth something. She wished for this, and knew that it wasn't so. With Rafik it had been different, he had raised her up, but Hassan had degraded her. She saw her hopes receding. Again she became the stained creature who threw herself at Hassan, for the little things he gave her.

"You came with nothing, you leave with nothing. You've been paid and fed for some time at least. You have decent clothes and a little slug of money."

"What of you and Rafik?"

"We're being put in the Islamabad house."

"And did Rafik say anything to the mistresses about me?"

"Nothing," Hassan said cruelly. "Not a word." He put his hands on the counter and looked directly in her face. "It's over. There never *was* any hope. I spent my life in this kitchen. Look at me, I'm old. Rafik's old."

So Rafik had renounced her. At the end of the month she had found another place, with some friends of Harouni, who took her because she came from this house.

Before leaving she said to Rafik one day, "Meet me tonight in the kitchen. You owe me that."

• • •

SHE FOUND HIM waiting for her, under a single bulb. He had aged, his face thin, shoulders bent. Worst of all, his eyes were frightened, as if he didn't understand where he was. K. K. Harouni had been his life, his morning and night, his charge, his wealth.

"What of the child?" she asked. "Will you help him? When he's grown will you find him a job?"

"I'll be gone long before that, dear girl."

"Say that once you loved me."

"Of course I did. I do. I loved you more."

WITHIN TWO YEARS she was finished, began using rocket pills, which she once had so much despised, lost her job, went on to heroin, leaving her husband behind without a word. She knew all about that life from her husband and father.

The man who controlled the lucrative corner where she ended up begging took most of her earnings. This way she escaped prostitution. She cradled the little boy in her arms, holding him up to the windows of cars. Rafik sent money, a substantial amount, so long as she had an address. And then, soon enough, she died, and the boy begged in the streets, one of the sparrows of Lahore.

Provide, Provide

Seated at a dinner in Lahore one winter in the late 1970s, for the third time in a week Mr. K. K. Harouni was forced to endure a conversation about a Rolls-Royce coupe recently imported by one of the Waraiches, a family no one had heard of just five years before. The car had been specially modified in London and cost an absurd amount of money, and the mention of it inevitably led to a discussion of the new Pakistani industrialists who at that time were blazing into view. Like other members of the feudal landowning class, Harouni greeted the emergence of these people with condescension overlaying his envy. He had capital, as he observed expansively. Why shouldn't he play along a bit, how difficult could it be?

Toying with the idea in the following weeks, then deciding, Harouni resolved not to do things by halves. He began selling tracts of urban land and pouring more and more cash into factories, buying machinery from Germany, hiring engineers, holding meetings with bankers. Caught up in these projects, he spent increasingly less time at his family estate in the southern Punjab, relying instead upon his manager, the formidable Chaudrey Nabi Baksh Jaglani. Tall and stooped, wearing heavy square-rimmed glasses, his face marked with deep lines of self-control and resolution, Chaudrey Sahib grew paramount in Dunyapur, the place along the Indus where the Harouni farms lay.

Thus, Chaudrey Jaglani's moment struck. The more money that Harouni sank into the factories, the more they seemed to decline in a bewildering confusion of debts and deficits, until finally his bankers advised him to fold. A few months after this catastrophic event, Harouni summoned Nabi Baksh Jaglani to his house in Lahore. When the manager went into the landlord's study, a dark place with a famous ceiling painted by the great surrealist Sadequain, and incongruously adorned with Indian miniatures and temple bronzes of dancing girls and Hindu gods, he found the old man sitting with his steno. Jaglani remained standing.

"Come on, Chaudrey Sahib," said his master. "After all these years you can sit down."

They enacted this scene every time Jaglani came to Lahore. He complied, not quite sitting at the edge of his seat, as the steno Shah Sahib did, but keeping himself rigid.

"How are things on the farm?" asked the landlord.

"The crops are good but the prices are bad."

"How are land prices?"

Jaglani had been expecting this and saw in a flash where it would take them. "Low, buyers get nothing from the lands, so they don't pay much for them. The Khoslas sold four squares at sixteen hundred an acre." He failed to mention that this land stood far from the river, at the tail of an unreliable canal.

"In any case we need to sell. Have them prepare powers of attorney so that you can arrange the transfers."

They spoke for a few minutes about a murder recently committed by one of the tenants, a matter of a girl. Jaglani knew to do this, in order to paper over the embarrassment his master must feel at having to sell land held by his family for three generations.

Walking out under the cool white verandah of Gulfishan, the name by which Lahore knew the great house, Jaglani reflected, *Well, there's plenty of it. He can sell for thirty years and he'll still have a farm.*

The chauffeur, Mustafa, stood by the car. Seeing Jaglani coming, he flicked away his cigarette and went around to open the door. A short man with a chipped tooth, a small, careful mustache, and wavy hair, Mustafa had earned Jaglani's confidence by his discretion and by his excellent qualities as a courtier. Although they spoke frankly and easily on the long drives to Lahore, Mustafa became mute in the presence of others, stone-faced as a chauffeur should be.

Getting into the car, Jaglani said, "Well, now the game heats up."

"Good news?" asked Mustafa.

"Not bad, not too bad."

ACCUSTOMED TO HAVING almost unlimited amounts of money, K. K. Harouni began selling blocs of land, sold it with the sugarcane still standing, the hundred-year-old rosewood trees on the borders of each field thrown in for nothing. Jaglani would receive a brief telegram, NEED FIFTY THOUSAND IMMEDIATELY, and he would sell the land at half price, the choice pieces to himself, putting it in the names of his servants and relatives. He sold to the other managers, to his friends, to political allies. Everyone got a piece of the quick dispersion. He took a commission on each sale. He became ever more powerful and rich.

Harouni's children, seeing their inheritance bleeding away, said to their father, "Jaglani's fleecing you. He's a thief. You should cut down your expenses. If you must sell, for God's sake sell at a proper price."

"If I believed that Jaglani had cheated me," said the father, "I wouldn't believe in anything anymore."

The old man sentimentally thought that the people of Dunyapur, the village in the heart of the Harouni lands, revered his family, whose roots had been in that soil for a mere hundred years.

THOUGH HE HAD become crooked on a large scale, Jaglani did not believe himself to have broken his feudal allegiance to K. K. Harouni, but instead felt himself appropriately to be taking advantage of the master's incapacity and lack of oversight, not seceding but simply expressing a more independent stance. He continued to run the farm extremely well and profitably, and continued sending money to Lahore, a larger share of the net in fact than he used to send, because he himself had developed other sources of income. As his political ambitions grew, he moved his family and household from the village to a large but plain house in the small city of Firoza, the subdistrict headquarters, in order to be closer to the courts and to the government administration. He kept his house in Dunyapur, and often spent nights there. An old sweepress cleaned the house, and he ate the food prepared in the *dera*, the administrative center, where many visitors, buyers and sellers, came and were fed and housed.

One spring day, while driving Jaglani from Firoza to Dunyapur, among the rising green sugarcane fields, with partridge and the migratory quail calling, Mustafa the driver, sensing his master's good mood, begged to speak.

"That's fine, go on," said Jaglani, who knew that the driver had chosen this moment to make some request. Mustafa rarely asked for anything on his own behalf, but often acted for other people who needed something from his master. He advanced carefully, asking only at the correct moment, when he knew Jaglani would accede; and Jaglani, who often sounded his ideas on Mustafa, did not mind this slight bit of manipulation. His own career had been built on calculations of give-and-take. Mustafa took care to make requests that reflected Jaglani's interests, or at least that would not harm his interests.

"My sister," said Mustafa, "just fled back from Rawalpindi, leaving her husband there. He works in 'Pindi as a peon in a bank. You were good enough to get him that post. She couldn't stand the city, the dirtiness, the bad food, the lack of friends or family. Her husband doesn't send any money, because he wants to starve her out and force her back to his home. You often have said that the food they prepare for visitors doesn't suit you. Viro, who cleans your house, is getting old. Let my sister cook for you and keep the house. Let her try for a week or two. If she doesn't do well, then please let her go. I beg pardon for troubling you with this."

Mustafa always managed to ask favors in a way that made Jaglani glow, choosing moments when his master felt satisfied, with work or with politics, the moment when the day seemed sweetest.

"That's fine," said Jaglani tersely, not wanting to show his pleasure at obliging his driver in this almost personal matter. "Tell the accountants to put her on salary, and put the old woman wherever they will."

THE NEXT EVENING Jaglani returned to Dunyapur at dusk, after a day spent on the farms, the jeep's twin lights poking into the night. Peasants bringing their buffalos back from watering at the canal stood aside and saluted, the heavy bells hanging from the animals' necks making a mournful hollow gonging. Some had old shoes tied around their necks, as amulets against the evil eye. Only Jaglani's house had electricity, and as they drove along the dusty main street of the village, lanterns glowed in the unshuttered windows and cook fires threw orange light on the mud walls. The village smelled of dung and dust and smoke and of the mango blossoms in the surrounding orchard.

Entering his house through a side door, Jaglani saw a woman

Daniyal Mueenuddin

crouched over the hearth in the courtyard lit by a single bare bulb, cooking *parathas* in clarified butter. She looked back at him and then covered her head, turning her face away.

"*Salaam*, Chaudrey Sahib," she said.

"*Salaam*, Bibi."

He went into the whitewashed brick house, the rooms over-crowded with ugly carved wood furniture. In his bedroom he took off the revolver that he always wore under his *kurta* and hung it on a hook, then washed his hands and face at a sink in the bedroom and said his prayers.

Returning to the courtyard, he sat down on a *charpoy* and put his feet up. She had already lit his hookah, and he began to smoke.

"How long have you been back in Dunyapur?" he asked.

"Two months."

"Are you staying with Mustafa?"

"Yes, he took me in."

"What's your name?"

"Zainab."

When she brought the food, four or five small dishes of curry on a steel tray, with the *parathas* in a woven reed basket covered with a napkin, he looked up at her suddenly, wanting to find out what kind of woman she might be.

Slowly looking down, she avoided his eyes. She had a hard pale face, angular, with high cheekbones, almost beautiful, but too forceful, reminding him of a woman who had been caught years ago on the banks of the Indus, a cattle thief. No woman had ever before been known to lift cattle, and people came from miles around to see her, sitting defiantly on a *charpoy* in the *dera*, waiting to be turned over to the police.

As Jaglani finished eating, Zainab slipped away. The food could not have been better. Smoking the hookah and listening to the village going to sleep, the last few voices, the animals bedded down, he decided he would keep her on.

IN LATE MARCH the wheat harvest began, and Jaglani moved to the village, as he did each year, in order to observe the weighing of the crop as it came in. That year he had planted seven hundred acres of wheat, and now he hired the villagers to cut it by hand, moving across the yellow fields and setting up the cut bundles into shocks, women and men working together. Their babies swung in cloths strung in the shade between trees, and the tractors pulled steel wagons, which bumped over the field rows and gradually filled with the loose sheaves thrown up by the men. The threshing machines ran all day and night, powered by tractors which idled or roared as they ran light or had to bear a load, when the man on the wagon threw a big armful of wheat into the hopper. The chaff, blown out to one side, would grow into enormous golden piles, until finally the men would uncouple the tractor and move the thresher to another spot. Jaglani sat much of the day in the *dera*, on a *charpoy* under a massive banyan tree, smoking a hookah and watching the trolleys come in. Two men would pull the burlap sacks down from the trolley along a wooden ramp, each holding one corner, dragging them over to the balance scales that hung from a far branch of the banyan. An accountant entered the weight of each sack into a ledger, and then the two men threw the wheat atop a growing pile, which they climbed, their bare feet digging into the hot grain, sinking to their knees, until they reached the top and upended the sack.

Once again neither hail nor winds had ruined the crop, and the fruits of Jaglani's management stood there beside him, growing, golden. This harvest mattered more to him than any other, more than the mangoes or the cane or the cotton. The men would be paid a portion of their wages throughout the year in wheat, which they preferred, saying that money might be spent, but as long as they had the monthly allowance of wheat their families would not starve. At noon each day Zainab sent out a tray of food to him, covered with a white cloth, and Jaglani ate under the breezy leaves of the banyan, while the men continued to work.

Late one evening, when he returned tired to his house in the *dera*, having spent the afternoon out along the river, dealing with a tractor that had foundered in a sandbank while returning to the farm with a load of grain, she brought him a glass of sherbet, as she now always did as soon as he walked in the door.

"Would you like me to press your feet?" she asked.

This too became part of the routine. He would lie on a *charpoy* in the shadowed courtyard of his house, smoking a hookah, leaning on one elbow, while she massaged his legs and feet, patiently, her hands red with henna. Her head scarf would slip down to her shoulders, and he admired her thick black hair, braided and oiled. She had strong hands.

Inevitably, one evening he reached for her and took her inside. Now often they would make love before she went home, if he was not too tired. She did this uncomplainingly, giving him whatever he wanted. He had little experience with women, other than the wife to whom he had been married by arrangement at the age of seventeen. Once or twice he had slept with the wives of peasants in the village, when the women threw themselves at him. He would give the husband a job, something that might as well go to one man as to another, but these women were unclean and crude, and once he entered his forties he stopped succumbing to them. He had two sons by his wife, and he continued to sleep with her when he needed release, though he didn't find her attractive, her slow mind and preoccupation with the household in Firoza, which smelled of cooking. Zainab by contrast knew how to please him. She wore no scent, but bathed always before he came home and wore attractive clothes.

WHEN THE HARVEST ended he still found some pretext to come every day or two to the farm. He would do his business and then go to the house, where Zainab would serve him the meal she had cooked earlier. He would bathe, she would massage him and feed him, and then they would make love. He said her name in a particular way, pronouncing the first syllable in his throat, and this became the emblem of their closeness, which otherwise they did not refer to. In the bedroom, with the lights off, she kissed him hard and soft and gradually persuaded him by her supple actions to lose his inhibitions. She had a way of falling on the bed, with her face buried in the pillow, on her knees. As he drove around the farm, or in the city, the vision of her giving herself so trustingly would come to him.

One evening at bedtime they quarreled. Next morning when she brought his tea, Jaglani reached around her waist and pulled her down beside him, wanting to be reconciled. "You never ask for anything. Let me give you some money. You can buy clothes."

"You buy me things and then later you'll think you bought me. I was never for sale," she replied, standing up.

"Stop," he called. He spoke in the voice he might have used with a servant.

She left, quietly closing the door behind her.

That evening they said nothing about this, but he left money on the table beside the bed. She did not take it that night, nor the next morning. He went to the city for a few days, and on the evening when he returned to the farm he found the money still where he had left it.

. . .

EACH TIME HE met her she approached him with the same reserve she had displayed the first time he saw her. She spoke to him formally, called him "Chaudrey Sahib." When he tried to kiss her, coming in at dusk, her lips would never be hungry. After they made love he would stroke her, run his hands over her slender body, tell her how much she meant to him. He never before had said these things to any woman. She did not caress him, and he felt that she herself was not touched in her core. She would lie on her back, while he nuzzled her neck and threw one arm across her body. Although she massaged him, cooked for him, cleaned his house, and made love to him, he found that after two months she still had not come any closer. She needed him, he knew that, but he had no idea whether she cared for him. Except when they made love, when she abandoned herself, a red patch of flushed skin brightening each cheek, he found no response in her eyes, except a willingness to serve him. He looked for contempt in her eyes, but did not find even that. He wanted more from her, for her to spend the entire night with him.

"Why do you care?" he asked. "Are you afraid the other villagers will find out?"

She laughed humorlessly. "The villagers! They knew the first night. They leave me alone because they're afraid of you. It's nice, it's a proof of just how much they do fear you. If you dropped me they would call me a whore out loud as I walked down the street."

"Then why not spend the nights?"

"Then I *would* be your whore. At least now we still pretend. Leave it alone, I've already said more than I wanted. Please."

. . .

IN JULY THE monsoon began, a strong monsoon, with rain and enormous clouds towering over the flat desert that fell right to the edge of the river. It had rained all day and all night, and Jaglani came to the farm in order to oversee the pumping of water from the cotton fields. Where the fields lay low the young cotton stood under four inches of water. Mechanics removed the turbines from the tube wells and powered them in the fields by shafts run from tractors. If the sun shone on the plants while they stood in the water, the reflected heat would kill them.

That night, late, the watchman from the *dera* knocked on Jaglani's door. He rose quickly and took his revolver.

"Sir, may we use the jeep? Loharu's son just got bitten by a snake."

Putting on his clothes, Jaglani sent for Mustafa and went to Loharu's house.

Lowering his head to walk under the lintel of the small door, stepping carefully in the slippery mud, he approached the family, an old woman and her husband Loharu, who had worked on the farm as a laborer since he became old enough to be useful. They were standing in the little single room by the light of a lantern, the woman quietly sobbing and dabbing at her eyes with her head scarf. A crowd of villagers stood around, some inside and some outside the hut. When Jaglani entered they murmured, "Chaudrey Sahib." Even in his grief the father fell into a posture of deference, taking Jaglani's hand and reaching to touch his knee.

The boy lay on a *charpoy* in one corner, very thin, just developing a mustache. Although still alive, his body had softened and lost all tension. A bit of white foam sat in each corner of his lips. Jaglani knew he would be dead soon, as did the villagers, who had seen this before. Only the parents refused to accept that their son would soon be gone. They heard the jeep coming along the muddy street of the village, splashing, whining in first gear. No one made a move to lift the boy, and after a few more minutes he died, curling now, his throat rattling, and then becoming limp.

The mother fell onto the body, quietly saying, "No, no, no, no, no."

Jaglani went outside. "What happened?" he asked.

"A cobra came through the window, the water must have filled its hole. The boy's hand hung over the edge of the *charpoy*, and the snake brushed the hand."

"Did they kill the snake?"

A man went inside and brought out the cobra, black, three feet long, dangling like a hose over the stick with which he carried it. It slid off into the mud, making a soft slapping sound.

BACK IN HIS house, Jaglani found that he couldn't sleep, that he wanted something, tea or some food. He hadn't known the boy, though he had seen him about. The father had worked on the farm for twenty years, since childhood. Now he was a heavy-featured man with a few days' muzzle of graying beard, his teeth almost gone, rather stupid, so that the other men made good-humored jokes about him.

Jaglani pushed the bell button, which rang out in the *dera* where the watchman could hear it.

"I'm not feeling well," he told the watchman. "Call Zainab and tell her to make me some tea. I've got a fever."

"Shall I send Mustafa for medicine?"

"No, in the morning I'll go back to Firoza. Just tea."

ZAINAB CAME INTO the room, walking quietly as always. "I'm sorry you're not well."

"Come here," said Jaglani. He took her by the wrist and pulled her down onto the bed. She didn't resist, but instead, with a single motion removed her *kurta*, pulling it over her head. As she came onto the bed she kicked off her shoes.

Rolling on top of her, he searched her face.

"I need you to be here in the house whenever I'm here." He looked directly into her eyes.

"I told you, I won't. I'll go away."

"Where can you go?"

"My husband has written three times. He says he'll take me back. I'll go there."

Jaglani lay on his back staring at the ceiling, his emotions tightened up almost unbearably.

"I'll marry you," he said.

"What about my husband?"

"I'll arrange it."

She turned and began kissing him, looking down on his face. He closed his eyes.

JAGLANI KNEW THAT his wife, who was also his first cousin, would try to turn their common family against him if he took another wife. In the next few days he didn't mention his offer of marriage again, although it lay between them. Zainab became harder and more emotionally inflexible than before. She did what he asked. Again and always in bed, sexually, she opened and became almost vicious, pliable, biting him, on his cheeks, his neck; but after they finished she withdrew into herself. Only sometimes, when they lay in bed, she would cough or feel cold and he would offer to do something for her, to bring water or to find a blanket, and she would say, "Yes, please," in a girlish voice that wrung his heart. Finally he could not deny to himself that he had fallen in love, for the first time in his life. He even acknowledged her aloof coldness, the possibility that she would mar his life. And yet he felt that he had risen so far, had become invulnerable to the judgments of those around him, had become preeminent in this area by the river Indus, and now he deserved to make this mistake, for once not to make a calculated choice, but to surrender to his desire.

In the beginning of September, after the monsoon, the immense Punjabi heat began to subside. One morning when Zainab brought his breakfast he said to her, "Your husband comes today."

"Why?"

"I've called him. He needs to sign the divorce papers."

"He won't do that."

Jaglani looked up at her as she leaned forward placing the tray of food on the table in front of him. "You still don't know me, do you?"

IN THE LATE afternoon Zainab's husband, a peasant named Aslam born in Dunyapur, entered the *dera*, a small figure advancing through the whitewashed brick gates, having walked from the main road, where the intercity bus dropped him off.

Jaglani sat under the banyan tree, signing cash vouchers passed to him by an aged accountant wearing spectacles mended with wire.

Aslam approached, said his *salaam*, and touched Jaglani's knee.

"Hello Aslam," said Jaglani. "I'll call you, go sit."

Seven or eight men sat in chairs under a verandah, all waiting to see Jaglani, with petitions of various kinds—a stolen ox, water issues, begging for jobs, needing letters to local government administrators.

Jaglani saw Aslam last of all, several hours later. The sky had darkened, and the *maulvi* in the plain but large marbled mosque built by the Harounis had finished the *maghreb* call for prayer, standing on a platform, his voice reedy.

"Aslam, you can't seem to control your wife," began Jaglani, without any preamble.

"No sir. She ran back to the village. I'm here, and I intend to take her home."

"I'm told she doesn't want to go. You better divorce her."

"Sir, no. My house is empty, every night I come home and it's empty."

"Why don't you have children?" asked Jaglani. "Didn't you live with her as her husband?"

"In the beginning we tried. We had no luck."

"That's grounds for divorce. I suggest you divorce her for being barren."

"Please, Chaudrey Sahib, you and I grew up together in Dunyapur, we played together as children. I beg you, don't take what's mine. You have so much, and I so little."

"I have so much because I took what I wanted. Go away."

The husband said, "Take her and be damned with her," but Jaglani ignored him.

The next morning one of the farm accountants presented Aslam with some papers. Knowing the husband to be illiterate, and wishing to spare him further humiliation, the accountant assured him that the papers simply gave Zainab permission to live apart. Aslam left Dunyapur with a letter to the manager of the bank where he worked in Rawalpindi. In the letter Jaglani requested that the manager, a dependent of the Harounis, give Aslam a raise and watch over him.

A FEW WEEKS later Jaglani secretly married Zainab. The *maulvi* from the mosque came quietly into Chaudrey Sahib's house one morning, bringing with him one of the old managers to act as a witness. The villagers bullied the *maulvi*, a timid man with a scrawny beard. He blushed when he spoke, and would ask the cook in the *dera* for little treats from the common pot to take home for his wife, as his pay barely covered their thin monthly expenditure. The manager, by contrast, cuffed his men about and had a voice like a baying hound. Coming across the courtyard of the *dera*, under the blowing trees, the *maulvi* turned to the manager.

"Won't Jaglani's sons blame us for this?"

"Don't worry," said the manager, "there's not enough blood in their livers to clog the foot of a flea. Even when the big man dies they'll be afraid to cross him. And she can take care of herself, she's like a hatchet."

When they entered the courtyard of the little house they found Jaglani sitting on a *charpoy* smoking his hookah. The two men sat down, and while the *maulvi* watched, Jaglani and the manager spoke of the September cane planting, just completed, and of the cotton just then developing bolls. The manager picked at a callus on his foot. After a few minutes the register of deeds, a man who owed his posting in the area to Jaglani, and who had collaborated in numerous dubious land transfers, entered with the marriage papers in a big ledger under his arm. He took from his pocket a gold pen worth several months of his official salary and began filling out the forms, writing in an elegant hand, and with a look of satisfaction on his face. He loved these forms, loved consummating rich transactions. Jaglani signed, the single witness signed, and then the *maulvi* rose and said a prayer, his hands cupped, speaking rapidly and with perfect memory. The other three required witnesses would sign later, if the need arose—the register of deeds had urged that they leave the document incomplete to this degree. Under the trees and with the birds calling, Jaglani felt extremely moved, felt his emotions to be like clear glass. He took the papers inside and Zainab affixed her thumbprint, leaning against him as they sat on the bed, her face soft. When he had insisted upon keeping the marriage secret she made only one stipulation—that they no longer would use birth control.

• • •

ZAINAB NOW SLEPT the night in Jaglani's bed. She brought many of her things, clothes and jewelry, her makeup, and put them about the house. Seeing these little tokens of her presence made him happy, made him feel that he possessed her. She asked him to buy a buffalo, and twice a day, at dawn and at dusk, the villager who cared for the animal would bring a pail of the rich milk and leave it just inside the courtyard, covered with a cloth. She made *ghee* and butter, and if some was left over she sent it to Mustafa's house, or to the house of one of the poorer neighbors who couldn't afford to keep a buffalo. Only in the mornings, when Jaglani wanted to hold her, to lie in bed with her and talk quietly, or perhaps to make love, she still would not stay with him, but became restless and would get up, saying that she needed to begin the day. Although she did not like being touched, except when in bed, he found that now she tried to accept his caresses, tried not to be cold to him. When he came into the house and approached her from behind as she stood doing some household task, cupping her breasts in his hands, she became still and turned her head, smiling, and only after a moment would she disengage from him. Even then she would hold his hand and lead him outside, seating him on the *charpoy* and bringing his hookah. He became familiar with the smallest aspects of her body. She cut her toenails one day, but cut too far, into the quick, an inverted half-moon, until one of the nails bled. He loved this wildness in her, evidence of hardness toward herself, contained violence.

She developed a urinary infection, and he took her into town. She rode in the back of his jeep, and as always her brother Mustafa drove. None of them spoke. She kept her head covered, and didn't look out of the window. Even this trip, their first together, became for him a significant memory. He wanted to take care of her, but often she would not allow him to. When he returned to Dunyapur after spending a few days in Firoza with his senior wife, as he drove toward the river he would feel a weight on his stomach. He feared Zainab, strangely enough, although he had made a career of fearing no one and of thereby dominating this lawless area. Sometimes he thought that it would be a relief to be rid of her, and yet his love kept increasing.

He became slightly complacent, finding her softer than he had imagined. After they made love she would lie next to him in the dark, tracing her fingers on his back and leaning down to kiss him. Before the marriage he always had been the one to caress her, while she lay with her back to him, curled into his body, her eyes open, rigid and seemingly resentful of having opened herself, not only physically but also emotionally, at least in the moments of sex.

SHE HAD BLAMED her husband for her failure to conceive. A year after her second marriage Jaglani arrived at dusk from Firoza. Mustafa drove the jeep into the *dera*, the headlights illuminating the banyan, the tractors standing in a row along the wall, plows and harrows and disks here and there. The watchman stood up, leaning on his long stick, and shielded his eyes with one hand. Another summer had passed, another monsoon. The jasmine planted along the high mud walls that enclosed the *dera* gave off its strong sweet smell. Jaglani liked flowers, and he also believed that the farm ran best when the roads were kept immaculate and smooth and the buildings whitewashed and adorned with flowers and trees. Order begat order.

Walking into the house, he found the fire out and the light off, although he had sent word in the morning that he would be returning to the farm. Inside Zainab sat in the dark on the edge of the bed.

"Why no lights?" he asked, flipping the switch.

She had not dressed up, but wore wrinkled clothes.

"Do you know what day this is?"

"No."

"The day we married, last year." She paused. "You know, I thought I didn't have children with Aslam because he couldn't. But it's me." She almost began to cry, but then stopped herself. Her face became hard. "I only married you because of that."

Cut badly, he said, "You had no choice. How long would your sister-in-law have treated you well? You came like a beggar."

"I never begged, but now I'll beg from you. I'll bow down. I beg you, give me one of your sons' children to bring up. Shabir has three daughters. The little one, give me her. He has his sons, he'll still have them and the other girls. The little one is only a few months old, she won't even know that I'm not her real mother. Give her to me, I beg you, and I'll never ask for anything again." She began to cry, through her teeth. "I beg you, I beg you, I beg you. I've served you. I belong to you, you know I do. Give me the little girl. Shabir doesn't even want her, you know he doesn't."

He refused. "I can't, my family doesn't know we're married."

THAT WINTER JAGLANI decided to run for office, for the provincial assembly. The local powers, the people above him, the Makhdooms, hereditary saints who controlled huge areas of land nearby and who could hand out Muslim League tickets, sent people to Jaglani and offered to help get him elected. He went to Lahore and received the blessing of K. K. Harouni. As a preliminary to the election, in order to prevent his opponent from using it against him, Jaglani disclosed the secret of his marriage to Zainab. He gave his wife and children no opportunity to respond—he simply announced it to them. The villagers had already guessed, but now had it confirmed. Others found out. No one thought anything of it, he ruled his area in the old way, with force. He had the prerogative of taking a second wife, a chosen wife. Flushed with his power, Jaglani went further. He brought his son's infant daughter to Dunyapur and gave her to Zainab, to nurse and to bring up.

ANOTHER YEAR PASSED. Jaglani had been elected to the provincial assembly by a wide margin, and thus spent his time either in Lahore attending sessions or at the farm, hearing the petitions and complaints of his constituents, the people from the area. His district ran along both sides of the Indus River, and the people on the far side came across on a wooden ferry, flat-bottomed and large enough to hold twenty people, pushed along on long sweeps by an old man, whose body had remained muscular, but whose skin hung off him wherever the muscles didn't extend.

One of Jaglani's first acts on entering office had been to move the ferry from another spot five miles downstream to a little bay on the river immediately next to Dunyapur, over the protests of those who found the original situation more convenient. The ferry had served the village of the man who stood against Jaglani in the election, and by moving it he showed the entire district his new powers. He had new bricked roads built to meet the ferry at each bank of the river, and these roads greatly increased the value of Jaglani's lands and the lands of his friends. Jaglani could order men arrested or released, could appoint them to government posts, could have government officers removed. He decided whose villages the new roads passed through, decided which areas got electricity, manipulated the flow of water through the canals. He could settle cases, even cases of murder, by imposing a reconciliation upon the two parties and ordering the police not to interfere. These new powers changed him. Because he had no higher ambitions, he became impartial. By temperament orderly, within this isolated area he sought to impose harmony and prosperity.

COMING INTO THE house one afternoon, Jaglani did not find Zainab in the little kitchen preparing his food. He called.

"Where are you?"

"In my room," she replied, speaking in her gentle voice, which he liked so much. "Come in, come see."

Jaglani walked through the room he shared with her and into her own quarters. Unlike the rest of the house, which was dark and crowded with furniture, Zainab's room had only a small low bed, padded with cotton, a chair, and a plain wooden table, on which she had arranged her makeup and combs, with a mirror in front of it, and in one corner a crib. A small cotton *dhurrie* covered the center of the brick floor. The high windows stood open, drawing light into the room, reflecting off the freshly whitewashed walls. The baby stood on the bed, waving her fat little arms, naked, her feet planted between Zainab's crossed legs. Zainab leaned against a pillow and, dipping a cloth into a bowl of warm water, gently washed the baby. The light from the windows reflected off the disturbed water in the brass bowl, throwing a pattern onto the walls.

"Watch," said Zainab. She tickled the baby, whom she had renamed Saba, under the chin, holding her around the waist. He noticed the strength of Zainab's slender arm, on which the veins stood out, and he noticed the sureness with which his wife held this baby. The baby giggled. Zainab laid her on the bed and bent over her.

"Say it," she whispered soothingly. Her pale manicured feet peeked out under her thighs, the soles reddened with henna. "Say it, little bunny, my little Saba."

The baby looked up at her, smiling, coral gums wet with spittle. She waved her chubby arms, fingers splayed. "Ma," she said.

"See?" said Zainab, turning to Jaglani, who sat on the little chair next to the table. Zainab had been worrying because the baby, nearly two years old, had not yet begun to speak.

Vulnerable, he watched the baby intently, smiling a shy smile, his features becoming gentle, the face of a sad boy, knowing and needy. "If only the managers could see this smile," she would say.

Zainab gestured. "Come, bring your chair over by us."

He carried the chair across the room and sat down, his elbows on his knees, looking into the little girl's face and at Zainab's hair, which fell over the baby.

FOR SEVERAL MONTHS Jaglani had been feeling unwell. A few days after this little scene with the baby, Jaglani learned that he had bone cancer, and that he would be dead within six months. When he didn't visit the village for a week Zainab went to see her brother Mustafa, who spent each Friday night with his family in Dunyapur.

"You better come inside," said Mustafa. He took her into a neat room, adorned with the fruits of his petty thefts, his inflated bills—a television and video player, a sewing machine covered with an embroidered cloth, a large garish clock with a plastic figure of a shepherdess that moved back and forth across the face—for like everyone else on the farm Mustafa trimmed out money where he could, a few rupees on the petrol, a bit of padding when he bought spare parts.

"What?" she said, as soon as her brother closed the door.

"He's dying."

She sat down, almost falling, and hung her head. "Oh my God. Of what? And now what do I do?"

"It's cancer. You better be sharp."

"He hasn't come in a week," she said.

"Don't count on anything anymore," said Mustafa. "His family's all around him now. He'll get weak fast. Don't forget, he owns twenty squares of land, just as a start. You'll be lucky to see him again, at least to see him alone."

"He's tied to me," she said, looking Mustafa in the eye. "He'll come."

Mustafa sat down and ran his hands over his face. "What a mess. He's going tomorrow to Lahore. He's trying to make sure that Shabir wins the by-election. That won't happen, the boy barely has enough spine to stand upright. The big guys around here will eat him up once Jaglani's gone. No one reaches out very far from the grave."

"You know what that means for me," she said. Brother and sister understood the enormity of her loss, the failure of her preparations against abandonment. "They're going to take Saba away from me, aren't they? She's too young, in a year she won't remember me. I'll get nothing."

JAGLANI FADED AWAY. Knowing how vulnerable his family would be to the enemies he had made in the course of a life in politics, he went to Lahore, seeking a sure seat in the Assembly for his son, the one who gave a daughter to Zainab, in the by-election that would follow his death.

The provincial party chief, a ward boss from Lahore who held the office of Punjab chief minister, received Jaglani just after sunset at his house, a large shabby building constructed on public land, formerly a park, which he had condemned and appropriated as soon as he attained office, throwing a wall around it.

Jaglani waited in the anteroom with twenty or thirty other supplicants, who gathered in circles or huddled together on grimy sofas, speaking in undertones, puffing cigarettes, and whispering into cell phones tiny as jewels. Two pictures hung on a wall of the dirty, smoky room, one of the country's founder, the Quaid-e-Azam, and next to it, just slightly lower, a photo of the party's leader. The other men in the room, mostly provincial politicians risen from the business classes, held their phones in their hands when not speaking into them, displaying this new status symbol recently introduced in Lahore and the other big Pakistani cities.

Entering the immaculate office, ushered in by a sleek-looking steno, Jaglani approached the chief minister, who sat behind a desk covered with green baize, reading a file. He looked up, narrowed his eyes, and rose.

"Hello, hello, Chaudrey Sahib."

He walked from behind the desk, his Western clothes, a pinstripe suit and gold cuff links and English shoes, distinguishing him from Jaglani and from most of the supplicants waiting in the anteroom. Taking Jaglani's hand, and holding on to it, he sat them down next to each other on a sofa.

"You're looking well," said the chief minister insincerely.

"Thanks to Your Honor."

"And how is Mr. K. K. Harouni?"

They began speaking of the political situation in Jaglani's district. The chief minister spoke little but listened, his face set in a shrewd expression, looking at the opposite wall and occasionally asking questions.

After ten minutes he looked at his watch.

"And how's everything else?"

"I've come with a request, sir. I regret to say I've been diagnosed with cancer."

"Well, well, I'm so sorry," said the chief minister, who knew all about it.

"Sir, I request that the party support my son in the by-election."

"Nonsense, nonsense," said the minister. "You're healthy as a horse. These doctors kill everyone off, everyone. You've still got twenty years ahead of you, bulling Dunyapur."

"If something does happen to me, however, will you support the boy? He's capable, he knows the area, and he knows all the people. I've served the party for twenty-five years, in one way or another, and I've always voted in the Assembly the way you asked me to." He played his only card. "We go a long way, Shujaat Sahib."

"We'll have to put the boy forward. We'll plan that. Don't worry, it's done."

"Will you call a meeting of the people from my area? We'll need to get them in line."

The chief minister rose. "Yes, yes. We'll have to do that." Walking Jaglani to the door and ushering the dying man out, the minister said, shaking an upraised finger, "Now remember, no more about this illness. You'll outlive us all, I know how you country people are, it's the food, it's the food." He had this habit of repeating himself when telling lies.

Jaglani walked through the anteroom, down the dirty steps, and out the gate. Mustafa stood in a line of cars parked along the sidewalk. He had failed. He went back to Dunyapur without seeing any of his old friends and allies.

THE CITY HOUSE in Firoza, with antimacassars and sofas covered with plastic liners and the constant smell of fried onions, depressed Jaglani, and yet its gloominess and air of resignation and finality seemed consistent with the great change coming over him. He felt the cancer as a tension in his stomach, a breeding knot that hurt sometimes but that never went away. He longed for the country and for Dunyapur, where he had been born and where he achieved all the successes that mattered to him now. He remembered the day when he became a manager, appointed by K. K. Harouni, who at that time still looked rich and clean and strong, different from anyone Jaglani had ever known. Jaglani once went with him hunting ducks along the river, floating on a barge, and he remembered still the softness of the landowner's white shirt and the way in which his collar touched the brown hairs on his neck. Harouni had carried a beautiful shotgun, very light, slim, almost like a toy, but deadly.

Yet Dunyapur had been spoiled for him by the presence of Zainab. He minded very much that he had given his sons a stepmother of that class, a servant woman. He minded that he had insulted his first wife in that way, by marrying again, by marrying a servant, and then by keeping the marriage a secret. His senior wife had never reproached him, but after Jaglani told her she quickly became old. She prayed a great deal, spent much of her time in bed, stopped caring for herself. Her body became rounded like a hoop, not fat but fleshed uniformly all over, a body thrown away, throwing itself away, the old woman sitting all day in bed, dreaming, muttering perhaps when left alone. He reproached himself for taking his eldest son's daughter and giving her to Zainab, transplanting the little girl onto such different stock. Secretly, and most bitterly, he blamed himself for having been so weak as to love a woman who had never loved him. He made an idol of her, lavished himself upon her sexual body, gave himself to a woman who never gave back, except in the most practical terms. She blotted the cleanliness of his life trajectory, which he had always before believed in. She represented the culmination of his ascendance, the reward of his virtue and striving, and showed him how little it all had been, his life and his ambitions. All of it he had thrown away, his manliness and strength, for a pair of legs that clasped his waist and a pair of eyes that pierced him and that yet had at bottom the deadness of foil.

ONE MORNING IN April, three months after he had been diagnosed and condemned to die, Jaglani woke feeling better than usual. Walking now with a cane, his face gaunt and improved by it, he went to the verandah and without telling any of the people in the house ordered Mustafa to drive him to Dunyapur. They arrived in the *dera* just at the time when the sun began to pour down over the roofs of the sheds onto the bricked threshing floor. Chickens walked about picking at spilled grain, and the odor of burnt oil that had soaked into the dust added to the sleepiness of the scene, a heavy baking scent.

Only a few people sat in the sun, two accountants, a watchman, and one or two others, loafers sitting around drinking tea. On the far side of the large open square an old woman with bare feet hunched over and swept the brick threshing floor, throwing up a cloud of dust in the sun. When the people sitting there saw the car they jumped up, saying, "Chaudrey Sahib, Chaudrey Sahib," as if they had something to hide.

Mustafa ran around to open the door, and Jaglani stepped painfully out, took his cane, and after receiving their obeisance went into his own house, without pausing to discuss business. The men had approached him not less deferentially than before but less fearfully. They knew he had come for the last time, and already their feelings about him were becoming sweeter and more genuinely respectful. With him an entire generation of men from Dunyapur would pass.

JAGLANI HAD LIVED an opportunistic life, seizing power wherever he saw it available and unguarded, and therefore he had not developed sentimental attachments to the tokens of his power, land, possessions, or even men. Walking into the silent dark house, he felt, for the first time, that he would regret losing a place, these whitewashed walls, the little windows. He had aged greatly in the past weeks as the disease bit into him. He had never loved his wife, his children were fools, and he had no friends. For him there had not been any great leave-takings, no farewells. He had spent his life among the farmers and peasants of the area, or among politicians. He liked some of them, liked their stories or their intelligence or cunning. Although he didn't laugh often, he played a part when the politicians or the strongmen from around Dunyapur gathered and talked. In the early years, Jaglani sat to one side, dark and acute, and in quiet moments added his shrewd remarks. Later, when he became important, he still mostly listened, but signaled to those around him that they could unwind and speak freely by making brief and slightly witty comments, speaking through lips almost clenched, resisting a smile. His social life had not extended beyond these diversions. He worked in concert with other men, or used them, or struggled against them. The rest did not interest him.

GOING INTO THE small living room, Jaglani saw a light in Zainab's room, and thought that she must be there with the baby. He wondered if someone in his household at Firoza had called and informed her of his arrival. He knew that she must have contacts among his servants in the city. She would want him to find her there, caring for the child. The darkness of the house, its dampness, the expectancy of the salt and pepper shakers carefully aligned on the table and the sadness of the toothpick holder, its pink plastic cover gleaming softly, waiting for his next visit and his next meal, reminded him of the days when he first realized that he loved Zainab, and she sensed that he loved her, and began to smile around him, to play as she served him dinner. He walked quietly to her bedroom. She lay on the white divan, with the baby next to her. He expected her to jump up, to make some reproach at his not having visited her for so long, but she put a finger to her lip, and then with gentle hands covered the baby with a tiny knitted blanket. She disengaged herself, rolled away, kissed the baby, and stood up, smoothing her hair with one hand and arranging her head scarf.

"*Salaam*, Chaudrey Sahib," she said quietly. "Let me bring you some tea." She showed no surprise at seeing him.

Without waiting for an answer she went out. He leaned on his cane, looking down at the baby lying splayed on its face, dressed too warmly, in socks, a sweater, and a crocheted hat. Tiring, he sat down heavily on a chair. He loved her still, he realized, noting it, as if painfully writing something into a notebook. (Lately he often found himself doing this, inscribing his experiences and thoughts, his final record, in an invisible notebook, never able to find a pencil, holding the pad in the air and writing shakily, illegibly.) He had come here to abjure his great love, and he found just this—just a small room lit by a single bulb, chilly despite the sun outside, and the woman he loved sitting alone, putting to sleep this stolen child that he gave her. He finally understood that she lived a simple life, and a wave of pity came over him. He had imagined her moving quickly from task to task, and only now did he perceive how lonely she might have been, waiting for him in the past years, never knowing when he would arrive. She had made so little of his coming that it had not occurred to him that all her days must have been directed toward that moment.

She carried in the tea things, the milk in the pitcher steaming, the sugar bowl covered with an embroidered cloth. From the smugglers' market in Rawalpindi he had bought her this flowery tea set, kept unused on a shelf with her other good dishes. She was the only woman for whom he had ever brought presents. She placed the tray on a table by the bed, then sat down on the floor, at the edge of the carpet, with her knees drawn up and enclosed in her arms. She looked up at him, holding her chin on her knees. He noticed the kohl on her eyes.

"They tell me that you're dying," she said quietly, as if smoothing it away between them.

"Probably."

She rose up on her knees and poured him tea, sweetened it, and handed him the cup. Watching her settle back on her compact haunches, seated on the carpet, he understood that he would never

Daniyal Mueenuddin

again make love to her, never again hold her nor see her face when she woke in the morning. They talked of nothing, she told him of the baby's little tricks, asked him about the farm. It surprised him that she didn't ask about her own future, about property or money.

Finishing his tea, he rose, making an effort not to lean on the cane.

"Goodbye," he said, looking at her. As he reached the door, leaving her sitting on the floor, he realized that he couldn't do this, that he must say more, although he had told himself that he wouldn't. He remembered the morning when he married her, quietly signing the papers while sitting under the mulberry tree in the little courtyard of this house, with the sounds of the village in the background, goats and a radio playing a song and tractors driving down the street.

"I've told the boys to give you something after I'm gone," he said, without looking at her.

"Fine," she replied, in a clipped voice.

Both of them knew that this meant nothing.

He walked out under the big banyan, where Mustafa toiled over the jeep, polishing it. The managers stood to one side, not speaking to each other. Jaglani got into the jeep and offhandedly said goodbye forever.

IN THE NEXT few days Jaglani intended to do something for Zainab, to put a house in her name, for he had several in the city, or to give her a square of land. His children would anyway have so much, and after his death Zainab would be attacked from all sides, by the villagers and by his family. But his illness progressed very quickly, and the constant pain kept him from acting. He chose the path of least resistance, and his family ensured that this path always led to them and to the gratification of their interests. The papers ensuring their inheritance readily appeared whenever he had the impulse to sign

90

them, whereas other documents, those that did not suit the two sons, were delayed indefinitely. The sons had agreed not to fight among themselves, but to divide the property equally. They also agreed to prevent their father from making any other disposition.

The servants moved Jaglani's bed into the living room of his house. They removed the furniture, except for one sofa, placing the bed in the middle, with a table covered with medicines next to it. On the floor stood a tin bucket, and then, contrastingly, two thin oxygen cylinders almost as tall as a man, with dented steel bodies, nickel fittings, and a profusion of clear tubes feeding him air through a cannula pinched onto his nose, the apparatus setting him apart from those who now surrounded him. Day and night, one or another of the servants would press his arms and legs. Jaglani grew angry with the servants, making cruel and untrue accusations, that they were hurting him, that they had always stolen from him. One of Jaglani's patrons, Makhdoom Talwan, paid a visit, a great landowner of the district, toward whom he had always been deferential. Now, when this man entered the room, Jaglani started up and told him to go to hell, began shrieking about stolen votes and stolen water, until he couldn't speak and lay panting. The family bustled the great man away.

EVERY DAY, AT some moment when the room stood empty except for the servant on duty, Mustafa would come to pay his respects, one of the few people whom Jaglani looked on with kind eyes. Mustafa would remove his shoes and stand just inside the door with bare feet. Jaglani would call him forward, to stand beside the bed, and would say a few inconsequential words, asking about Dunyapur. Mustafa answered the questions very briefly and would stand beside him until he fell asleep.

Jaglani became weaker and angrier, until everyone wished he would die. One day he heard a commotion in the anteroom, raised

voices and doors slamming. Zainab had come, taking a *tonga* from
Dunyapur and then a bus, walking solitary up to the house, past the
gatekeeper, who had become slack and who watched her without
bothering even to get up from the chair where he sat smoking a
hookah. He knew her, for like all the servants Jaglani had chosen him
from the village.

The sick man heard her in the anteroom say to Shabir, the son,
who had rushed to intercept her, "Get your hands off me, you little
piece of shit. I'm his wife. Don't touch me." Jaglani reached painfully
and rang the bell on a cord that lay by his pillow. Shabir came in,
locking the door behind him.

"Tell her to go away," said the dying man. "I don't want to see her."
She had spoken in the most vulgar Punjabi, like women screaming
over the common wall of their village huts.

Lying alone, unable to sleep, Jaglani had for days been renouncing
Zainab. He had done wrong to his sons and to his senior wife, whom
he didn't love, had never loved. His first wife and his sons belonged
to another time, to his days of strength, when the world stood open
to him. He remembered the river, the way it glittered in his youth
and in his manhood. He married his first wife at seventeen, when he
still earned a salary of only forty rupees, and she rose with him, made
his meals, and now old, an image of his mother, wore smudged glasses
and with teary eyes stood over him when he ate. She would die soon,
would never again be happy. She hadn't been happy for years. Zainab
would go on, she had life in her, vitality, many years ahead. He didn't
want her to live on after him.

Mustafa took Zainab outside and walked her back through the
gates of the compound and out into the busy street, where no one
cared that Jaglani lay dying in the big house, or if they knew of it,
thought only of the changes to come, new men up, old men down,
Jaglani's adherents thrown down.

Zainab wept quietly and kept saying to herself, "And they didn't even offer me a cup of tea."

TWO NIGHTS LATER Jaglani died. The cancer had spread to his lymph nodes and to his brain, and he died in great pain, despite the morphine. A man from the city came and laid him out, bathing his body, tying his mouth shut with a strip of gauze. At the burial, held by custom before nightfall, the two sons stood next to Jaglani's patron, Makhdoom Talwan, the dominant landlord and politician in the district, a member of the National Assembly. Makhdoom Sahib said to Shabir, "So now it's your seat to lose in the by-election." Immediately after the burial his driver brought his big Land Cruiser jeep right up to the gates of the old cemetery, blocking the flow of mourners. Shaking hands with the two sons, looking with penetration at each of them, he drove away into the falling night, having said nothing more of the elections, offering no support.

Nevertheless, Shabir went to see the great man. Preparations for the by-election had begun in earnest, groups of men were gathering and going around together, forming alliances, bartering votes, but few people came to see Shabir, and the ones who did were lightweights. The gatekeeper at Makhdoom Talwan's house leapt up on seeing Jaglani's car, but Shabir found that the further he penetrated into the sanctum, the colder the reception he received. Talwan's personal assistant went so far as to suggest that Shabir should come back in the morning, at the time of general audience. Finally gaining admittance, Shabir was seated in a dark room and asked to wait. A servant brought him a glass of lemonade, then left him alone. Ten minutes later Makhdoom Sahib's enormous bulk pushed through the door, in an immaculate white *kurta* and a turban tied so that a flap hung down along the side of his head, fringed, like an egret's wing.

"Hello, young man," he said rather casually, sitting down heavily with a little puffing exhalation, smoothing his hands down his belly, as if brushing away crumbs. "So how are you? How are things settling out?"

He placidly asked a few questions, listened, seemed to approve when Shabir called him "Uncle." Then, at a pause in the conversation, just at the moment when Shabir was about to launch his plea, Makhdoom Sahib turned with a hard look.

"My boy, our friendly relations are one thing, politics are another. I want to give you an understanding of the position." He paused to think. "Let me tell you a story. You may remember Jam Rasheed, the famous chief minister of Sindh. He ran an entire province more strictly even than your father ran Dunyapur, with a whip made of good thick buffalo hide. Top to bottom everyone obeyed, and the ones who didn't died in police encounters or disappeared or lost their lands or their factories. Now, right at the height of his power, he arranged the wedding of his daughter. On his lands the Public Works people made a huge city of tents and pavilions for the guests—they spent crores of government money. Madam Noor Jahan came out of retirement, Nusrat played, everyone. The preparations were immense, on a royal scale.

"Jam Sahib had his creatures and creations, as such men do—freshly minted princes of industry and millionaire bureaucrats from humble families—and these gentlemen were made to understand that luxury vehicles, customized Mercedes limousines or the very latest models of jeep, would be acceptable gifts. The vehicles duly paraded in on the new-laid roads and were parked in a special compound, for all to see. Then, the second day into the festivities, while presiding over a magnificent dinner, Jam Sahib suddenly fell to the ground in front of the whole assembly. A stroke had left him incapable of speech and paralyzed on one side. That night, under cover of darkness, a strange procession slipped out from the tent city. The vehicles that had been brought as gifts crept away, never to be seen again by Jam Sahib or his daughter."

Makhdoom Talwan stood up. "Think about this story, and then think about your position. Your father is gone, but you're nevertheless a fortunate man, your father left you with a great deal of land and money. Enjoy what you have and learn to know your level. Most of all, don't let what now belongs to you be taken away. The first thing for you is to be safe. I'm speaking as your elder, and I offer you this counsel as repayment for the many years of support your father gave me. Goodbye."

A FEW DAYS later Makhdoom Talwan sent a group of lesser politicians to Shabir, requesting him to step aside during the by-election in favor of another man, a sleek lawyer from the city. They all promised to back Shabir in the next election, if he would just for now withdraw, and even prevailed upon him to take part in one of the lawyer's political meetings. The crowd, trucked in from the surrounding villages and in the mood for fun, munched on peanuts and sweets—for years on end the politicians ignored or abused the peasants, and then in election years the people abused the politicians. Called to the podium, removing his glasses from a case and putting them on, Shabir looked out on a shoal of grinning and unfriendly faces. He had barely begun his little speech, urging support for the lawyer, when someone in the back made a loud farting sound, silencing him. Two men, on far opposite sides of the crowd, began shouting back and forth to each other.

"Hello brother. What do you have there?" bellowed one of them.

The other man held up an enormous cucumber. "Do you know what they say? The world is like a cucumber. Today it's in your hand, tomorrow it's up your ass."

"Now that, my friend, is pure poetry. Kind of a metaphor—

something you're sharing with the honorable speaker up on the stage, I suppose."

The two went on in the same vein until finally the lawyer-candidate stood up and took Shabir by the arm, hustling him off the podium and toward the cars, apologizing and saying they would definitely find out who had arranged this outrage, get to the bottom of it no matter where the trail led, and punish the guilty ones thoroughly.

As he was driven out of the stadium, Shabir's skin crawled with shame, his face itched, and in order to relieve the silence he drummed with his fingers on the windowsill. His eyes were unwillingly drawn to Mustafa's opaque expressionless face—this sole companion of his father's triumphs. "First thing tomorrow," he promised himself, "I'm going to fire this man."

About a Burning Girl

am a sessions judge in the Lahore High Court. I should tell you
at the start, so that you understand my position regarding these
events, that despite my profession I don't believe in justice, am no
longer consumed by a desire to be what in law school we called "a
sword of the Lord"; nor do I pretend to have perfectly clean hands, so
am not in a position to view the judicial system with anything except
a degree of tolerance. I render decisions based on the relative pres-
sures brought to bear on me.

A few more words about myself. My wife, to put it in the clearest
terms, is a shrew. She quite truthfully insists that without her I would
still be a lawyer without briefs, roaming the courts looking for clients,
or clamoring at the bar and groveling at the feet of judges whose
greatest ambition, when they wake each morning, is to sell themselves for a good price. The car I drive is another of my trials. I fit
inside of it like an orangutan in a shipping cage; but for the moment,
on a gazetted salary of fourteen thousand rupees, I do not presume
to get a bigger one. The British built the large but run-down house

in which I am quartered. My wife got this residence allotted to us by spending a month camped in the living room of her second cousin, a deputy additional secretary, and our greatest fear is that someone senior to me will see it and covet it and take it. I look out on the little brown lawn, without flowers, for we don't wish to make too much of a show by hiring gardeners, and hear my brats making a mess behind me, and such are my evenings.

There are three servants in my house, a cook, a sweepress, and a bearer. All three have the mute expression of servants in a modest household such as mine: lordly dishonest valets, the sort who are immune to colds but are martyrs to dyspepsia, work for ampler men than me. I believe the cook has a *setting*, as they say, with the sweepress, although he has a wife and children somewhere up by Kohat. The bearer, named Khadim, is a boy of twenty, from one of the villages in the valleys near Abbotabad. He has no personality whatsoever. He cleans, takes care of the children, washes the car, waters the few plants arranged along the driveway, brings lunch in a tiffin carrier to my office, lays out my clothes, and does all this with a lugubrious expression consistent with the tone of the house, which smells of cooking and damp walls, and which my wife has decorated with small glass objects, a constant source of discord, for the children are always breaking them. The bearer is gentle in a bovine sort of way and he works at half speed but consistently. He has no opinions and no dissipations, at least that I know of, although as a judge I am often amazed by the behaviors of seemingly mild people. In short, he is the ideal servant.

Khadim is permitted one week's vacation each year, which he spends at his village up in the mountains. One day I came from the office, went for my walk in the Lawrence Gardens—I've put on weight—and settled down with the paper. The boy brought the tea, straightened the napkin, asked if he should pour me a cup, and generally drew attention to himself. He wouldn't leave, and finally I looked at him over my glasses, a habit I've acquired in the courtroom, and asked if he wished to say something.

"Sir, I must go home," he said.

The "must" sank in. "Perhaps," I said, "you don't feel the need any longer for your position in this household?"

"I haven't been home for many months, sir. My mother isn't well."

"I see, a supplement to her annual illness. I don't care, go ask the lady of the house—though it won't do any good."

Strangely, she agreed, though she usually requires months of notice before giving leave to the servants. I hardly know how he earned this great dispensation—nor do I care. The boy is handsome; and you need only see her disjoint a roast chicken to know the depths or heights of her carnality. (Thinking back almost twenty years to our first little house, the bare rooms and the kisses—kisses!—I bestowed on her, I consider how little I knew this iron lady, or knew myself for that matter.)

TWO DAYS LATER I received a phone call from the boy's brother, a useless sort of fellow who periodically comes to Lahore and sponges off the kitchen.

"And how, I ask, do you presume to interrupt me in my chambers?"

"Sir, forgive me. Khadim is in Abbotabad jail for the murder of my wife. He is accused of pouring kerosene over her and setting it aflame."

"Ah, well." I paused, thinking. "That's an old story. The exploding stove. What can I do about it?"

"Sir, Khadim served you since before he began shaving. The police are under pressure to beat him."

"I suppose he'll confess."

No reply.

I told the brother to take the next bus for Lahore and rang off.

WHEN I WOKE next morning, no eggs. The cook had not got them. He told me that Khadim always bought the eggs. I sat eating toast with marmalade, poured a second cup of tea, and then picked up the *Pakistan Times* and took its crisp virginity, inhaling the scent of damp ink and newsprint. I enjoy this paper because it gives me absolutely no information except that which is sponsored by the government. It never disrupts my morning.

Shaved and showered, glistening, as I like to think of myself, I paid my respects to my wife, who lies in bed each morning, sipping tea and planning operations for the day ahead, and then proceeded out into the verandah where the car stood in the cool gloom. The key to my mornings is order. Thus, I went out precisely five minutes earlier than usual, in order to speak with Khadim's brother, who as I expected stood waiting for me.

This man is of a type I often encounter in my courtroom, distinguished by a glossy mustache, excessively clean and pressed clothes, and a battered and invariably maroon-colored portfolio held in one hand, from which he produces volumes of papers to bolster his arguments, papers that only further confuse the matter. One of my small indulgences, now that I am a member of the judiciary, is to allow myself airs with people who need favors from me. I gave him my hand with a loose wrist, as if expecting him to kiss it, and stood on one cocked heel.

He began to make the usual obeisance, asking after madam, the children, my health.

I cut him off. "Yes, yes. So tell me what happened. I only have a few minutes." (An enormity! I intended to spend the morning, as I often do, drinking tea and being really thorough about reading the rest of the newspaper. My personal secretary does most of my work.)

"There was a robbery in my family's house, Your Honor."

"And what did you lose?"

"All my father's money."

This could hardly come to much. The boy's father cooks for some landlord family, a type I know well—all punctilio and no pence. The servants in those households have the rapacity of vultures. Still, how much could he have pocketed?

"Amounting to . . . ?"

"Three hundred thousand rupees and four sets of gold jewelry."

My god, I thought. The old man should have been a policeman, not a cook. That's a good sum to pack away, even if the master is a fool.

"But of course. The fruits of long and faithful service, no doubt?"

The man said nothing but only looked at his feet.

After letting him stew for a long moment, I asked, "And what happened?"

"Sir, my father worked for the same people for fifty years. He put away money, and with some of it he bought gold, and he kept all of it in a tin trunk in the house he built in our village, hidden among seven trunks full of clothes."

"Where all of you left behind kept a close eye on it. But not close enough."

"Yes, sir. As you know, sir." He held his hands crossed in front of him, one holding the maroon portfolio. I decided to let him tell the story, and to spare him the peppering of questions that I often use when reducing idiots like this to absurdities.

"Well, sir, one morning we woke up, that would be Tuesday, two days ago, and someone had broken into the trunks, which we kept in a little kitchen, and had taken the money and the jewels. The police came and asked some questions—we phoned them as soon as we found out the loot was gone. At the end they talked to my wife, the deceased, but they hadn't finished before dark. There's no good road to our village, way up in the mountains, and they left, saying they'd be back the next day.

"That night as usual we went to sleep on the terrace in front of the house. In the middle of the night I woke and there was my wife sitting on the ground next to me. Beside her the empty bottle of kerosene, and in her hand the match that set her on fire. A painful sight, Your Honor, just burning like fireworks. She had committed suicide. I ran to get help from the neighbors. In front of the house there's a steep slope, and she fell down this, flames right up into the trees, and then she finally fell down on the ground, on her side, kind of spinning around with her legs, like a clock's hands. When I returned she wasn't even human, covered with sticky fluid, but she was still alive. We carried her to the road and then took a loader truck to the hospital in Abbotabad. She just would not die. A few hours later her father and brother came, and brought some policeman. The policeman registered a false statement from her, saying that Khadim set her on fire, and now he's sitting in jail. Her family paid the police to beat him, but we also paid, so they've done nothing so far but kick him around a bit."

"Hmm," I said, putting my joined hands to my lips to indicate deep thought. "So, how many rooms in your house?"

"Two, and then the terrace where we sleep in the summer."

"Were the trunks locked?"

"Yes, sir."

"And how many people were sleeping on the terrace on the night the trunks were rifled?"

"All of us. Me, my wife, my brother—he'd just arrived that night on leave from Your Honor's house—and his wife, and five children."

"And of course the same people were there the night of the suicide."

"Yes sir."

"What really happened?"

He offered a little sigh before plunging in, as if regretting the folly of the world.

"My wife and her brother, who lives in the next village, stole the money. I wouldn't have thought it of her, sir. She is, or was, very weak, weak in the head. The police scared her, and she got afraid of what they'd do to her. Plain fear and shame is what it was. Everyone knows what happens to women in prison."

"And what are you suggesting I do?"

"Sir, you are a judge, if you say a word to your fellow judge in Abbotabad, he will see the true merits of the case. Khadim has eaten your salt."

"And who will pay for all this? The judge, no matter how well disposed to me, will need to be oiled if he is to work. And then you'll need a lawyer, court fees, tips to the judge's readers, and most of all, something really magnificent for the police."

"My father works for Mr. K. K. Harouni's nephew, up in Islamabad. You must know them, sir. His wife is American, and she already promised to help in whatever way she can."

"Oh yes, I know of the Harounis. Excellent. Your father works for the proverbial foolish son of a rich father. Enough. For me, as you know, this is a family matter. Tell your father to come see me. And go back to your home. Call me the day after tomorrow, at ten in the morning, exactly."

Turning, I walked to the car. He trotted after me, no longer so composed, and as I opened the door he fell to the ground and put his hands on my feet.

I raised him up. "I'm going to ask you two questions, but I don't want you to answer them. First, in a house of two rooms how could someone break into seven trunks without being heard? Merely knock on a trunk made of tin, much less break its lock, and it resounds like thunder. Second, why didn't you try to put out the flames? Your wife must have burned for a long time, and she must have been scream-ing bloody murder throughout, so that you can't possibly have slept through it. Her first screams should have woken you, before she so badly injured herself. Why go for the neighbors instead of helping her? Think about it."

WHEN I RETURNED punctually at five from the office, my wife called me into the living room, where she sat with an old lady, one of her projects, someone from whom she wanted something. Judg-ing from the guest's enormous Land Cruiser parked in the verandah, she must be the wife of a *big fish*. This is the phrase; also, a *big gun*. Imagine my wife as being the poor man's Lady Macbeth and you will have the entire picture.

The guest went away, having been stroked to a silky fineness, and my wife turned her eyes, now in repose, upon me.

"What word from Khadim? Any news?"

I explained as briefly as I could.

"And what shall we do?"

"First of all I suppose we should spread some of young Harouni's money around. A fool and his money, etc. Second, it is of course no suicide. *Somebody* murdered the poor woman. The police have a deathbed confession. False or not, he'll hang for it."

"No, no," she said, tossing aside the facts. "Nonsense. Good servants are impossible to find." She thought for a minute. "You must, and you will immediately, send Mian Sarkar."

And so, the next morning my reader, Mian Sarkar, lambskin cap, imitation leather briefcase, spectacles, and three-piece suit, boarded the air-conditioned bus to Abbotabad, a ten-hour journey. He would only have done it for her.

· · ·

THE TWO STEEDS pulling my career rapidly forward along the treacherous road of the Pakistani judiciary are my wife and Mian Sarkar. Each is, in a different sphere, absolutely matchless. My wife you already know. Mian Sarkar deserves not merely a thumbnail but a biography in two volumes—if it were possible to find out anything at all about him except his present rank and station. So far as I am aware, Mian Sarkar wore a cheap three-piece suit and a pair of slightly tinted spectacles of an already outmoded design on the day that he emerged from his mother's womb. When he leaves the office in the evening, exactly at five, he doesn't turn a corner or get into a cab or a bus, he simply dematerializes. No one knows even what quarter of the city he lives in, much less his address. He drinks nothing but milk, one careful glassful each day at lunch, and because of his digestion he eats each day only a single cheese sandwich, on white untoasted bread, with the crust cut off, brought to him by a boy from a tea stall. They must stock the cheese for him especially. Before speaking he clears his throat with a little hum, as if pulling his voice box up from some depth where he secretes it for safekeeping. His greatest feature, however, is his nose, a fleshy tubular object, gorged with blood, which I have always longed to squeeze, expecting him to honk like a bus.

That would be a fatal act! There is nothing connected with the courts of Lahore that he has not absorbed, for knowledge in this degree of detail can only be obtained by osmosis. Everything about the private lives of the judges, and of the staff, down to the lowest sweeper, is to him incidental knowledge. He knows the verdicts of the cases before they have been written, before they even have been conceived. He sees the city panoptically, simultaneously, and if he does not disclose the method and the motive and the culprit responsible for each crime, it is only because he is more powerful if he does not do so. Locked in his impenetrable bosom are all the riots and iniquities of the past, and perhaps of the future, and when his mild figure steps out of the law courts of an evening and is lost in the crowds along the Mall, I am irrationally reminded of Lenin disembarking at the Finland Station in 1917. He is a man of secret powers, and a mover of great events. This is the bacillus my wife sent to resolve Khadim's case as she wanted it resolved. Mightier men than I fear him.

THE NEXT EVENING, when I drove through the gate of my house, a sagging wooden affair once painted green, once perhaps in colonial days a swing for little English children, I found an old man standing by the portico with the timeless patience of peasants and old servants, as if he had been standing there all day. He wore a battered white skullcap, soiled clothes, a sleeveless sweater, and shoes with crepe rubber soles, worn down on one side, which gave each foot a peculiar tilt. The deep lines on his face ran in no rational order, no order corresponding to musculature or to the emotions through which his expressions might pass, but spread from numerous points. The oversized head had settled heavily onto the shoulders, like a sand castle on the beach after the sea has run in over it.

I opened the car door, closed it carefully, and rounded upon him. He put his head down, looking up at me under his brows, and quickly and pathetically saluted me, with a hand balled together.

"*As-salaam uleikum*, Baba," I said.

"*Salaam*, Sahib."

"You are the father of Khadim."

"Yes, Your Honor."

By his language and his manner I knew him to be a serving man of the old type, of the type that believes implicitly in his master's right to be served. They are impossible to get now, unless you own land and bring a man from your own village, and even then you have to choose a simpleton, a real feudal peasant.

I waited, but he said nothing. "You've come," I volunteered, "about your boy? You wish me to intervene?"

"You can do anything, sir. I don't understand. They took my money, sir, all of it. I'll starve to death."

"Who took your money?"

"God knows, sir."

"What happened?"

"My daughter-in-law, she became insane. She killed herself."

"What should I do, how can I help?"

"The girl's family, if they agree the police will release my boy."

"And will they agree?"

"Never, sir, not in a thousand years."

I began to lose patience. "What about the girl's statement that Khadim killed her?"

"The father told her to. They told her to." He began sobbing, his face long and dark like a cab horse in the rain. His shoulders shook but no tears came to his eyes and he didn't raise his hands, which hung at his side.

"O God, O God, I'll starve, I'll die, I want to die."

I couldn't bear it, I put my arm around him. He reminded me of the old man who brought me up, whose lap held me, who had callused hands and wore a ring with a cheap red stone, who took me to the zoo and showed me the deer, put me on his shoulders so that I could see over the fence.

"Don't cry, Baba, don't cry." I felt embarrassed. "Your boy will be all right."

"He's a good boy, he's the only one, the other is no good." He wiped his eyes, now full of flat tears, like splashed water. "They took my money," he sobbed, head bowed.

"Wait, one moment. Is your master really willing to lay out a lot of cash?" I had to ask.

"I've served fifty-eight years, for the big sahib and now the small one."

"Go in back," I said. "They'll give you some tea. I'll fix it."

He walked away from me without shaking my hand, without thanking me, his shoulders fallen, shuffling, still crying.

THE NEXT MORNING but one Mian Sarkar came into my office at his usual time, as always arriving exactly five minutes after I did, and seated himself primly at his desk. (Arriving after me, although by this same small margin, is his one extravagance.) He did not open the files arranged in front of him, though he would answer with exactitude any question I might presume to put to him about them.

I treat him always with the greatest refinements of courtesy. "Mian Sarkar, I trust you had a comfortable journey?"

"The roads might be better, sir."

"Indeed. And on returning you found everything well in your home?"

"No surprises, sir."

"Of course."

I retreated into my chambers, in order not to seem impatient. Half an hour later I called him in.

"Mian Sarkar," I began, "would you be so kind as to explain the situation in . . . what was the name of the village?"

"Parian, sir." Putting his hands on his knees, which he held clamped together, he cleared his throat. He has a habit of sitting always at the edge of his seat, as if at any moment prepared to spring up. "To be brief, sir, the deceased did not commit suicide. She was killed. The boy, however, is not the murderer, although he was present and did not interfere."

"Excellent, or rather, good. And the—"

"The husband killed her. As always there had been trouble in the family. The old man threatened to remove his money and to retire in Islamabad. The elder brother called the younger home, in order that they might steal the money together and neither feel compelled to take the father's side. Husbands and wives all took part in the theft. Of course I entertained no doubt that the sons had stolen the treasure and murdered the girl. Only the question of why they killed her remained. The harsh method they selected to practice upon her I left aside as immaterial.

"The facts presented themselves as follows. The police, who had been called by the brothers merely to conduct a pro forma investigation of the theft, saw the possibility of exploiting the situation, of taking the lion's share of the stolen goods, and began to act with unwonted energy. When the husband saw his wife breaking down under questioning, he prepared an elaborate dinner with which he lured the constables away, urging them to continue their inquiry the next morning. They acquiesced, sensing an opportunity to negotiate in private. That evening the boys decided to kill her. Not only must they silence her, they also needed a victim, someone to whom they could ascribe the theft, and who would not talk. They panicked. Criminals are fools. The husband was the prime mover. He is, sir, a nefarious fellow. A man of very poor morals."

"Undoubtedly." I paused, not wishing to seem importunate. "Would it be indiscreet to ask how you unraveled this, and unraveled it so quickly?"

"Options, sir. For every lock there is a key. Take hold of your man, sir, and give him options. Contrary to popular belief, there is no honor among thieves. The elder brother quite expected young Khadim to be presented with the black warrant and to swing. He of course would thereby reap the younger brother's share. The victim's deathbed statement went against him, and in these inflationary times to escape murder charges is ruinously expensive. I explained to the gentleman, however, that if the unfortunate death were to be called a murder, neither you nor the generous Mr. Sohail Harouni would allow the younger brother to absorb the blame. The younger was after all the father's favorite. Why then, I asked him rhetorically, shouldn't the less favored one make the sacrifice? In Pakistan all things can be arranged—and surely the girl's family could be mollified. That evening he came and laid open to me not only his heart but also his overflowing purse."

After pausing again, in order to let this sink in, I asked, "And so, what is the solution?"

"I took the liberty of making inquiries regarding the willingness of the deceased's family to settle the case. It seems they were attached to the girl and wish to see the young man hang. They nominated him as the subject of the alleged deathbed confession because he is the most beloved of the father's offspring. They want blood rather than gold."

"That looks bad."

"Madam most particularly desires to retain the services of the young man. I had money in hand. It happened that the district superintendent of police and I became well acquainted, almost in fact as if we had grown up in the same village, as he rather poetically phrased it. He had informed me already of the costly treatments his aged mother was undergoing—a heartbreaking tale. His men belatedly reported that they did not distinctly hear the confession, due to the extent of the deceased's injuries. This confession is the only evidence linking the boy to the murder.

"I also happened to strike up a second acquaintance. A respected doctor from Abbotabad, another similarly disposed though less effusive friend, happened to be in the hospital that night, and this gentleman suddenly recalled that he had looked into the room where the woman lay. He is willing to testify that due to her burns, which covered ninety percent of her body, and which had incinerated her cheeks, her lips, her teeth, her tongue, and even her gums, there is not the remotest possibility that she could speak. Furthermore, he testi-fies that she would not have been in her right mind at the time."

"How dreadful!" I interjected, and Mian Sarkar cast his hooded eyes upon me, as if to say, Ah! Pieties!

"And so . . ."

"Judge Aftar will preside over the case. He graduated from the Academy five years after you did. His wife is second cousin to Mrs. Arafa, Brigadier Kuloo's niece, who came under obligation to madam, your honor's wife, at the time of Bibi Kamo's death—you recall, I am sure, the dancing master and the emeralds. In any case, you may wish to speak with the judge."

And that, of course, is exactly what I did.

In Other Rooms, Other Wonders

Husna needed a job. She stole up the long drive to the Lahore house of the retired civil servant and landlord K. K. Harouni, bearing in her little lacquered fingers a letter of introduction from, of all people, his estranged first wife. The butler, knowing that Husna served the old Begum Harouni in an indefinite capacity, somewhere between maidservant and companion, did not seat her in the living room. Instead he put her in the office of the secretary, who every afternoon took down in shorthand a few pages of Mr. Harouni's memoirs, cautiously titled *Perhaps This Happened.*

Ushered into the living room by the secretary after a quarter of an hour, Husna gazed around her, as petitioners do, more tense than curious, taking in the worn gold brocade on the sofa, a large Chinese painting of horsemen over the rosewood mantel. Her attention was drawn to ranks of black-and-white photographs in silver frames, hunters wearing shooting caps posed with strings of birds or piles of game, several of women in saris, their hair piled high in the style of the fifties, one in riding breeches, with an oversized dedication in looping script. To the side stood a photo of Harouni in a receiving line shaking the hand of a youthful Jawaharlal Nehru.

The door opened, and Mr. Harouni walked in, a mild look on his handsome golden face. Placing a file on the table in front of him, the secretary flipped through the pages and showed the old man where to sign, murmuring, "Begum Sahiba has sent this young miss with a letter, sir."

ALTHOUGH HE HAD an excellent memory, and knew the lineage of all the old Lahore families, K.K. allowed Husna to explain in detail her relation to him, which derived from his grandmother on his mother's side. The senior branch of the family consolidated its lands and amassed power under the British, who made use of the landowning gentry to govern. Husna's family, a cadet branch, had not so much fallen into poverty as failed to rise. Her grandfather had still owned thirty or forty shops in the Lahore Old City, but these were sold off before the prices increased, when Lahore grew in the 1950s and 1960s. Encouraged by K.K., given tea and cakes, Husna forgot herself, falling into the common, rich Punjabi of the inner city. She told with great emphasis a story about her mother, who remembered having fallen and broken her teeth on the steps leading into the courtyard of a lost family home, which were tall and broad to accommodate the enormous tread of a riding elephant, emblematic of the family's status.

Husna was silent for a moment, then narrowed her eyes, collected herself. "In this world some families rise and some fall," she said, suddenly cold rather than postulant. "And now I've come to you for help. I'm poor and need a job. Even Begum Harouni agrees that I should have a profession. My father can give me nothing, he's weak and has lost his connections. Everyone says I should marry, but I won't."

• • •

OUTSIDE THE DRAWING room, overlooking a side patio, a gardener switched on yard lights, illuminating a cemented swimming pool half filled with rainwater and leaves. A servant came in with an armful of wood, threw it with a crash into the fireplace, then took a bottle of kerosene and poured a liberal splash. He threw in a match and the fire roared up. For a minute he sat on his haunches by the fire, grave before this immemorial mystery, then broke the spell, rose, and left the room.

A car drove into the long circular driveway, and a brushed-looking elderly couple entered the room. Coming up and kissing Harouni on the cheek, the woman said in a husky voice, "Hello, darling." The man, gray beside his brightly dressed companion, mustache trimmed, waited to one side.

"Hello, Riffat," said Harouni, kissing her on the top of the head and then going over to the wall and pressing a bell. "Will you have a drink, Husky?"

The man glanced at his wife. "I'll have a small whiskey."

The woman eyed Husna, as if pricing her, and Husna shrank into herself. She hadn't been prepared for this. The visitor wore a pinkish *kurta*, too young for her but certainly very expensive, finely printed with a silver design.

"This is Husna," said K.K. to the woman, who had taken a seat on the sofa beside the young girl. "Husna will graduate soon and is looking for a teaching position."

"How interesting," said the woman, her voice confiding and smoky.

They had been speaking in English, and Husna exposed her poor accent, saying, "It is very good to meet you."

Two servants carried in a tea trolley and placed it before the newcomer, and Rafik, the butler who had seated Husna in the secretary's office, brought two whiskeys on a small silver tray.

"Cheers," said Husky, taking a sip and very slightly smacking his lips. "How nice to have a fire."

Riffat Begum poured out tea, offering a cup to Husna. The conversation wandered, and Riffat looked meaningfully at Husna once or twice. When she went out in society with Begum Harouni, Husna was not a guest, not even really a presence, but a recourse for the old lady, to fetch and carry, to stay beside her so that the begum would not be left sitting alone. Unable now to meet the occasion, Husna followed the conversation from face to face, sinking, the skin around her mouth taut as if frozen. Abruptly she stood up, catching a foot on the tea trolley, rattling the cups and saucers.

"Thank you, Uncle, for your help and your kind advice," she said, although K.K. had given her no advice whatsoever. She meant this as an opening to him, at least as a reproach.

"Let me have the car drop you." He followed Husna out into the verandah, while the driver brought the car. "First of all, you need to develop some skills," he said. "Why don't you learn to type? Come tomorrow and I'll arrange for Shah Sahib to give you lessons."

As she got in the car he gave her a fatherly kiss on the cheek.

When he returned to the living room, Riffat raised an eyebrow and pursed her lips. "Naughty naughty," she said, exhaling a cloud of cigarette smoke.

K.K. took a sip of whiskey. "At my age, my dear, she's in no danger."

HUSNA CAME EVERY few days for typing lessons. She would sit in the dark little office off the living room, inconveniencing Shah Sahib, the secretary, who could not continue his own work till she had abandoned her weak efforts. He tried to show her the correct technique, but she refused to learn, and insisted upon typing by hunt and peck, getting through her daily half page as quickly as possible. One of the servants would bring her a cup of mixed tea, which she drank with Shah Sahib, who also at that time received two slices of grilled cheese toast, a treat that made his stomach growl, and one that he ensured by being of service to the cook, passing his bills without question.

K. K. Harouni, who had been a polo and tennis player until he suffered a heart attack seven years earlier, took a walk morning and evening, totaling exactly four miles each day. Usually he went from end to end of the serpentine back garden, but a few days after Husna began her lessons, a winter rain wet the grass. Mildly enjoying the break in routine, that evening he walked on the brick-paved front driveway, looping around a circular lawn and through a carport in which a misplaced glass chandelier cast a friendly yellow light.

At dusk he heard a rickshaw enter the drive and park at the far end, next to the gatekeeper's shelter, its two-stroke engine crackling. After a moment a figure stepped from the door of the secretary's office and tripped rapidly down toward the gate. Lengthening his stride, K.K. came up behind her.

"Hello, Husna," he said.

She stopped and turned. As before, she wore too much makeup and clothes too bright. She held her large white purse on a long chain over one shoulder, and had covered her hair with a *dupatta*. "Hello, Uncle," she said, her face involuntarily stretching into a broad smile.

"You're very cheerful. And how are your lessons?"

"Thank you, Uncle," she said.

"Why don't you walk with me?"

"My ride is waiting." She spoke timidly, for she felt ashamed to be seen taking a rickshaw, which only poor people used.

"Tell him to go, and later the driver can take you."

• • •

THEY BEGAN WALKING, Husna taking two strides to every one of his, clicking along in her heels. Her feet began to hurt, and whenever they came to a puddle he would step aside and allow her to go first, so that she had to hurry awkwardly in front of him.

"Those shoes aren't good for walking," he said, looking at her from behind as she skirted a puddle. "Your feet are hurting, aren't they?"

"No, it's fine, really it is." She didn't want to lose this chance of his company.

"Why don't you take them off. Don't be shy, there's no one here."

"You're joking with me, Uncle."

Hesitating for a moment, she reached down and undid the straps, her hand tentatively on his shoulder.

When they came to the next puddle, he stopped, amused. "And now that you're barefoot, let's see you jump over the puddle."

Quickening, she glanced at him sideways, still a girl at twenty, still playing tag with her cousins in the courtyard of her parents' home; and yet now aware of men's eyes flickering over her as she walked through the lanes of the Old City.

He took her hand and swung it. "One, two, three, over you go!"

She hesitated for moment, refusing the jump, then leapt, landing just at the edge and splashing.

"Try again, the second one!" he urged, and she jumped the next puddle, clearing it with a bump, then turning to face him, laughing.

"Well done! I've had ponies that couldn't do as well."

"Now you *are* joking with me."

RAFIK CAME OUT to the drive and reported a telephone call from K.K.'s youngest daughter, Sarwat, who was married to a tremendously wealthy industrialist and lived in Karachi. He went inside, walking unhurriedly, and Husna sat down in one of the chairs placed in the verandah for the petitioners who came each morning, asking the old man for letters to government officials or asking for work on his farms.

Rafik stood next to her, relaxed, looking out into the night. He glanced at her bare feet but made no comment.

"So, Husna Bibi," he said, "how are the good people over at Begum Sahib's house? How is Chacha Latif?"

Chacha Latif played the corresponding role of butler in the house of K.K.'s estranged wife, and Rafik maintained cordial relations with him. As a matter of comity they kept each other informed of household gossip.

Understanding this oblique reference to the fact that Chacha Latif treated her with little ceremony, as an equal, Husna sweetly replied, "He's well, Uncle, thank you."

"Give him my regards, young lady," said Rafik, settling the matter.

K. K. Harouni came out and resumed walking with Husna. Finishing two measured miles, twenty rounds, he invited her to dinner, asking for it on a trolley in the living room, which would be less intimidating for her.

AS SHE RODE home in the back seat of K.K.'s large if old car, looking at the back of the chauffeur's immense head, Husna's complex thoughts ran along several lines. Given to fits of crushing gray lassitude and then to sunny, almost hysterical moments, she had always believed she would escape the gloominess of her parents' house in an unfashionable part of the city. She would escape the bare concrete steps, layered with dust, leading up into rooms without windows, the walls painted bright glossy colors, as if to make up for the gloom, the television covered with an embroidered cloth. She had spoiled herself with daydreams, until her parents were afraid of her moods.

She despised them for living so much in the past, retelling the stories of their grandparents' land and money, and yet at the same time she felt entitled to rejoin that world and felt aggrieved for being excluded from it. Her pride took the form of stubbornness—like others who rise above their station, she refused to accept her present status. Taking service in an ambiguous position with Begum Harouni had been the greatest concession she ever made to her mediocre prospects, and having made this concession increased her determination to rise, although she had no idea how to go about it.

Husna knew that she could never hope to marry or attract a young man from one of the rich established families. Wearing clothes just better than those of a maidservant, she saw them from a distance at the weddings to which she accompanied Begum Harouni. At that time, in the 1980s, the old barons still dominated the government, the prime minister a huge feudal landowner. Their sons, at least the quick ones, the adapted ones, became ministers at thirty, immaculate, blowing through dull parties, making an appearance, familiar with their elders, on their way to somewhere else, cool rooms where ice and alcohol glowed on the table, those rooms where deals were made; as she imagined them blowing through foreign airports, at ease in European cities that she read about. She would even have sought a place in the demimonde of singers and film actresses, bright and dangerous creatures from poor backgrounds—no upper-class woman would dream of entering those professions—but she had neither talent nor beauty. Only determination and cunning distinguished her, invisible qualities.

The chauffeur, knowing without being told that Husna would not wish to be seen coming home late at night in the old man's car, dropped her just inside the gate of the house in fashionable Gulberg. K.K. gave this house to his wife when finally and uncharacteristically he made a firm decision and told her she must leave. Unable to keep Harouni's attention, barely out of *purdah*, she had tried amulets, philters, spells—he joked to his friends that she would end up poisoning him by accident. But one day she came into the verandah off his bedroom, where he and a lady friend were having tea and innocently playing rummy. A woman with a sharp temper, she stood humped and spitting in Punjabi, "Leave my house, leave my husband alone, you witch!" And Harouni's friend, a convent-schooled society woman who barely spoke Punjabi and had only a vague idea who this lady might be, kept asking, "But what's she saying, K.K.? Should I leave?" He had not, however, divorced his wife, having no intention of remarrying and no desire to humiliate her. Old Begum Harouni thereafter lived in a state of suspended equilibrium, hoping to be recalled to her husband's side. She would naturally have been furious to learn that Husna had just eaten dinner alone with K.K.

Husna cautiously walked up the straight, long drive, bordered with bougainvillea and jasmine. She went to the back, where the servants lay in a courtyard under blankets, and slipped through the open kitchen door, through the filthy kitchen, which smelled of garlic and curry, and into the heavily carpeted dining room. Over the fireplace, which had not been lit in years, she saw her face in a mirror. The irregularity of her features, her straight, dry hair, her small mouth, all caused her to cringe inwardly and suddenly to feel vulnerable, to feel the stupidity of a few remembered comments that escaped her that evening. She felt the immensity of her encounter with K. K. Harouni. The old lady didn't wake when Husna crept in, but almost at dawn called her, saying she couldn't sleep, and told the young girl to massage her legs.

HUSNA CONTINUED GOING for lessons, and thrice in the first weeks walked with K.K., who then sent her home in the car. She tried to limit these encounters, fearing that Begum Harouni would discover the growing relationship and would send her away, back to her parents.

On the days when she allowed herself to see him, Husna would sit in the office after the secretary left, beside a window that overlooked the long garden where K.K. walked. She didn't read, but sat at the desk surrounded by books both in English and Urdu, her chin resting on her hands. She did not even plan, but floated through images.

Seeing a girl her age stepping from a large new car in Liberty Market, among the expensive shops, or glittering in a pair of diamond drops at a wedding, Husna's mind would hang on these symbols of wealth, not letting go for hours. She sensed that all this might come to her through Harouni, if she became his mistress. In the Old City where she grew up, the neighborhood pointed with shaming fingers at women from less than respectable families who were kept by merchants. The eyes of these creatures glided over the crowd as they rode on *tongas*, emerging untouched from dark streets where sewage flowed in the drain, prominent as targets in brightest red silk, lipstick, gold. Husna's mother ground out remarks of the price to be paid, broken relations with family, broken old age.

The young girl's fear of Harouni had dissipated, and she let herself be seen, critical, quick-witted, sensual, and slightly crude. Not despite but because of his sophistication, he found her manner piquant. She behaved and spoke unlike the women he normally met, for she had always inhabited an indefinite space, neither rich nor poor, neither servant nor begum, in a city where the very concept of a middle class still found expression only in a few households, managers of foreign banks and of the big industrial concerns, sugar and textiles and steel. As a boy Harouni slept with maidservants; lost his virginity to one of them at fourteen. Husna evoked those ripe first encounters.

SIX WEEKS AFTER Husna's first walk with K.K., Begum Harouni announced a pilgrimage to the holy places, in order to perform the *hajj*. Husna decided that evening to bring the begum's impending departure into the conversation, before guests came and interrupted them. She had begun to understand the management of the old man, how to introduce subjects.

When he entered the living room for afternoon tea, K.K. heard the typewriter clacking in the background. It stopped, and then Husna knocked, opened the door, showed her head without entering.

"Come in, my dear."

Her cultivation of the butler Rafik had progressed, to the point that, without being asked, he included an extra cup on the tea trolley. She drew herself forward and made K.K.'s tea exactly as he liked it. A boy passed a plate of biscuits, while Rafik stood back on his heels by the door.

"When I'm here," said Husna, "everything is so nice and everyone is pleasant. These biscuits, the tea. Shah Sahib tries so hard to teach me the typing, though I can't seem to learn." She held out her hands and spread the fingers in front of him, like a cat stretching. "My hands are so tiny, I can't reach the keys. But then all of me is small."

She wore a fitted *kurta*, showing the cleft of her breasts, which jutted out from her muscular youthful torso. Their eyes met; they both saw the joke, and he allowed himself a tight-lipped smile, his normally placid expression becoming knowing and avid.

"That's what I've been telling you about," purred Husna, putting her hand on his arm. "Your crocodile smile, the one I like."

After pausing for a moment to clear the air, she lowered her eyes and said in a meek voice, "But soon I won't be able to come here. The begum is going on *hajj*, so I'll have to be in charge of her house."

"Not *hajj* again!" said K.K. "It's becoming a vice with her. But darling, don't be ridiculous. If she's away you can come even more regularly."

"When the begum is gone they don't cook any food at all, just the servants' food. I go sometimes into the bazaar to eat. And Begum Sahiba doesn't like me to use the electricity."

"You poor thing," said K.K. "And you ask so little."

Husna's eyes became moist. "Yesterday Begum Sahiba had gone out when I got back to the house, and she had locked all the doors and taken the keys with her. I stood under the trees in front for three hours. And if I eat anything from the refrigerator she becomes angry at me. And when she's gone on *hajj* the servants will take liberties, they make jokes and want me to sit with them. She won't leave me any money." She wiped her eyes with her *dupatta*, head cast down. "When Begum Sahiba is harsh, what can I do?"

"Come, little one," said K.K., patting the sofa next to him. "Come sit here. Don't cry." K. K. Harouni avoided unpleasantness at all costs, for he lived in a world as measured and as concentric as that of the Sun King at Versailles. He did not like to see her cry, because it upset him. She stepped out around the tea table, wiping a tear with one arm, and then slipped into the place next to him and nestled under his arm, still tearful, but now muffling her face in his sweater. He stroked her hair.

"Now stop," he said. "Why don't you come stay here while the begum is on *hajj*? I'll have them fix up the rooms in the annex."

Husna looked out from under her eyelashes and smiled weakly. "Oh, I would like that too much. Then I could keep you company when you're alone and make your tea for you. And I would practice typing every day for a long time. And I'll study for the M.A. exams."

K.K. cared nothing for what his wife or the servants thought. He ordered the annex to be prepared, a suite of rooms built over garages at the far side of the compound. The rooms had been refurbished several years earlier, when important guests from India came for a long stay, and so Husna would live in better quarters than ever before in her life, with uninterrupted supplies of good food, servants who more or less did her bidding, and occasional use of the car. To Husna it felt like a validation, almost like revenge, and yet with the bitterness of triumph after humiliation.

Husna simply disappeared from the house in Gulberg. Begum Harouni learned of her departure from the servants. The old lady stormed in to see her husband but found him impervious to her outrage.

"I'll never take that little . . . *thing* back into my house," said Begum Harouni. "Imagine! I picked her from the dirt, from nothing, and I fed and clothed her."

"It reflects well upon you, my dear," responded K.K. placidly.

HUSNA BROUGHT OVER her shabby luggage to the house on Danepur Lane, a brown suitcase bulging and strapped. She had clothes and shoes, not much else, arriving in a rickshaw, the facts soon communicated through the house among the snickering community, washermen, drivers, sweepers, household servants. After Begum Harouni had gone on the pilgrimage Husna asked K.K. for the use of the car, and went back to the house. At first the butler, Chacha Latif, would not let her in, but Husna raised her voice and became abusive, and the servant, knowing that she might later be in a position to injure him, let her do what she wanted. All the closets had been locked, but she found a few of her things, a pile of Indian movie magazines, a little dish with an image of the Eiffel Tower that her grandfather brought home from a European tour in the 1920s. When she went out, she found K.K.'s driver speaking with Chacha Latif.

"What does he say?" said Husna to the driver as they returned along Jail Road, driving in and out of shadow under flame-of-the-forest trees planted a hundred years ago.

"Nothing, Bibi," said Samundar Khan.

"Nothing? Not anything at all?" replied Husna, speaking in sharp Punjabi. And then, leaning back in the seat, patronizingly, "You drivers are always the clever ones."

• • •

A WEEK AFTER she moved into the annex, Husna slept with K. K. Harouni. He had visitors for lunch, a State Bank governor, another old civil service friend, and his cousin, the retired General Karim, along with their wives. They took lunch in the room known as "the White Verandah," shaded by a pipul tree and overlooking a little side garden. Already, in early April, the ceiling fans barely kept the room cool. Husna remained in the annex, reading a dull and badly printed history of the Sikh Wars, in which K.K.'s ancestors fought, then set it aside. Though she wanted to make herself interesting to the old man, reading serious books, she never finished what she began, instead lapsing into daydreams or reading secondhand fashion magazines that she bought from a used book stall. A servant boy brought her a tray of food, the same food that the cook served to K.K. and his guests.

From her perch in the rooms above the garage Husna watched the guests emerge into the portico, continue speaking to Harouni for what seemed to her an interminable period, then drive away. Soon afterward, a servant came to ask Husna if she would join Harouni for green tea in the garden. She walked past the formal dining room and along a corridor hung with darkened portraits of his ancestors and with photographs of him and his family in the first half of the century. She felt intimidated by this house, by its heavy gloomy air, which contrasted with K.K.'s light manner, and looked almost uncomprehendingly upon the strange and numerous objects scattered about, the ivory scabbard of a Chinese sword, a carved walnut love seat from Kashmir, numerous brass and copper figurines of Hindu gods. The house smelled of dusty carpets and disinfectant and wood polish. K.K. sat under a tree in an old railway chair, with two cups of green tea on a table. She took one and sat down.

"Hello, girl," he said, pleased to see her, fed and mellow. "How lovely it is." Old trees were scattered around the receding lawn, creating areas of shade where the grass wouldn't grow. A row of mulberry trees just ripening at the far end attracted sugar-heavy bees, which sipped the purple berries hanging from the branches and littering the ground. Overhead, in the bleached sky, kites and vultures wheeled at a great height on the afternoon thermals, as if the sky itself were slowly turning.

Draining the tea, he said, "Well, my dear, it's time for my rest."

"Let me massage you, Uncle," she suggested, blushing. Though her ambition always tolled in the background, she had come to respect him genuinely, his unstudied fairness, his gaiety, his integrity and openness, plain and light and valuable as a metal unknown in her world. She wanted to keep her part of the bargain, and had only herself to give. It hurt her that it was so little; she imagined that her body, her virtue, meant almost nothing to her.

She followed him into his bedroom. Rafik had already closed the curtains and laid out his pajamas.

"You needn't wake me," he said to Rafik, who stood by the door and who knew very well the routine to be observed on such an afternoon.

Of course she was a virgin, and that touched him. Letting him do exactly as he wanted, throughout she wore a look in her eyes that he misunderstood as surprise and shyness, and later identified with moods that verged on madness—sequences of perplexity and focus in her eyes, expressing her hooded rage to get what she wanted. She had expected this to be as simple as the signing of a check, a payment. Instead, for a moment the romantic girl awoke, who would have accepted another man, one her own age, from her own station.

Goodbye to the life she would never have, a life she despised, economies that she would never make as she cooked and kept house for a clerking husband in the Old City, one of the boys who might have accepted her hand. She and that husband might have gone away, might have moved out to the new suburbs of Lahore—the ones out past Model Town, grids of streets laid out in wheat fields or untended orchards, no houses yet built. The moment with K. K. meant a great deal to her, but not in the way that he understood it—without meaning to, she had given herself completely. She could pretend later to be a virgin; or someone would take her even knowing she wasn't. A marriage could always be arranged, it was always a bargain, a deal. But she knew then that she wouldn't have another man, because any man after this would have to be a compromise, a salary man.

Late in the afternoon she put on her clothes, languid and shy in her movements, and slipped away to the annex. This nap became their routine.

WHEN HE HAD no guests, K.K. ate lunch with Husna. Rafik served the food with care, the dishes on from the left, off from the right, the napkins starched and arranged like a fan by the plate. In May now the air-conditioning had been turned on. In this room, the coolest in the house, Husna felt most intimidated. She sat at his right, at the far end of the long table that could seat eighteen, and spoke little. Over the past month she had learned which utensils to use, but still did not use them gracefully. K.K. chewed his food exactly ten times before swallowing.

As Rafik brought in a cheese soufflé one afternoon, a car drove into the portico behind K.K. He had his back to the window and did not turn. They heard the creaking of the carved swinging doors, taken from K.K.'s ancestral home in the Old City, and then the visitor, a middle-aged woman, pushed into the dining room.

"Hello, Daddy," she said. "Isn't this cozy!" She had a tinkling laugh which, while it did not seem entirely genuine, by its musicality caused the hearer to join her in a heightened response, like a painting that one knows to be good, although unmoved by it.

K.K. rose, seeming suddenly frail and old next to her vivid personality, and kissed his youngest daughter on the forehead.

"Hello, darling. When did you get in?"

"Just now, on the eleven o'clock flight. I'm here because Pinky's daughter got secretly engaged. Don't ask!"

They sat down, including Husna, who had also risen.

"This is Husna," said K.K., "Mian Nasiruddin's daughter."

"Yes, yes, I know," said Sarwat maliciously, looking not at Husna's face but at her person, hunched across the table. "I met her at Mummy's."

Rafik brought in a mat and laid a place for Sarwat. "Good lord, Rafik," she commented, rearranging the cutlery, "you're getting even fatter."

Sarwat settled back into her chair. She wore an understated tan sari, a gold watch, several unusual rings, a star sapphire and a Burmese pigeon-blood ruby. Her salt-and-pepper hair, worn up in a high chignon, lengthened her still beautiful face; and her slender manicured body suggested lotions and expensive soaps, a hairdresser and a masseuse, idleness and ease. In all she looked rich and sleek and voluptuous. Even at fifty she still had admirers, and it had become a convention among the circle in which she moved to speak of her lovely gray eyes.

"I am very glad to meet you," said Husna. "I have heard so much about you." Her head had sunk into her shoulders.

Sarwat looked down at the girl with a wolfish grin, almost spoke, then turned to her father. "You look well, Daddy."

He had resumed eating, and with his mouth full, raised a fork, as if to say, You can see for yourself.

"Tell me, what do you know about the Talpur boy, the son of Bilqis Talpur? Mumtaz went off and got engaged to him, and Pinky's absolutely livid. That's why she called me here. I can only stay for a minute, I told her I'd be at her house just after lunch."

K.K., who took these matters seriously, put down his fork. "I spent time with his grandfather when I was posted to Leiah. The old man had a bit of a temper, and of course you know about the father. You should speak to Wali, the boy was at Aitchison with him, a year before or a year after."

Husna broke in. "He is very handsome."

Sarwat looked at her in amazement, as if the furniture had spoken. "Tell me about the land," she said to her father.

"It's good land, on the river. The family used to hold a big parcel near the city, and that would be enormously valuable." He looked at her, raising a warning eyebrow. "But then they say that Adnan spent the last thirty years drinking it away."

Finishing the meal, they rose to have green tea in the living room.

As they stood, Sarwat said to Husna, "I'd like to be alone with my father, please," and then proceeded through the door without waiting for a reply.

K.K. FOLLOWED HER into the living room. Sarwat sat down on a sofa and tucked her feet under herself, leaning against a large pillow. "Really, Daddy," she began. "I can imagine keeping her around, but to sit and have lunch with her, that's too much. You're becoming eccentric, you really are."

"She comes from a good family," said K.K. "Her great-grandfather owned more land than yours. But for a few twists of fate she might be in your place, and we might be living still in the Old City."

"But we're not," said Sarwat. "That's the point, we're not." She tried another tack. "And what can you possibly find to say to her? Sheherezad told me she came for tea the other day, and that this unfortunate little thing sat without saying a word, just listening, like a frog in the corner. It's indecent."

"She too would have wished for your advantages, my dear, your schools and clothes and friends and property."

"Please, Daddy. I doubt if this is a humanitarian mission."

"And I'm lonely, Sarwat. You're in Karachi, Kamila is in New York, and Rehana hasn't even spoken with me in ten years. My friends are dying off or don't go out anymore. She keeps me company. She's no genius, if you like, but she can play cards and so on. Why don't you spend more time in Lahore? You have a lovely house here, friends here. I would much prefer to see you than her, but you're not available."

"What about Riffat or one of your other old girlfriends? Why choose someone like this, she's neither pretty nor presentable."

"At my age, what I need is companionship, and Husna can give that to me. Riffat can only come for tea or for a few hours, but Husna is here whenever I need her."

They sat back in silence, neither satisfied with the other. After a few moments, Sarwat put down her cup. "Daddy, I must go. I'll come this evening. Please, at least tell her not to come out when I'm here."

THAT AFTERNOON WHEN Husna entered his room, summoned from the annex, K.K. felt abashed, creating a tightness in his face and causing his mouth to become dry. Irresistibly drawn to the one subject that he wished to avoid, he said, "It's wonderful to see Sarwat. I hope you and she will get to know each other." He had been sitting on the edge of the bed, and now he rolled over, tucked himself under the sheet, and put a black mask over his eyes, to screen out the light.

Snarling, her face contorted, she exploded. "She's mean and rude. She treated me like dirt." Husna's seething voice broke, out of control, pouring from her. "Why don't you get her to come live in the annex and to play cards with you and make your tea?"

"I can't have you speak like this," said K.K., removing the mask, face drawn and imposing. "You're upsetting me." He spoke in a measured voice. "You've upset me."

"I'm leaving this house," she said, standing up on the bed, looking down at him. "I gave you everything I had, but you give me nothing in return. I have feelings too, I'm human. She made me feel like dirt, and you didn't say anything to stop her." She began to cry hysterically, still standing on the bed, and when he sat up and tried to touch her leg she shrieked and stepped back. "Even the servants here treat me as if I'm nothing. When I ask for things they tell me that they don't have time. I have to crawl even in front of them. Yesterday Hassan swore at me."

"I'll speak with him," said K.K. "Now stop. You know the doctor's orders. Do you want me to have another heart attack?"

She saw that she dare push him no further, and so gradually became quiet. Lying down on the bed, she wouldn't get under the covers, but held herself rigidly beside him.

When K.K. woke Husna said, "Talk to Hassan now. I won't stand the servants' treatment of me anymore." Knowing she couldn't at this point win the larger battle, against Sarwat, she wanted at least to consolidate her smaller gains. She insisted that K.K. speak to Hassan in front of her, though he would have preferred not to humiliate the old servant.

The grizzled cook stood with his shoes off, having left them at the door, and with his lambskin hat clutched in his hand. He looked down at the floor, at his splayed bare feet planted on the polished rosewood parquet.

"Bibi says that yesterday you swore at her."

Husna had been waiting for some concrete provocation and had pounced when Hassan, in his habitual foul temper, called her a bitch under his breath.

"Yes sir," said the old cook. "I mean no sir."

"Well, Hassan, did you or didn't you?"

"No sir."

Husna became shrill, which injured her cause. "I asked him not to put chilies in the omelet, and he swore at me. Ask the sweepress, she heard."

Hassan looked at her squarely. "You and the sweepress."

"You can go," said Harouni, not raising his voice.

When Hassan had left, Harouni said to Rafik, who had been impassively watching this performance, "See that this doesn't happen anymore."

Husna gloated from the sidelines. Rafik responded without expression, "Yes, Mian Sahib." He paused. "Shah Sahib is here. Should I send him into the living room?"

While she knew that now at least the old servants would be decided against her, Husna felt she could afford their ill will, for her position in the household grew stronger daily. The attitude of the servants changed after Rafik gave them the word. Only a few, the old ones, covered their insolence with glacial politeness, while the younger became either servile or friendly to the point of taking liberties, thinking thereby to win her favor.

HUSNA BEGAN TO enjoy the advantages of her new position. The secretary, Shah Sahib, handled the household accounts, writing up all the expenses in a complicated double-entry bookkeeping system, so complicated in fact that K.K. couldn't and wouldn't take the trouble to understand it. For years the books had been larded with excessive expenses. The drivers, Hassan the cook, all of the others except Rafik, lavishly inflated the bills they submitted. After Husna had a few times complained of not having money, of wearing torn clothes and broken-heeled shoes, K.K. instructed that she should be given a tiny allowance. In old age he had become tightfisted, although the household hemorrhaged money, and he spent two or three hundred thousand rupees a month without knowing where it went. Shah Sahib soon enlisted Husna in his system, since he didn't want her to begin making inquiries, as women in a household have a tendency to do; and so her allowance monthly grew larger and larger, inflated in various ingenious ways.

She had the use of a car, bought herself clothes, even small bits of gold jewelry. In her rooms she kept one, then two locked steel trunks, which she filled with everything from raw silk to electric sandwich makers. She would come to K.K. with some special request, wanting to buy something, and he would ultimately agree. She wheedled, petted him, became frosty, became nice. Giving in, he would be unable to look her in the eye, himself embarrassed. She said to him, speaking plainly, "Scratch a man and find a boy."

A FEW OF K.K.'s old gentleman friends, mild landowners with courtly Punjabi manners, came to the decision that they had no reason for isolating the young girl. They called her "daughter" and looked forward to her lively, flirtatious company. Among this group, who now in old age constituted K.K.'s closest friends, he had always been the fast one, the sportsman and lover. They envied him the possession of Husna, while at the same time being slightly relieved on reaching their lugubrious houses after a few hours in her company. Her striving wore on them. She flattered them, asked about their harmless projects—a Union of Punjabi Landowners, a pipe-dream society for tort reform—and so wielded them into a circle, with herself at the center. She teased them, sitting at Harouni's side during bridge games, and would try to peek at his opponents' cards. Playing rummy for small stakes with whoever was dummy in the bridge game, she cheated, and when caught laughed and denied it.

• • •

THE AIR CONDITIONER in the annex didn't work properly, and on that pretext Husna moved into a study adjoining the master bedroom, with communicating doors. This new proximity proved at times inconvenient for Husna, because it exposed her use of sleeping pills to K.K., who strongly disapproved. For several years she had found it difficult to sleep at night. Her mind raced during episodes of hysteria, when she barely could govern herself, and so she had developed a dependency on sleeping pills, which were available from the pharmacies without any prescription. Occasionally, desiring complete oblivion, she would take a double dose—it was almost a game with her, a flirtation with the dangers of the pills. She did not sleep the night with K.K., but invariably at some point withdrew to her own room, saying that his tossing movements disturbed her. Sometimes in the morning, when she had taken a stronger dose, she didn't answer when the servant knocked at her door, and then K.K. would himself come and shake her, wearing his pajamas and an old silk robe. He would look down at her sleeping face, in repose and therefore cleansed of all ambition and anxiety and spite, qualities that he forgave her because he felt that the conditions into which he had thrust her brought them out. Seeing her there, he sometimes thought that he loved her, loved her brightness in these last years of his life, when he had become so lonely. Old General Hadayatullah, the retired chief medical officer of the army, had told K.K. that his heart might at any moment carry him away. K.K. feared death with all the terror of a perfectly rational man, who took no comfort in religion, and knew death to be his final end. He wanted so much to live!

Gradually Husna would wake, late in the morning, and K.K. would hurry to her room.

"Suppose something happened to me in the night?" he asked, as she sipped her tea, lying in bed, her face drained and pale. She looked prettiest then, emerging from drugged sleep, erased.

She would cry and ask him not to speak of such things, and at those moments he felt that she too genuinely loved him, something that he often doubted, despite her professions of love. He craved her presence and reproached himself with a phrase that he once repeated even to her: *Too old to be roused by pleasure, I seek pain.*

IN AUGUST THE monsoon broke. The rains came up from India, sweeping the Himalayas, filling the rivers of the Punjab, pouring down water on the Hindu Kush and on the plain that extends from the Khyber to Karachi. In the gardens outside K.K.'s room, crows sat in the dripping branches of ancient trees, bedraggled, and the lawns filled with water.

One night the bell in the servants' quarters rang, and Rafik rose, dressed, and hurried to K.K.'s room. The master sat up in bed, in the glare of the single light.

"Something's wrong," he said. "My pulse is racing. Wake Husna."

Husna came into the room, wiping her face, adjusting her clothes.

"What is it, Uncle?"

"Telephone General Hadayatullah. It's my chest."

K.K. sat in the bed, scared, his face thin and worn, and distracted himself with meaningless banter, falling into Husna's mode of speech, which had become for them a private language.

"So, Bibi, for a while you won't be plucking me clean at rummy. Or they'll give me bedrest, we'll play even more, and soon you'll have salted away a nice fat dowry." In the past he would have found this kind of joking in poor taste. He had begun teasing her, saying that she was seeking a young husband—leaving him—and almost convincing himself that she was. In fact, as he mimicked her brassy manners and slang, saying in joke what couldn't be said outright, she steadily drew him onto her own ground, where she could engage and control him so much more effectively.

Servants had crowded into the hallway outside the room, perhaps twenty of them, barefoot and speaking in whispers, coming into the house by ones or twos as they learned that something had happened to the master.

The general swept in, a tall anglicized officer, his trimmed mustache and even the cut of his slightly military clothes reflecting purpose. Rafik, who knew the general well, brought a stool. Administering an ECG on a portable machine, the general took the tape to the light, and said, "Go immediately to Mayo Hospital. Carry him out in a chair." He very precisely clicked shut the lid of the machine and put the tape away in the pocket of his vest, wearing a thoughtful expression.

For a moment Husna and K.K. looked at each other, his face lined and grave, hers puffy with sleep. For the first time he thought of her as a grown-up, as a woman; and for the first time she thought of him as a lover, sick and possibly dying.

ALL THE SERVANTS, the gardeners, the chauffeurs, the junior ones who saw K.K. only from a distance, wanted to help carry the chair through the corridors of the house, where only a few lights burned, throwing shadows. K.K. sat impassively on the chair, raised above the crowd, then lowered at the doors, like an awkward king, a king onstage.

As Husna prepared to get into the car, the general stopped her. "You need to be here. People will be coming to ask about him. He's probably going to be all right, but you should call Sarwat and the others. Kamila should come back from New York. Have them call Rehana also." Rehana, the middle child, had broken with K.K. when he separated from his wife. Husna began to cry, shaking, and he stood back and looked at her shrewdly. "Don't, this isn't about you. Prepare yourself now. Remember who you are."

. . .

BY MIDMORNING PEOPLE had begun to call at the house, friends of the family, for in Lahore word traveled quickly. Husna received them, sitting in the living room. She had dressed up too much, wearing an embroidered black *kurta*. Several of the guests asked pointedly about the daughters.

Sarwat had ordered that a car wait at the airport and meet each flight from Karachi, as she would get a seat as quickly as possible. Just before lunch she came through the door into the living room, narrowing her eyes. An elderly couple, who had been sitting with Husna, stood up.

"What's happened?" she asked, addressing Husna. "What are you doing here? Where's Daddy?"

Husna explained. The old couple quickly took their leave.

"Please," said Sarwat, "this is a time for family. I've asked my cousin Bilqis to come here and receive people. Go up to your room and stay there."

Husna didn't dare tell Sarwat that she had moved next to the master bedroom. A servant turned on the air conditioner in the annex, and all day Husna stayed there, sitting on a chair and looking down through the window at callers arriving and leaving. Hassan sent up some food, but she didn't eat. She knew she would not be allowed to attend K.K. at the hospital.

IN THE MIDDLE of the night she fell asleep, still sitting in the chair by the window. Suddenly waking in the morning, she looked down on the driveway jammed with cars, the line of them running all the way out to the massive gates of the compound. Not even putting on a head scarf, she ran down the stairs and into the servants' area. Rafik sat on a chair sobbing unnaturally, as if racked with coughing, his head in his hands, his elbows on his knees. She saw very distinctly the old man's bare head, bowed down, the gray thin hairs, the scalp. She knew, of course, that K.K. had died. Two other servants, young ones new to the house, sat uncertainly on their haunches nearby. They looked at her with curiosity, but said nothing. She turned, her eyes filling with tears, and walked out and up into the annex, into the cooled rooms overlooking the driveway, shaded by tree branches. She lay down on the bed, her feelings concentrated at the forefront of her mind like an immensely weighted black point, incomprehensible. She felt afraid to cry aloud, to draw attention.

IN ISLAM A body must be buried as soon as possible, ideally before nightfall. When Husna emerged from her bedroom and looked again out onto the drive, she saw men putting up a tent, where the male guests would sit to mourn during the *jenaza*. The women would sit inside the house with the body. Among the things that she had not carried over to her room in the main house, Husna found a suit of clothing that she brought with her when she came into the household, a cheap *shalvar* and *kurta*, with a simple white head scarf. Wearing this costume, she entered the packed living room. The body of K. K. Harouni lay on the floor, wrapped in a white cloth, his jaw bound closed with a white bandage, the knot tied jauntily near one ear. His dentures had been lost, and so his cheeks had caved in. His body had shrunken, lying among rose petals scattered there by the servants. Sarwat stood up from her place at the head of the corpse, touched Husna on the head with both hands, but said nothing. Husna went to the back of the room and sat down as far away as possible from K.K.'s old wife, who was telling a rosary, a stunned expression on her face. All sorts of women had come, women from all phases of

K.K.'s life, and kept arriving, clicking under the portico and through the front vestibule in high heels, spilling out into other rooms. From various places soft or loud sobbing would break out and then subside, as is the custom. Two society women sat uncomfortably on the floor next to Husna, whispering, gossiping, and she heard one say to the other in English, "Oh, isn't that *delicious*."

Of course you don't care, thought Husna, who wouldn't cry in front of them. She felt that only she truly cared, that she had lost more than all the others.

And yet she wanted to be like them, they were what she had lost.

FOR THE NEXT two days Husna stayed in the annex, without once going out. People came day and night to condole with Sarwat and Kamila. Rehana, the estranged third daughter, had arrived from Paris, where she taught some esoteric form of Islamic women's studies— but she pointedly stayed with her mother rather than at K.K.'s house. Husna felt that they had forgotten her, and she wanted to be forgotten, to stay here alone in these rooms, with rush mats on the floor, bits of scavenged furniture, and an air conditioner that almost kept the apartment cool, that dribbled water onto the pavement below. On the third day a servant came, early in the morning, before there were any callers, to say that the sisters wished to speak with her. They waited for her in the living room, all three wearing saris, relaxed, Kamila sitting with her feet curled under her on a sofa, Rehana and Sarwat in high-backed chairs.

They got straight to the point, Kamila, as the eldest, speaking.

"My father allowed you to live in this house. However, he would not have wanted you to stay here. Tomorrow afternoon the car will be available to take you wherever you wish to be taken. I suppose you'll go to your father's house. There will be no discussion on the subject." She settled back, finished with the problem.

Husna, who had taken a seat halfway through this monologue, though she had not been invited to do so, looked down at the floor. Tears welled up in her eyes.

"Did Uncle say anything about me before . . . before . . . ?"

Sarwat broke in. "No," she replied with finality. "There was and is nothing for you."

"That isn't what I meant," said Husna.

Kamila softened. "Look, whatever you had with my father is gone now. If you took care of him in these past months, you were rewarded. You're young, you'll find other things. You think that you'll never heal, but you will, sooner than you think. Go on, go back to the annex."

Now Husna stood. She had reached the bottom, her pride arose, her sense of wanting to be dignified now, to accept the inevitable. For her, dignity and pride and memory would be all and everything from this moment forward. "I have no power. You are important people, and I'm nothing, and my family is nothing. I have to obey." The finality of this rang true, the absence of appeal, countering their dismissal of her.

Just as she approached the door, Rehana called to her. "There's one other thing. They tell us you have a number of trunks in your room. We will not ask what you have in them. You may take those with you. But nothing else."

Reaching the annex, staggered, Husna sat on the side of the bed and buried her face in her hands. She had hoped that Rehana, the foreign one, the aggrieved one, would take her side—yet it was she who pronounced the harshest words. At the end their estrangements were less than their contempt for her. They had closed up against her—family, blood. She tried to tell herself that she had gone to the sisters hoping for nothing, with nothing in her heart but sadness at the death of their father, who had loved her. She should have said something cold, should have refused their last insulting offer.

"For him I should have said, 'I came with nothing, I leave with nothing. I leave with the clothes on my back. I served your father, when you were far away. The shame be on your heads.' "

But she could not afford even this gesture. The next day two men loaded the trunks onto a horse-drawn cart and carried them away to the Old City.

Our Lady of Paris

ohail and Helen had begun dating two years earlier, at Yale, where she was an undergraduate and he at the law school. After graduating the previous summer he had returned to his home in Pakistan, while she completed her senior year. They had agreed to put the question of their future in abeyance until she finished school—not the question of whether they would be together but of how: in Pakistan, New York, or somewhere else. Sohail had vaguely committed himself to joining his father's sprawling business—a sugar mill, farmlands, and much else. The degree had been a way to put off this step.

He lived that fall in the family's Karachi mansion, a rambling pile large enough that he could bear the rub of his parents, who occupied what was called the Old House, leaving him to an annex under an enormous banyan at the far end of the garden. When he announced to his mother that he would be going to Paris for Christmas, to meet Helen, she pursed her lips but said nothing.

A few days later, he found her alone in the living room, having tea, waiting for guests. She had been a famous beauty, from a prominent, cultured Lucknow family. Now at forty-five she knew everyone of a certain class in Karachi, went to dinners and to the polo and to all the fashionable weddings, flew often to Lahore and Islamabad, and summered in London.

In winter her rooms were warmed by a fire lit at dusk; in summer her rooms were kept ice cold. On her bad nights, as she called them, she took sleeping pills, which left dark shadows like bruises under her eyes. A portrait that hung in the formal dining room showed her reclining on a chaise longue, one shoe dangling from her long, elegant foot, skin velvety and evenly white; she seemed indolent and dangerous, as if she were waiting in ambush, with herself as the bait.

"Hello, darling," she said. "Come have tea with me." She was sitting on a divan in a green silk sari with her feet tucked under her, her black hair pulled tightly back. "I don't see you enough."

He had been avoiding her, unable to abide her questions about his future—he was still "settling in," going every couple of days to the headquarters of the family business to write emails and read the *New York Times* online. During this time, with his confidence faltering, he found her overwhelming. He fixed on the cucumber sandwiches, devouring one after another.

"Why won't you ever use a plate? Your manners are even worse since you went to America." She took a plate, put a napkin under it, and gave it to him. "Sohail, I'd like to ask a favor." She blended these articulations together—following the maternal scolding, her request almost flirtatious.

He raised one eyebrow, nibbling at another sandwich.

"I want your father to take a vacation, he's pushing himself too hard. He's always bored in London. I thought we might come to Paris." She said this brightly. "Only for a week, I know you'll want to be alone. Do you remember when we were in Rome, how nice it was? Your father mentioned it just the other day, how much he'd liked that."

"I haven't seen Helen since June," responded Sohail carefully. "Wouldn't it be sort of like taking your mother on your honeymoon?"

"Oh, we wouldn't be in your way. And I'd like to see her. You'll hardly know we're there. I've found an apartment."

He acquiesced, because he generally ended up doing as she wanted, and because he would inevitably and soon have to introduce Helen to his mother, in order to move the relationship forward.

SOHAIL HAD BORROWED an apartment on Île Saint-Louis from one of his childhood friends, also a Pakistani industrialist's son, who had spent much of the last two years in Paris being a writer—though not actually writing. Arriving in Paris two days before Helen, Sohail cleaned the apartment, made the bed with new sheets he bought at Galeries Lafayette, and picked up food and wine from the tiny overpriced shops on the Rue Saint-Louis-en-l'Île. After collecting Helen from the airport, Sohail carried her bag on his head up to the sixth-floor garret, hitting it on the turns of the narrow stairwell. She had come to love this in him, his playing, his willingness to be slightly ridiculous. At the top he dropped the suitcase, panting, and with a flourish produced a strange circular key, unlike those in America.

She paused at the door, a pretty girl, unmistakably American, her short hair held back with a tortoiseshell barrette. She had lived among and through books, in high school and then college, won a scholarship at Yale. Paris had been a dream from her childhood, when her single mother could not take her places, not to Europe. Walking across the room and opening the window, she looked out over a cloister, then across the Seine to the Panthéon and the city beyond. A phrase came to her mind—*my barefoot need*—another phrase from a book. She did not want Sohail to see this. It had begun raining again and the slate roofs opposite shed streams of water.

AT DUSK THE following day, Sohail sat watching Helen dress for their first dinner with his parents. He wore a sports jacket, a black cashmere turtleneck, and pleated trousers; she rolled black stockings over her legs, which were pink and damp from the shower. Walking to the closet, naked but for the stockings, she removed a black dress, stepped into it, pulling it over the flare of her hips. She turned her back to him, and he zipped it, then stood for a moment holding her close, inhaling the scent of her hair.

THEY WALKED PAST the halfhearted Christmas tree in front of Notre Dame and then along the left bank of the Seine, among the headlights of scooters and cars, the crowds rushing home into the twilight, the tourists everywhere taking pictures, the Parisians with buttoned-down faces. The wet streets glittered. Helen walked beside Sohail, keeping up with him, her heels clicking. She drank in the city around them, moving so quickly, so differently.

A barge passed, going upstream, long and fast, smoking into the night, the lit cabin cozy and cheerful above the cold black water.

"You know," she said thoughtfully, "the Seine doesn't divide Paris, it keeps the city together. It's just the right width, not a little stream but a public place in the heart of the city."

Sohail leaned down and kissed her. "That's a great image, the river *not* dividing Paris."

"It's yours," said Helen. "For your next poem."

His parents were staying in an apartment on the Quai des Grands

Augustins, overlooking the Seine. Sohail and Helen went up to the second floor, found the door, and he had just touched the bell when a voice called, "Coming."

"Hello, darling," said his mother, presenting her cheek to kiss, looking past him to Helen. She had a husky, attractive voice and was dressed quite plainly, a long white cotton tunic embroidered in white over slim-fitting pants.

Helen extended her hand, palm flat, and looked Sohail's mother in the eye, directly and ingenuously. "Hello, Mrs. Harouni. I'm Helen."

"And I'm Rafia. Welcome." She had fixed a stiff smile on her face.

Sohail's father stood to one side, a smallish man with a little mustache, precisely dressed in a thick brown tweed suit with a vest and muted tie and brilliantly shined shoes of a distinctive tan color. As he took Helen's coat he said, "Welcome, welcome. Thank you for coming." But his statement appeared to be reflexive, without connection to his mental processes. Putting the coat on a hanger, he looked at her closely, with shrewd eyes. Sohail had thrown his coat on a chair near the door.

"Very nice," said Sohail, looking around at the apartment, which had high ceilings and diminutive fittings. A woman on the stereo sang in French, and his mother had lit candles.

"It belongs to Brigadier Hazari," said his father, sitting down again in front of the fire.

Rafia and Helen had moved into the living room. The mother leaned down and looked at Helen's necklace, an Afghan tribal piece, silver with lapis.

"Isn't that pretty."

"Sohail gave it to me. It's one of my favorite things."

Rafia said to Sohail, turning and smiling at him, "Will you get Helen and yourself whatever you want—it's in the kitchen." Then to Helen, "Come sit here by me."

• • •

SOHAIL BROUGHT A drink for Helen and one for himself. His father sat back in the sofa, his drink on his knee, and looked sedately about the room. Rafia began.

"I promised Sohail not to embarrass him, not to say how much I've heard about you." She had little dimples when she smiled. "But it's true, he keeps telling me about you, it's sweet."

"Ma, please. That makes me sound like I'm fifteen," said Sohail.

"It's the simple truth. And why shouldn't I say it, it's nice to see you happy. But please come help me with dinner. Bring your drink."

As mother and son went into the kitchen, Helen heard Rafia whisper to Sohail, "But she's *so* pretty."

HELEN WAS LEFT with Mr. Harouni, who did not seem disposed to conversation. He looked complacently at the fire, his glass sweating. After hesitating to have a drink, Helen had accepted a white wine, reminding herself that she was an adult. Now she took a sip of the wine, trying to relax. She had been sitting up erect, halfway forward in the seat.

Still looking into the fire, Mr. Harouni observed speculatively, "Sohail was very happy at Yale." She waited for more, but the father seemed to be content placing this statement on the table between them, a sufficient offering.

"He really was, Mr. Harouni. He's been happy as long as I've known him." She wanted to be as straight with his parents as possible.

"Please, call me Amjad." The thick tweed of his suit and the smallness of his hands and feet made him appear to Helen like an expensive toy. He spoke very quietly.

She decided to press on, to maintain even this slight momentum of conversation. "His life in Pakistan is so different, at least from what

I know. But he has an American side, what I think of as American. He's very gentle—I don't mean Americans are gentle, they're not. But it's easier to be gentle in a place where there's order."

She paused, took a sip of her wine, waited for a moment.

"Go on," said Mr. Harouni.

"He and my mother got along well, even though—she's a secretary in a little Connecticut town, and she has a house with cats and a garden. He liked that. At first I thought he was pretending, but he wasn't."

"It's a wonderful country. There's nothing you people can't do when you put your minds to it. I admire the Americans tremendously." He sipped from his glass, the ice cubes clattering. "So many of our young people want to live in America—I suppose Sohail as well."

"He talks about it," she said cautiously. "But he talks about Pakistan a lot too. When he and I first met he told me stories about Pakistan for hours."

"And what about you? What would you like to do?"

"I want to be a doctor. I just sent out my applications to medical school." She blushed as she said this, the color unevenly creeping up her fine-grained cheekbones.

"On the East Coast?"

"In New York, maybe. When I was little my mother would drive me to the city, to the Museum of Natural History or the Met, or sometimes we would just walk around looking at the stores and the people. I've always wanted to live there." She paused again, conscious that she might sound pathetic. "It feels like the center of everything. And it's not the way it used to be, it's safe and clean, you can walk through the park at midnight."

The father looked at her with an expressionless face. "Perhaps Sohail can set up a branch of our company there."

Sohail had come in and heard this last part of the conversation. He sat down on the arm of Helen's chair, put his hand on her shoulder, and said, "Now you've seen it, Helen. That's as close as my father comes to humor." He leaned forward, took his father's empty glass, and stood up. "I warn you, this man has more factories than your mother has cats. Watch out for him. Stick to name, rank, and serial number."

Mr. Harouni smiled appreciatively.

"We both want the same thing—what's best for you," said Helen in a flirtatious tone quite new to her. "Why would I need to be careful?"

THEY HAD DINNER at a small table under a spiky modern chandelier painted with gold leaf, Mr. Harouni sitting at the head and filling their bowls with bouillabaisse, saffroned and aromatic. Rafia tasted hers from the tip of her spoon and said, "It's good. It's from Quintessence—that's the new chic place, supposedly." Sohail poured the wine and then turned down the lights, so that the table was illuminated by candles.

A *bateau mouche* glided by on the Seine, its row of spotlights trained on the historic buildings along the quay, throwing patterned light through the blinds onto the living room wall. For a moment they carefully sipped the hot stew.

Helen felt she should break the silence. Just as she was about to begin, Rafia turned to her.

"Do you know, Sohail was almost born in Paris?" She sipped from her spoon, looking at Helen sideways. "I was in London to have the baby, and I was enormous and felt like an elephant—so I begged Amjad to come over with me and let me pick out some outrageous outfits. I thought I'd have my girlish figure back the day after I delivered."

Sohail beamed across at Helen, his face framed by two wavering candles. "You can tell this is one of my mother's tall tales—by the simple fact that she's never begged my father for anything. If she had said she ordered my father to Paris it might have been true."

"In any case, you were almost born here, in the Hôtel d'Angleterre."

"I wish it had happened," said Sohail. "For a Pakistani being born in London is about as exciting as being born in Lahore. Paris would be glamorous."

Rafia tilted her head toward Helen. "Where would you have liked to be born?"

"I've never thought of that. The first time I met Sohail he asked me where I'd like to be buried."

"In seven years of dating, that line has never once failed." Sohail appeared to be saying the first thing that came into his head, filling up the gaps in the conversation.

"Don't be flip, Sohail. Amjad, where would you like to have been born?"

The father, who had been drinking his stew with the equanimity of a solitary patron in a busy café, looked up from under his brows.

"I suppose in the happiest possible home. And not in India, I think. And not in Europe. Perhaps in America."

This interested Helen, relieving her irritation at the conversation between mother and son, which seemed too practiced, as if they were performing together, and in their display excluding her.

"Why America?" she asked. Her oval face reflected the light of the candles.

Placing his forearms on the table, still holding his spoon, Mr. Harouni looked for a moment over his wife's head at the opposite wall. "You know or you correctly assume that I was born into a comfortably well-off family. All my life I've been lucky, my business succeeded, I've had no tragedies, my wife and I are happy, we have a wonderful son. The one thing I've missed, I sometimes feel, is the sensation of being absolutely free, to do exactly what I like, to go where I like, to act as I like. I suspect that only an American ever feels that. You aren't weighed down by your families, and you aren't weighed down by history. If I ran away to the South Pole some Pakistani businessman would one day crawl into my igloo and ask if I was the cousin of K. K. Harouni."

Rafia touched his arm. "Darling, you're too old to be menopausal. Americans aren't more free than anyone else. Just because an American runs away, to Kansas or Wyoming, doesn't mean that he succeeds in escaping whatever it is he left behind. Like all of us, he carries it with him." She turned to Helen. "Let me ask you. Do you think you're free?"

"I'm not old enough yet to know. I think that at twenty-one many girls think they are."

"Brilliant!" said Sohail. He poured more wine for himself and for his parents; Helen put her hand over the mouth of her glass.

After a moment Mr. Harouni stood up and began gathering their dishes. He prevented Sohail from rising to help him, saying, "No, no, you sit, let me do this."

"You have to admit, my dad's pretty evolved," said Sohail. "He even likes to cook."

Her mind cooling, prickly from the wine, Helen listened to Sohail and his mother talking about their plans for the next few days, museums and the ballet on Christmas Eve. Rafia had a slight British accent, but softer than that, more rounded—as if the accent had been bred by the personality, as one of her individual characteristics. *So this is how Sohail grew up*, Helen thought. She wondered what lay beneath the angularities of Rafia's character—a woman so imposing not only in her speech but in her manner, the way in which she moved her hands, the angle at which she held her head. In any case, Helen would manage with Rafia, they would make their peace.

• • •

AS SOON AS they finished dessert, Sohail got up to leave, refusing coffee.

"You don't have to go yet," said Rafia, her voice tentative. "It's only nine-thirty."

Mr. Harouni looked out of the window and then insisted upon loaning Helen a scarf. "It's very cold, you know. And it looks good, the red suits your dress." He showed her how to tie the knot in a new way.

Outside it really had become very cold, and even though it was early the streets were empty, the restaurants along the quay deserted.

"That was nice," said Helen, intending it as a question.

"I wish, I wish they hadn't come. It's too much."

"Your mother loves you a lot, you know. She wanted us to stay, it was almost pathetic. She's afraid I'll take you away."

"God, and my father with his scarf. When I was little I went into the drawing room every evening to say good night to my parents—they always had guests—after my bath, with my hair wet; and my father would send the servant for a towel and rub my head with it. That's it, that was his parenting. And he did it so badly, roughly, just because he didn't know how to touch me."

She took his arm, squeezed it, and leaned in to him; they walked quickly along the river, across to the Île de la Cité, Notre Dame looming overhead.

"Did they like me? Did I do all right?"

"You did beautifully, my love. I was proud of you."

She knew that he wasn't being perfectly sincere. "I feel like Sohail's country-cute girlfriend."

"It's not at all like that."

The apartment felt warm at first, and they threw off their coats and lay back on the futon. Then it became too hot. Helen lit the candles on a little table near their heads, and in the orange light they both softened.

They made love, gently. When they finished Sohail opened the window and a delicious cold air blew in, billowing the lacy curtains and flickering the candles. A light rain fell. He stood by the window, naked, looking out at the city, and she watched him and knew that she loved him very much.

THE NEXT MORNING Helen and Sohail walked along the cold Seine. Among the cobblestones of the quay little puddles had frozen, rough at the edges and black at the centers; as the sun hit them, the ice softened and broke underfoot. The hard blue sky stood enormously tall over Paris. Helen wore high-heeled boots and a long wool skirt. Her friends at Yale each had loaned her something, the reefer jacket she wore that day, some little bits of jewelry, and other simple things. Sohail wore what Helen called his interesting shoes—he had a dozen pairs—jeans, and a long camel-hair coat.

They stood in front of a wooden houseboat painted cream, black at the waterline, the interior visible through latticed windows cut into the sides.

"Let's buy one of these soon and live on it," he said.

"I know," she said playfully. "And we'll raise sheeps and rabbits and live off the fatta the land." Helen often used this line from Steinbeck. She put her little mittened hand into his, turned to face him, and kissed him on the tip of his nose. "You make too many impossible plans."

They left the quay at the Pont de la Concorde and turned down the Champs-Elysées. Under the trees the fallen leaves smelled bitter from the previous day's rain. They passed a young man selling chestnuts, warming them over coals in a tray cut from a tin barrel, standing on a piece of cardboard for insulation and stamping his feet.

Sohail pulled Helen close and whispered in her ear, "He's one of mine, from Pakistan, from Punjab."

The young man, stamping his feet and shivering in his inadequate coat, held up a packet of the chestnuts.

"I'll try some," said Helen. She took a euro from her purse and paid.

They emerged from the little park onto the sidewalk and could see down the Champs-Elysées to the Arc de Triomphe, humped unnaturally large over the avenue.

"There's a line from Merrill," said Sohail, "it's on the tip of my tongue, something about a 'honey-slow descent of the Champs-Elysées.' " Sohail had an excellent memory, which had compensated for his indifferent work ethic in law school. After a moment, he began reciting.

> *Back into my imagination*
> *The city glides, like cities seen from the air,*
> *Mere smoke and sparkle to the passenger*
> *Having in mind another destination*
> *Which now is not that honey-slow descent*
> *Of the Champs-Elysées, her hand in his,*
> *But the dull need to make some kind of house*
> *Out of the life lived, out of the love spent.*

He finished and sat down on a bench. The sun had come out brightly.

"That's beautiful, sweetie. Say it again."

While he recited she looked at him, his handsome dark profile, and ran her hands through the thick black hair at the nape of his neck.

"What does it mean?" she whispered.

THE NEXT NIGHT was Christmas Eve, and Rafia had gotten tickets for the ballet, *Sleeping Beauty* at the Garnier. Helen changed first her dress and then her shoes, so that when they arrived at the Opéra they found the Harounis waiting in the lobby, Rafia wearing a midnight blue sari of shot silk, a long heavily worked pashmina shawl, and earrings made from cabochon emeralds, green drops large as grapes. Mr. Harouni looked at his watch pointedly.

"It's fine, darling," said Rafia, in response to Helen's apologies. "We've been people-watching. The clothes are wonderful."

Helen had settled on a pale apricot dress and ornaments that Rafia had given her as an early Christmas present, dangling white earrings. Her agitation was reflected in her girlish brimming face.

Rafia smiled, showing her dimples. "You make me wish I were twenty again."

They moved up the stairs among the crowd, Helen very conscious of her long dress, afraid she would trip on the hem, particularly in the reflected attention drawn by Rafia.

The Harounis had the center box in the second loge. "You ladies sit in front," insisted Mr. Harouni, standing in the vestibule at the back of the box and placing his Burberry overcoat carefully on a hanger.

Helen protested and then gave in, arranging herself into one of the small, uncomfortable chairs upholstered in the same muted red velvet as the walls. The musicians in the pit were warming up, the sharp sounds of the string instruments cutting through the murmuring of the crowd.

The ballet began—Nureyev's choreography, the production finespun and brilliant. At first Helen had trouble following the story, which was darker and more adult than the version of *Sleeping Beauty* she had known; but gradually she became absorbed in the precision of the dancers' movements. When the intermission came she blinked and for a moment didn't know where she was.

· · ·

THE CROWD STOPPED clapping, and the silence in the box became prolonged.

"Well, it's absolutely first-rate," said Rafia, with a finality that did not invite further opinion. She rose and positioned her shawl, flipping it around her neck in an economical little movement. Looking at Helen, touching her elbow to guide her out, she said, "I was watching you—I could see it all reflected in your face, the freshness of your impressions. I'm so glad you like it."

They walked out onto the balcony, and Sohail drew Helen over to the banister, where they could see the crowd emerging from the orchestra.

"I love you," he said, kissing her on the neck.

"I love you too," she replied. Everything in this world seemed to her finer, more defined, more weighted. The lights blazed above them in immense chandeliers, and the people walking up the Garnier's famous stair seemed themselves to be gravely dancing, moving in unison, chatting fluently and with choreographed gestures.

Standing behind her, Sohail whispered in her ear, "Let's have a glass of champagne."

The Harounis wanted coffee—"Your father's falling asleep," said Rafia—and so the two couples separated.

Helen stood by a tall golden window overlooking the Place de l'Opéra, gazing back into the elaborately decorated room, watching Sohail approach with two flutes of champagne. She felt shy, her senses alive.

As the ushers came through to call the audience back into the hall, Sohail asked, "Can you find it? I have to go to the bathroom, I'll be right there."

Helen climbed the stairs to the curving wall set with the doors to the boxes. The first door she opened was wrong, and a strange couple stared at her, as if she were trying to slip into their seats. Confused, she peeked gingerly through the next door, which was half open.

Stepping into the vestibule, she saw Rafia and Mr. Harouni seated together in the front seats, looking down at the orchestra, intimate in a way that she had not seen them before. She immediately sensed they were speaking about her.

"I suppose that depends on who is being fascinated," said Mr. Harouni.

"Not really," answered Rafia; and then: "Look at that couple, aren't they superb. Look at the way she carries herself."

Just then Sohail burst through the door behind Helen, his face splashed with water. "Hello, hello," he said, carrying Helen forward into the front of the box.

She felt naked and ashamed as Sohail's father rose quickly from her seat. "Please, Mr. Harouni," she implored. "Please sit in front."

He wouldn't hear of it, and so she sat exposed by the bright lights until the curtain rose, studying a program, her face burning.

When the ballet ended Helen couldn't look at Rafia and pretended to be fumbling with her little beaded purse. Her chest felt tight, and it all seemed false to her, the people shuffling down the staircase and out through the lobby, each one to a particular evening, the wood moldings painted gold, the massive and elaborate chandeliers. As they emerged into the cold Paris night she thought, *It's Christmas Eve.*

SOHAIL AND HELEN decided to rent a car and spend New Year's Eve out in the country. Upon their return to Paris the Harounis would be gone. Both felt constrained—in college they sometimes fought, as couples do, but each night they came back to each other. Helen would say, "Let's not go to sleep angry," and they would stay up and talk and sometimes make love to drive away whatever had hurt them. But in the days following the ballet they had begun to guard their thoughts. They agreed it would be better in the country, in another place, staying in a little hotel room with a creaky bed and eating a country dinner in a rain-washed town overrun by cats—that was the way Sohail described it.

Sohail had seen his parents apart from Helen, respecting her desire to have a little space, as she put it. On Christmas Day they had dropped in at the Quai des Grands Augustins apartment to exchange presents, and saw the Harounis for coffee several days later at Rafia's favorite café, La Palette.

As they were parting, Rafia said to Helen, "I'll see Sohail in ten days. But let's you and I meet for a girls' tea, just to have a little time alone." She suggested the next afternoon at the Hôtel George V. Sohail and Helen would pick up their car the following day, early in the morning, and drive to the Loire Valley to celebrate New Year's in Montrésor, which would be empty of tourists this time of year. They would walk along the little stream Sohail described and have champagne beside the pond at midnight.

HELEN HAD BROUGHT to Paris the suit she bought for medical school interviews, a conservative blue jacket and knee-length skirt, and she wore this to tea, with cream-colored stockings and a fitted white T-shirt to make it less formal. She looked armored, cool, and efficient, exactly as she wanted to feel. After walking up Avenue George V, past decorous stores, under a warm sun, Helen was not intimidated by the liveried doorman who quickly assessed her and welcomed her in English. Although she had timed her arrival five minutes early, looking across the large airy room, she saw Rafia sitting at a corner table, reading a magazine.

"I'm sorry," began Helen, hurrying across the carpet.

"No, no, I came early, I like to settle in." She stood up and kissed Helen on the cheek. "How *are* you?"

Rafia wore Western clothes—tailored brown slacks, brown high-

heeled boots, and a white cashmere sweater with a thick turtleneck—
which surprised Helen, this collected, hip look.

"Have some petits fours, Helen," Rafia said, as the waiter approached
the table. "They're delicious." She sat back and lit a cigarette, looking
at Helen with a hint of a smile, a friendly, appraising expression. "So,
you're going to the Loire," she began.

"Though it's strange to be leaving Paris—when I spent so much
time wanting to be here."

"Sohail's like that—he always wants to do the extra bit, the flourish. You'll be back in Paris another year. I'm glad for you."

Rafia was gentler than she had been at their previous meetings—
even the clothing was less assertive.

"Somehow it's difficult for me to think of myself as someone who
will do all these things, travel and live in other countries."

"One of the things that I like about you, Helen, if you don't mind
my saying so, is that you *don't* assume those things. But I know you
will have a life in the big world. You're the right kind of American,
the Americans who went to the moon. And the Americans of Hawthorne and Robert Lowell—the Puritans and the prairie."

"Hawthorne and Lowell are more Puritan than prairie."

"True. I suppose you are also."

The waiter brought the tea and a silver dish with a selection of
delicate petits fours. Rafia took one, holding it distinctly with her
long fingers.

"Would you like to talk about Sohail?" asked Helen.

"Yes. Though that's not the only reason I asked you here. I also
wanted to have a real moment with you. Quite aside from Sohail, I
respect you, and I envy your freedoms. In your life you'll have solid
things, and you'll have them more solidly than I did."

"And we both wonder where Sohail fits in."

"You tell me." Rafia said this softly. "Is he one of those solid things?"
She placed her elbows on the table, joined her hands together, and

touched her lips with her fingers, the gesture masculine, her eyes bright. Watching her, struggling to keep up with her, Helen marveled at how quickly Rafia could transform herself.

She had known that the question of her future with Sohail would be at the center of this meeting, but now it seemed that any words she spoke would be too final, irrevocable.

"Sohail and I haven't *really* talked about it. Of course we've walked around the subject, a million times. He's so good at ignoring things that bother him. I can't help being the responsible one. I brood."

"And where does this brooding lead?"

"It depends on the day. I try to live in the present, not to ask so many questions."

"I owe it to you to be frank, even more because I like you and I respect you. Sohail is gentle—not weak, soft. That's one of the reasons we both love him, and it's also his greatest flaw. My husband never missed a meeting or a day of work in his life; and I've spent or misspent my life helping my husband's career and more or less having a career myself, as someone who knows where the power lies and how to focus it. Sohail doesn't have that mettle in him. He gets by on intelligence, that's why he's still successful."

"Perhaps he won't need to be hard."

"Because of his money? He'll need it more because of that. Even I can remember when everyone knew everyone in Karachi. Pakistan isn't like that anymore, there are many powerful men who would look at Sohail and his property and see a lamb fattened for the slaughter. And then, it's as difficult to have a meaningful life with a lot of money as without. But my point is, he'll follow you and do what you decide. I can't do anything about it—if I could I probably would, because I don't think you can make him happy, and I know he can't make you happy. You would hate Pakistan. You're not built for it, you're too straight and you don't put enough value on decorative, superficial things—and that's the only way to get by there."

"He could live in America."

"And how would that be? He would be emasculated, not American and not with any place in Pakistan, working at a job he wouldn't like. I see these boys come through Karachi on two-week vacations—the boys who settled in America—and they always have this odd tamed look, a bit sheepish. It's so much worse after 9/11—they more or less apologize daily. Sohail's background will always be a factor, when he flies out for a deposition to the Cracker Belt or the Corn Belt. He's proud of who he is, but they would knock a bit of that out of him. In any case, for you he would do it, join a law firm in New York. He would even stay with you, if that's what you wanted. But I promise you, he wouldn't be happy, he wouldn't feed the best part of himself."

Helen looked at Rafia squarely. "And in Pakistan will he feed that best part?"

"I don't know," cried Rafia, startling Helen. "I don't know."

"And would you be willing to let him go?"

Rafia leaned back in her chair and lit another cigarette, her hair, which was drawn back in a bun, cutting across her temples in two gleaming black bands. "Yes. But that's a different concern. I've said my piece, and now I trust you to do what you will. I trust you, it's as simple as that."

"That's almost blackmail, Mrs. Harouni. Suppose I don't agree with you."

"Then you'll do what you will."

Now Helen leaned back in her chair and looked out onto a little courtyard. In summer the hotel would serve tea there. "I also had something to say, Mrs. Harouni."

Rafia laughed, the sound easy and pleasant. "After all that, I think you should call me Rafia."

"Thank you. Rafia, then. I guess I just wanted to thank you for making Sohail what he is. He's been everything to me, he's been good to me. I think a lot of the things that he showed me, you showed him first. Just his way of looking at things, I mean, the good part of it. And books and pictures." She stopped. She could go no further in being gracious. It was dawning on her that Rafia had driven her to say more than she wanted, and perhaps more than she meant.

Rafia narrowed her eyes. "I can't decide if those are or aren't the words of a future daughter-in-law. There's something valedictory about them."

"Maybe of a daughter-in-law from the prairie. We *are* ingenuous, you know."

This broke the tension. Helen knew the interview was over. They began speaking inconsequentially, of an exhibition they had seen, separately, at the Petit Palais.

When they had finished their tea, they walked out together, down streets drowsy in the warm, still afternoon.

"I'm going to walk," Helen said.

"And I will take the Métro."

At the entrance Rafia embraced Helen closely and then leaned back, holding her forearms. "Thank you."

And before Helen could respond, Rafia turned and skipped down the stairs, in her impeccable high-heeled boots, went through the turnstile, and disappeared into the station.

AT FONTAINEBLEAU SOHAIL exited the motorway in the direction of Orléans, among the little towns with narrow streets. Helen observed the mossy orange-tiled roofs, the weathered stucco walls, the drives leading to the large summer homes of Parisians. Now in December, the day before New Year's Eve, the towns were shuttered. Helen played with the radio, alternating between classical music and French pop, and they spoke only of the passing countryside.

She felt comfortable with him, the car warm, the windshield

wipers throwing off the rain that began and then stopped. As they reached the city center of Orléans the sun emerged among strips of cloud. The blueness of the sky struck Helen as she uncurled herself from the car. Immaculate puddles reflected the brightening light.

They walked on the washed pavement, among crowds going to a fair in the main square, with an ice-skating rink and booths selling crafts. Weaving in and out of the people, holding hands, they broke apart and then came back together again, hardly aware of doing it, under the façades of nineteenth-century municipal buildings that crowded shoulder to shoulder around the square. Inhaling the rough scent of pine boughs, they passed between lanes of temporary plywood shops hammered together. Heavy orange electrical cords lay tangled underfoot, feeding the many lights.

They shared a crêpe, chocolate with bananas, and then bought a Nina Simone disc. The people around them were in a holiday mood, many of them old, the country aging.

Helen stopped at a booth selling candy, sour balls and gummi bears, jelly worms striped green and yellow, chocolate almonds, peanut brittle, each type in a little glass cookie jar, each to be weighed separately.

"Can we get some?" Helen would sometimes eat a whole bag of candy, then become sad and childish, with a headache.

Sohail pulled at her leather-gloved hand. "Let's get it at the grocery store, we need water anyway. It costs four times more here."

"But I want this."

"Why? It's the same thing."

She walked away, angry for a moment, and then her cheeks burned at the thought that she was spending his money. She had hardly any of her own for this trip, no savings; at school she lived on nothing, always had a job, even after she met Sohail.

They passed through a little alley to reach the car, and when they were in the shadows he turned to her and buried his face in her hair. "I'm sorry, I'm sorry."

She comforted him, his face wet.

"I can't believe I didn't buy you that fucking candy. I know I'll remember it, that I didn't."

He wanted to walk on, but she wouldn't let him, and held him. "You always give me nice things. You've taken such good care of me."

In the grocery store he laughed brokenly, sun after rain. "They really don't have the same candy."

They sat for a moment in the car. She leaned over awkwardly from her seat and kissed his neck. She kissed him on the lips, her tongue in his mouth, his face tasting of salt.

"I'm okay," he said, pulling himself together. "It's okay." He unfurled the map.

She picked randomly. "Let's spend the night here. I like the sound of it, Beaugency. It's on the river."

She took out the guide and read aloud to him about the town as they drove through the streets and then along the Loire, the sky becoming dusky, the clouds first orange and then red.

AT THE AUBERGE Maille d'Or in Beaugency, an old posting inn hovering between tight-lipped poverty and seediness, with the plaster cracked and paint chipping on the iron bed frame, their room looked onto a courtyard paved with cobblestones, with a fountain at the far end and, in the gloom along the wall, green plastic crates filled with empty beer bottles. They were the only guests and had what would pass for the best room, at the end of a long gallery on the second floor, with big windows. "I love run-down hotels," Sohail said. He turned on the TV and found a channel showing cartoons, dubbed in French. Helen moved about the big bare room putting away her things, her toiletries in the bathroom, hanging up her clothes.

At dinner they ordered a second bottle of wine. Helen became giggly and afterward asked him to drive her along the river, which glittered and then ran dark under the arches of an old stone bridge. Back at the hotel, a fat black kitten with white paws stuck its nose around the door of the reception desk.

"Look, it's our country cat," she said, tipsy, looking down at it. She knew she was looking pretty, she had been flirting with Sohail all evening, and now she wanted to hold the little kitty, it would suit her. The kitten looked up with wide green eyes, intent, face uplifted like a little black bowl, its feet splayed. It turned and raced out the door, skidding on the tiled floor, chubby tail standing upright.

"Viens, viens," she called, rolling the unfamiliar French word on her tongue, playing at being a little girl.

The kitten slipped behind the beer crates and would not emerge. The long courtyard shaded away into darkness, its silence broken by the splashing sound of the unseen fountain.

Helen sat on her haunches, calling. The kitten came out toward her a few feet, but when she moved forward it scrambled away again, its little white paws flashing.

She sat back and looked up at the stars, at the moon framed by the pollarded branches of a lime tree, stark without leaves. The same stars lit the snowfield behind her house in Connecticut. She would never again be twenty-one in an old hotel in the Loire Valley in France. "I can't believe Paris is over," she said, very softly, because she knew that Sohail was nearby, watching her. Fluidly she stood up, made a kissing sound toward the kitten, and walked back to him.

In their room she led him onto the bed and pulled his clothes off, threw off her own, raising her legs in the air to push off her panties, biting him, his nipples. The loose bedsprings made long rusty sounds, like a knife leisurely sharpened on a whetstone.

Afterward, she stood in the window with a blue-printed cotton scarf wrapped around her body like a sarong, looking out over the courtyard. The kitten ambled on the path beneath their room, on its fat clumsy legs. She called to it, "Hello, kitty cat."

IN THE MORNING a heavy mist lay over the winter fields. They drifted south on narrow country roads, Helen driving. She drove fast, not smoothly but with a kind of angularity, from point A to point B. A hare burst from the woods on their left, crossed the road, and then bounded over a plowed field. Helen stopped the car, and they watched it lope far across the field and into the woods on the other side.

At Chenonceaux rain began to fall lightly, as if the mist were dissolving. The brown wooded bank on the far side of the river Cher set off the quirky, light château, which seemed too playful to be a house, too fantastical, its towers and filigree, its position astride the river. The current as it flowed through the arches, rippling and white, appeared to Helen to be towing the château out to sea.

A fire burned in the guardroom, and they stood in front of it. Through the windows they could see the gray water flowing underneath. Helen wandered away from Sohail and up some stairs into a dark room—a bedroom—belonging to some widowed queen. She stared for a long time out the window, west, down the river as it flowed to the sea. Soon she would be going back there, to classes, to the snow in New Haven, to the old beaten-up car that she loved. Every few weeks she drove into the country to visit her mother, who would open a bottle of sparkling wine to celebrate. *Now,* she thought. *Now, now it's time. It can't wait any longer.*

She found him in Catherine de Medici's little study, which hangs out over the water like the cockpit of a plane, glassed on three sides. "I've been looking for you, baby," said Sohail.

Helen leaned her body against him, put her head on his shoulder. "Let's go home," she said.

"Do you mean to the inn in Montresor?"

"No, I mean Paris."

"What about New Year's?"

"Let's be in Paris. I need to, I really do. We'll walk along the Seine. It's only three hours away."

He didn't ask why. Returning to the car, Sohail insisted on stopping to see the maze. The hedges stood only to waist level, and so she watched him as he worked his way through it. It wasn't fun, she knew it wasn't fun for him, but he had to do it, pretending to play. He looked so beautiful in the rain.

Wearing an odd, determined look, he took a long time to get through, then succeeded and stood on the little platform in the center. "Look, I made it," he whispered, just audible.

Almost with horror she watched him approach her, then stand in front of her, looking into her face, and she hardened herself to meet him, eyes dimming, seeing through him, willing herself to remember the centuries, the kings and their queens who had walked here, seen this river, this wet forest—and now their loves blown away, their pain.

Lily

Part I: Islamabad

L̲ily had been to parties all week, month, endlessly, drinking, rarely having dinner. Walking back across the lawn from the bar with a glass of champagne, she stopped to look around her, at the gathering party, the DJ setting up his booth, the waiters in white coats, and felt as if she were an actress in a traveling theater company, once again tonight to go through the same emotions, the same intoxications. For this evening, themed as "Night of the Tsunami," her friend Mino's servants had brought in truckloads of sand to make an artificial beach beside his newly built weekend home at Simly Dam— where Mino sat holding court, sprawled on a *dhurrie* by the water, leaning against a pillow. She found Mino tiresome, though he was perhaps her best friend, found the whole group of them shallow and false—she included herself in the indictment—drifting from party to party, flying out of Isloo, as they called it, to Karachi, to Lahore, on the circuit in the spring weather, jet-propelled.

There were only a handful of houses out at Simly Dam, an hour from Islamabad on bad roads, and all were empty, unlit, except this one. The place looked unfinished, the landscape all boulders, red clay hills, rock cliffs falling down to the lake.

"Oh my *God*, these people!" Mino waved dismissively at a couple nosing off to the bar after saying hello. "Did you see those two? Daddy-O and his little girl. You'd need dynamite to get him off her." Mino wore an embroidered cashmere shawl draped over his well-fleshed arm, his look finished with an extravagant diamond ear stud—*a rich jewel in an Ethiop's ear*, he said when asked about it.

Leila, or Lily as her friends called her, sat perched on a stool, her slender legs held in her bare arms, chin on her knees, looking out at the water. Not yet thirty, she was unusually pretty, her hands and feet and small upturned nose—her high cheekbones, her lips—sharply defined and yet giving the impression of softness, as if she had been trimmed out of soft brown velvet with fine scissors. Her hair, worn long and with bangs, and skin that turned reddish brown in the sun, gave her a sleek appearance, the whole effect being that of a fastidious cat, tail wrapped around herself in repose, independent.

"Seriously, Mino," she said, flicking the stub of a cigarette far out into the water. "You've got some real prizes on your guest list. She's about sixteen, and he looks like he breaks kneecaps for a living."

"Oh, chill out. It's not like I invited them, he's probably some film producer, and she's about to be a star. Let the kid enjoy herself."

"That's your solution to everything, my love. You always tell me to chill out."

The sun had just gone down over the distant line of the dam, leaving a pink band on the horizon. Light flashed off the waves blown up by a slight breeze, chip chip chip, silver. The light seemed familiar—when had she been here before, on a night like this?—and then it came to her, a memory of an entirely different place. As a girl her father took her to the mountains once, to the Kaghan, where he fished for trout with a retired English brigadier, an old colonial. She remembered the dry spice of the pine trees in the air, the valley falling vertically down to the river, and the shallow curve of a stream, an eddy, with trout rising at dusk, pockmarks on the still water.

THAT WINTER SHE had been in London for a wedding, not a close friend but the wedding of the season, the daughter of some bureaucrat who made a crooked pile on the privatization of a steel mill and couldn't return to Pakistan because of cases against him in the National Accountability Bureau—"nabbed," as they called it, almost a mark of distinction. Late at night after the *mehndi*, riding through London in someone's hilarious car, she'd been in a bad accident. She woke at dawn in the hospital, severely concussed, and watched a rare snowfall from her bed, a thin drift on the sill, perceptibly gathering as the large flakes settled out of the gray first light and pressed against the window. She couldn't remember anything at first, where she was, why she was there, sleeping all through the day, until it began to come back, but changed, the experiences of another person.

She had a dream. Flying alone in an airplane, high above the clouds through an ice blue sky, the wing caught fire, orange and flickering. Metal flew off in sheets, the machinery coming apart. A panel above her opened, crumpling back, throwing her out into the slipstream, and her parachute shook out like hair falling loose, streaming lines, then a canopy overhead. The plane spiraled away below her, until it became a speck and hit the ground with a jet of flame, as she drifted down alone through an enormous sky. She woke at dusk in the little hospital room, the snow still falling quietly outside as the sky grew dark in the window, so cold outside, so warm inside.

For the first time, painfully, Lily got out of bed and went over to the window, the ridiculous hospital gown not hiding her nakedness. A visitor had brought candles, and now she lit one and turned off the lights. It seemed to her that the jet falling away was her past, and that she had been forgiven, believing it with all the intensity of the dream, like the intensity and purity of love in a dream. She would forgive herself, for the wrongs she had done and the wrongs done to her, the pain she had caused her parents, who maintained the proprieties on her father's Burma Shell pension, forgive herself for money she had thrown away, the men she had slept with, refusing intimacy, imagining there would be no cost. A few others blamed her, friends she had abandoned or guilelessly betrayed, friends thrown over, and acquaintances treated cruelly. She might not have survived the car accident. Only her barest self had gotten through, and for a while she absolutely believed that she had been freed.

She lay in the hospital bed at twilight after a day of snowfall and allowed a change to come over her, absolving herself.

THAT WAS TWO months ago. Since then she had given a total stranger a blow job after taking Ecstasy at a party—several years earlier a wave of Ecstasy swept through Islamabad, and still hadn't crested—and had another time quite tenderly slept with an old lover, who was visiting from his new home in Mississippi, of all places. But she held on to a little bit of that cleansed self, for evenings when she stayed at home, though she had places to go, sitting in front of the fireplace in the cool of a winter night, looking into the glowing orange flames and seeing mountains and valleys, storms, horses, huge crowds of men, in the flame that burned her cheeks and face. She had slowly begun to turn away from her friends, looked at them, at their conversation, their jokes, from a slight distance.

Her parents left her alone, as she had so harshly taught them to, although she lived in a cottage built in the large garden behind their house. They had almost no money—worrying about electricity and gas, about the car breaking down, and kept only a cook and a bearer—but her father had bought this large plot in Islamabad in the 1960s, when they were to be had for nothing. Today worth eighty or ninety million rupees, on Margalla Avenue, the most fashionable place to live, this property allowed them to maintain a position in the world of their birth, one of the old feudal families from Lahore, but with the land all sold in the previous generation.

NOW AT THE party, with a breeze off the lake gliding down the slope of the hills to the east, she rose and took her wrap. The ancient bartender, a retired servant from the regimental mess of Probyn's Horse, who served at all the parties, and whose leathery glum face made him look as if he had been pickled in gin, poured her a glass of champagne without being asked, taken from the stock being kept for the inner circle.

"For madam."

Presuming slightly, he added, "So many new people here, little people. They steal cell phones and cameras and make trouble."

"So I hear, Khan jee. Once upon a time we were the new ones." Taking the bottle that he had placed on the table, she poured a glass and handed it to him. "There, drink that to the way we used to be, old man."

She walked up toward the swimming pool, which had been built on a headland away from the house, with views over the water and the lawns below. She could be alone there for a moment, to compose the face with which she would meet the evening. A few more glasses of champagne, and she'd be fine, she knew, would enjoy it, people, personalities looming into view and disappearing, characters—and then, dancing. Sitting on a chaise longue at the far end of the pool, she lit a cigarette. Below, in a pavilion by the bar, music played, not yet loud, Césaria Évora, the voice calling, the beginning.

She heard a footstep behind her, and a man emerged from the darkness of a verandah.

"I'm sorry, do you have a match?"

She looked at his face, half visible in the blue shimmer cast by underwater spotlights. Plain dark suit, white shirt. Light framed, thin lips and a fine long nose with a distinct hump, as if broken and improperly reset, the break offsetting the feminine lips.

"Tell me that's not a pickup line." She took a lighter from her little beaded handbag and passed it to him.

He smiled, the impression held back for a moment and then spreading across his face. "No, I actually needed it. You don't remember, but we've met—at Bugoo Moono's place. I'm Murad Talwan."

"Oh God, not Bugoo's place. So you must be the son of Makhdoom Talwan. From Multan."

"His nephew. And from Muzaffargarh. You were close."

"That's not close at all."

"For a girl from Islamabad it is. I suppose the only time you're aware of our famous Punjabi countryside is when you fly over it."

She laughed, cocking her eyebrow. "And what do you know about me? Maybe my finest hours are spent giving polio drops to villagers' babies."

Looking out at the scene, the flickering lamps below, the lit DJ booth far down by the water, she asked, "So tell me, Mr. Murad Talwan, nephew of the great Makhdoom Talwan, friend of the less than great Bugoo Moono—what do you do when you're not loitering by the swimming pool trying to get a light? Are you exceedingly rich?"

The man sat down, placed his cigarette in an ashtray on a table beside him, and rubbed his hands together. "No, that would be my evil uncle, the famous Makhdoom Talwan as you call him. I'm actually a kind of businessman. I have some land, and I'm setting up greenhouses to grow vegetables. There's only one other man in Pakistan doing it."

"So you're the entrepreneurial type. Gift of the gab and lots of new ideas."

"I'm not sure. Probably there's a reason I've got only one competitor."

"I was being serious. I like people who actually do something useful, though I don't seem to meet them very often." She allowed that he had crossed the first barrier. "But anyway tell me about something else, something interesting."

"First, can I get you another drink? And I'll bring one for myself."

On the verge of excusing herself, she looked at him, his thin supercilious features and silver-minted look, which she had once admired in young rich Pakistani men and long outgrown—and then against that, the appearance of strength, of vigor, reflected in his posture, sitting relaxed and looking agreeably out into the night.

"All right. Champagne. Tell the bartender it's for me, otherwise he'll say he's run out."

HE DIDN'T MAKE a pass at her—in that evening's mood she would have rebuffed it with a jet of ice—and when they had talked for more than half an hour, quite easily, until she found herself laughing, on a whim she gave him her cell phone number.

"And now let's go dance," she said, putting down her glass, which had long been empty.

"I don't dance. I stopped when a girl told me I look like a chicken wading through melted tar."

She laughed. "Well that's sad, because that's pretty much *all* I do. Goodbye then." And she walked away, down the steps, and into the crowd, into the party.

SHE VAGUELY EXPECTED him to call the next day or the one after that—their conversation had been more substantial than such

encounters usually are, and she had volunteered her phone number—
but when he didn't she shrugged it off, saying, *"Tant pis."*

As it happened her phone rang on one of her alone evenings, as
she was sitting by the fire, a cup of tea beside her, reading—nothing,
chick lit, something easy.

"Hi, it's me," he began, and she rolled her eyes, simultaneously
taking a lock of her long straight black hair and curling it around her
forefinger. When she didn't respond, he added, "I meant to say, this is
Murad."

"Actually I recognized your voice."

"That lets me off the hook, I suppose." Then, after a pause, "Are
you busy?"

"Not really. I'm sitting in front of a fire, reading an extremely bad
book."

"I'm surprised, I assumed I'd hear pounding music in the background when you picked up."

"Not tonight. I'm alone, drinking tea, and generally practicing to
be an old maid."

"Look, this may seem a bit sudden, but remember you told me
about going to Kaghan with your father? Well, I thought about
driving to Attock and going for a picnic along the Indus. It's pretty
interesting, the Kabul River flows in, and it's brown, and for a long
way downstream it stays separate from the blue Indus, so they run
side by side, like two stripes. Right where we'll go they start mixing
together."

"A metaphor, I suppose." She said this more evenly, less ironically
than she intended. Sitting by the pool at the lake party, she had told
him about fishing in Kaghan as a girl—it had been on her mind, and
she had let herself go to that degree.

"You don't know me very well. But I can bring a certificate of good
moral character from my grandmother if that would help . . ."

"That's fine, I'll take your word for it. I'd love to. When?"

"How about this Saturday?"

"How about the next one."

"At eight. Or no, you're probably not up. At ten. I'll pick you up. I know where your parents' house is."

And abruptly, he hung up, just as she was about to say, "That sounds a bit creepy."

Putting down the phone, she cringed, thinking of her old maid comment, which sounded self-pitying, and worse, sounded as if she were sitting alone dreaming of matrimony.

"THIS IS A rather posh vehicle—for the poor nephew of a rich Makhdoom."

They were driving along the Grand Trunk road, under the eucalyptus trees planted by some briefly energetic government.

"I couldn't do without it. I live in this thing."

"It looks brand-new."

"It's ten years old. My driver takes brilliant care of it. Back and forth we go, to my farm—I stay there a couple of weeks, and then I start going crazy and I drive back to Islamabad for R&R. Ten hours on bad roads."

"Ah, the famous vegetables."

He looked over at her, smoothly changing gears, driving very precisely in the heavy chaotic traffic, buses swaying past with passengers on the roof and hanging from the doors, terrifically overloaded trucks grinding along, painted with elaborate scenes of a mountain paradise, snow-capped peaks like a child's painting, Shangri-la, or of fighter jets, babies, pneumatic film actresses.

"Indeed, the famous vegetables."

She had decided on Western clothes, white linen bell-bottom pants, a fitted emerald-colored blouse, which suited her complexion and her black hair, and sandals rather than something more practical—like a girl in a commercial for Bacardi rum, she told herself, looking in her dressing room mirror. Now she put one foot up on the dash, keeping it there for a long moment, glossy red nail polish, high arch. Rolling down her window, she put her bare arm out, the breeze soft, fragrant with eucalyptus blossoms, fields of yellow mustard blossoming out to the horizon, then the beginning of the hard country, the Frontier.

"So, do you often invite bad girls for picnics along the Indus?" she asked.

"Oh no. You're actually the first bad girl I've known well enough to ask."

"Very funny. Do you know, I've done some research. You went to college at Princeton, where you drove around in a Porsche. Your mother passed away two years ago. Your father and your uncle haven't spoken for years, your uncle sits in the Assembly—and your father is bedridden."

"Not guilty on the Porsche. Even if I had had the money, I'm not quite that much of a twerp."

"And you're either stuck up or shy—I heard both versions."

"Or maybe just schizophrenic, playing it both ways."

"Not in the report. Though it does occur in the family."

"My God! Is this stuff available on the Web or something? Paki-desigroom.com."

She folded her arms, shaking her head, saying in a kittenish coy voice, "That's it, I'm done. A complete description of the specimen." And then, having set it up, slyly, "I won't ask what you've heard about me."

"Well, that you had a bad accident, and that it changed you."

"What a gentleman. Anyway there are plenty of people to tell you lies about me. And truths for that matter. I hope you don't think I've been going around boasting about my near-death experience."

He turned off the Grand Trunk road, under the bridge leading to

Peshawar, through a little village. Passersby turned to look at them, the large gray jeep with a pretty girl wearing enormous white-framed sunglasses, and a man in Western clothes. They turned down onto what seemed like a streambed, Murad driving with concentration, working the car through difficult sections, backing up and trying a different route. The smell of dust filled the jeep, and soon a fine white layer covered the plastic of the dashboard. Continuing, following a more or less usable track, they came out on a sandbank broad as a football field ceded by a curve in the Indus. Murad drove partway across and turned off the engine, facing out to the water.

"There it is."

"It's amazing. How did you find this? It's like a secret hidden valley."

He had stepped out of the jeep, taken a pair of binoculars from the back seat, and was scanning the hills all around. She noticed the worn strong leather case for the binoculars, earlier had noticed a pistol in a tooled leather holster lying concealed between the seats. She liked that he had well-used solid things, this car, the gun and binoculars, and she liked that he carried a gun, but without making any display. In an emergency he would be solid, would take care of the problem.

"An army friend flew over in a helicopter and told me about it. It took me a whole day to find a way down, following these dry watercourses. Even goats can't find much to eat here."

Walking out onto the sand, she took off her sandals and carried them in her hand. The place seemed immense and empty, a huge bowl of rock, with the cool river running through it, the blue and white stripes of the two tributary rivers beginning to mingle, a confusion at the middle of the stream. A breeze blew off the water, increasing the loneliness, rolling up a tube of sand, which snaked in front of her, rustling softly.

She looked around, at the hills, bare all around, the parked jeep seeming to glow, tiny against the backdrop. "You know what's amazing, we're actually alone here. That never happens in Pakistan."

"I'm pretty sure we *are* alone. That's what I was checking with the binoculars."

Throwing herself down on the soft sand, wriggling to make herself comfortable, she said with a little laugh, "You're a real belt-and-suspenders kind of guy."

He brought a rug and a basket from the car, placed the rug carefully on the sand, and then poured them each a glass of white wine.

They drank, looking out at the river, silent.

Taking sand in her hand, she let it stream out between her fingers, blown away by the wind.

"I'm really moved. Thank you for bringing me here."

"I was afraid you wouldn't like it. You probably don't often go out of the city."

"I don't, but I wish I did. I'd like to live in the country. Sometimes I think I'd like to live alone on an island."

He opened the picnic basket, had clearly made a great effort, a baguette from the French Bakery, expensive cheeses, grapes, chocolate, nuts, little chicken sandwiches, and then Pakistani food in containers, more food than they could possibly eat.

After lunch, he went behind the jeep and came out wearing shorts, carrying a towel, his body slender and brown, legs muscular, a thin trace of hair below his belly button. His head was mounted well on his shoulders, the shoulders set back. Walking far upstream, he disappeared around a pile of enormous boulders, while she sat musing, the sun warm on her back.

Silently and very fast, he came sweeping into view out at the middle of the river, his head small and black against the dark green water, caught in the boiling current. Sheltering her eyes with her hand, she watched, knowing she could do nothing to save him, feeling irritation and regret wound together, at this abrupt sinking of her frail butterfly hopes, this stupid ending, the mess. As she lunged up to run across the sand, panicking, he waved to her, floated on his back for a moment, turned over, and began to swim in toward the shore with a precise motion, turning up his head to breathe at every second stroke. He took a clever angle against the river sweeping him away, and at the far point, where the curving bay ended, he splashed ashore.

Approaching, walking on the harder sand at the edge of the water, he stood above her, almost dry, glistening from the sun. "That was pretty goddamned cold," he said. "I'll admit that!"

She threw him the towel, squinting up at his face, which seemed black against the sun behind him. "You scared me. I thought you were drowning."

"Not this time. There's a bit of Persian poetry that my father quotes: *Standing there on the shore, / What do you know of my troubles, / As I struggle here in midstream.*"

He sat down, facing almost away from her. "You have to admit, that's a pretty apt quotation."

"Very impressive. Or maybe it's a bit too literal, if I wanted to be picky." After a moment she said, "I'm not going to sleep with you, you know. I decided that, while you were swimming or drowning or whatever you were doing."

"I must say, for a girl from a good Punjabi family you say the most astonishing things. Let me guess: you swore to God that if I survived you would renounce me forever. Or I should say, swore to some unspecified life force."

"I know, *The End of the Affair*. I saw the movie. But it's sort of true. I really did think you were finished. And I doubt I could get home alone in your car. Not to mention the scandal. Imagine explaining what we were doing together in this place. I wouldn't even bother to try, I'd dump the body outside your parents' gate at night."

He laughed. "I'm glad to know you were focusing on the really important aspects of the problem."

"Not at all. I didn't push you in the river, you were showing off. You're a grown-up."

"Very laissez-faire. You do your thing, I do mine."

"Exactly. Companions on a social venture."

"I see. Well, let's have another drink."

As she sipped from her glass, watching him over the rim, she said, "Or maybe not for a long time."

"You keep bringing it up. And how do you know I'll sleep with you?"

"Oh, that's easy. It's written all over your face."

He lit a joint, and she wished that he hadn't, looking over at him as he passed it, wanting him not to get drunk, not to smoke, to do drugs. Of course, he'd been at Princeton, he must have more or less gone through all that, rich Pakistanis at school in America almost invariably did—in her single year at NYU, failing, not even taking the spring semester exams, she herself received an entire parallel education, going around with an Iranian boyfriend three years older than herself, who took bumps of coke all day and night. As Murad sat facing the river, aloof, the breeze raising goose bumps on his bare arms, the towel pulled tightly around his shoulders, she felt immense tenderness toward him.

THE EXPERIENCE OF that day stuck with her, strange as if seen through warped glass. The scent of fast-moving water, the immense flow of the Indus, the dry flat light reflecting off the sand—all this seemed alien and harsh and therefore consistent with the intensity of Murad's approach to her, which was not in anything he said, but in the way that at every point in their interactions he seemed to maintain contact with her, to be interested in her, and to have planned his responses to her. He reassured her, held her up to a standard that she didn't quite understand, an unconventional standard, raw and entirely between them—and then found her sufficient by it. If initially his fixation on her had appeared menacing—she had been excited by it—now she saw in it something benign and heartfelt, a spontaneous resolution that he had made in her favor, an impulse to belong to her and be with her. It struck her that she had been alone with him by the river, no human being for miles around, after spending at most half an hour chatting with him at a party—and yet she had been perfectly comfortable. How many Pakistani men would that be true of?

HE DIDN'T PRESS her—the day after the picnic he left for his farm, where there was no phone, no cell phone service.

A week later, he called. "I'm back."

"So you are. I'm glad."

"What are you up to?"

"I'm getting dressed, some Norwegian Telenor guy is having a party. I'm going to Mino's first."

"That's too bad."

It struck her that she wanted very much to see him. "I guess I get plenty of those guys, and you're farm-fresh. Come over, and I'll make some excuse with Mino."

"That's rather nice of you. I promise to be really bursting with flavor."

She dressed carefully but very plainly, no makeup, jeans, a gypsy top with long sleeves, white—wanting to appear pretty but wholesome, as she felt. Examining herself frankly in the mirror, she acknowledged wanting to meet his image of her, not just to be pretty, but to show him a cleaner better side of herself. Another note sounded, a shrewd voice, telling her not to trust this enterprise, which required her to change her dress, her self-presentation—but then, wasn't that exactly what she wanted, a new life, and so a new look?

On the phone she had told him to drive around behind her parents' house, to her cottage at the back of the long garden. Now she called from an upstairs window that he should let himself in. When she came down the stairs after a few minutes, barefoot, she found him already in her little living room, standing and looking at the bookshelves.

"You've made yourself right at home."

"You have *no* idea." And then, when she looked puzzled, "You must have seen *The Lion King*. The cub says to his evil uncle, 'You're weird, Uncle Scar,' and the uncle says, 'You have *nooo* idea.' I was trying to be funny."

"If you say so. Actually I knew that, I've seen *The Lion King* way too many times."

"Proof of compatibility," he suggested.

"Or proof that I'm a Sunday afternoon stoner. How about you?"

"Arrested development. I watch brainless movies at the farm sometimes, when I start losing it."

Sitting on her haunches by the fireplace, she took a match and lit the rolled newspapers. She thought of doing this watched by another man a few weeks ago, feeling his eyes on her, admiring her, judging her body, back held straight, her blouse tight around her slender waist, the evening in front of them, the seduction and the dance, both of them easily prepared for this encounter—half drunk, snuck away from some party. It wearied her that this memory came now, as she turned and stood, appraising Murad's clothes, loafers with unfortunate tassels, pressed jeans, white shirt tucked in—resembling somehow an army officer out of uniform, the effect touching to her, sincere, a gentleman calling on a lady.

The fire took, slowly at the edges, as she went to a side table and poured two glasses, without asking what he wanted.

"We'll have whiskey," she said.

"All right."

Murad took an etching from a stand on a table, of a man lying in a boat, stretched out under a cloak, with a lamp burning at the prow, the boat floating downstream unpiloted.

"That's by Chughtai," she said. "It's my favorite thing."

Sitting down close to him on the floor, her finger tracing the figure on the glass, she asked, "Why the lamp? It's so strange, I don't know if he's being swept away or if he's just sleeping like that, and letting the boat go wherever it wants. I bought it for almost nothing. It's damaged in the corner, see, it must have been stored somewhere and got eaten just there by termites. I like it because of that."

He stood up and replaced the etching on the table. "You're more of a romantic than I am, and that's saying a lot."

"Are you trying to be smooth with me, Mr. Talwan?"

"I mean it."

"Come on, what do you know about me?"

He swirled the ice cubes in his glass, looked into the fire.

"Can I tell you a story? About the first time I saw you?"

"Do I want to hear it?"

"I think you do, actually. Do you remember, last fall there was a party up in the mountains, at the house of Sohail Harouni?"

"I remember. Were you there?"

"I was. It was an odd time for me. A couple of months earlier I'd gone to my farm, sick of everything. My mother had passed away two years before, my father had taken to his bed, my aunts trying to marry me off to 'suitable girls.' I was so goddamned bored, in my father's incredibly gloomy house. I would go to visit relatives and sit there for hours saying nothing. I really don't like my friends from Aitchison anymore, they all work in banks or do something in textiles, becoming politicians, or doing nothing if they can afford it. I hated myself, and I hated my life.

"So I went to my father's farm and swore to myself that I'd stay there for three whole months, without leaving. Before that I would go for a week or ten days, then retreat. Now I began the vegetable project, building the greenhouses, and I ran every day along the canal, until the villagers even got used to it. At the beginning they thought I'd gone barking mad, sprinting till I was red in the face. I would come home after running and lie on my back on the lawn and watch the day end and the stars come out. Have you ever done that? Staring straight up with the sweat trickling down my face and the mosquitoes hovering in a little formation, and I would think about how space goes on forever, and how little I mean, and how little my problems matter. Real popcorn philosophy, I know.

"A servant was coming to the village on leave from my father's house, and he delivered an invitation—to Sohail Harouni's Halloween party. My three months weren't over, and the party was just two days later. They brought the envelope out to me while I was lying on the lawn, and I realized how happy I felt, how alive, looking up at the sky. I had the farm running well, I'd been exercising, reading good books at night, now I wanted people, I wanted life. Right then I told the cook to pack some food, called my driver, called the farm managers from their houses to give them parting instructions, and a few hours later we were on the road, the driver and I taking turns at the wheel. The sun came up while we were still driving, smoking cigarettes, cruising on the motorway, over the Salt Range, into Islamabad. I love that moment, coming past the United Bakery, the jewelers, past Old Book Corner, the streets full of diplomats' cars, the farm and its problems far far away."

He held up his drink. "I'm sorry, I began sort of at the beginning. I'm boring you."

"No, I like it. I bet I'm about to enter the picture."

Going to the table, he made them each another drink. Sitting with her chin on her knees, she looked into the fire, which blazed now, the room soft and dark around them—she had turned off all the lights except two lamps, sentinels, on tables flanking the door. When he handed her the drink, she took it languidly, drank, and then again put her chin on her knee.

"I drove up to that massive house, with its views almost forever, over Rawal Dam. You remember, with a couple of hundred people there. His wife Sonya, the American, is very sweet, she was almost the only person I spoke with all night. She told me about leaving America as a bride and growing up suddenly when she came here, and then she told me that I seemed a bit lost—but said it in a way that I didn't feel imposed on. I'm not sure why, but for me the air was magic that night, I felt secure, perfectly unruffled merely sitting by myself on the terrace, looking out at the view, fifty kilometers down to Islamabad, to 'Pindi, the lights of the cities. When you're like that, sure of yourself, people take it quite for granted that you're all right, they might say a word to you, and then they move on.

"I walked down to the swimming pool, along the paths lit so beautifully with fires in metal pans, and I sat down in the shadows, on a bench placed under a little grove of chinar trees, beside the pool. People walked down toward the pool, but they kept veering off to the big lawn, where the famous Nizami Sahib was playing the sitar."

Lily began to get up, to put another log on the fire. He took her arm, touching her with just the tips of his fingers.

"Wait, I'm almost done. I sat there for perhaps half an hour, listening to the breeze in the pine trees. And then, a woman came down, but instead of going to the music she continued down to the pool. It was you, of course. You were wearing a long white tunic and a light blue shawl, your arms were bare, your hair was shorter then. You knelt down by the edge of the pool, do you remember? They had put candles in blocks of ice and floated them."

And she said, "I didn't see you, but I remember sitting there. I remember that I wanted to disappear into the water. I could see the moon reflected. Something had just happened, something bad, humiliating. I wanted to die, just for that moment."

"Don't tell me what it was. Hear me out. You splashed the water so that the reflection of the moon broke up and then became whole again. You kept doing it, so much longer than I thought you would, looking so amazingly pretty, pale as you were, in the moonlight. Then some people came down, and I wondered if you would stay and talk to them, and I wanted so much that you shouldn't. And quickly you stood up, so gracefully, and before they could see you, melting away like a wild animal, you disappeared, into the trees, away from the sound of the party. And after a moment I went home."

Neither of them spoke, and then she said, "That's the nicest story I've ever heard about myself."

SHE DRANK MORE than he did, though neither drank very much, bringing the bottle and the ice bucket beside them on the floor. He told her about his farm, about the characters living there, the loneliness he felt, and also how he felt whole and committed only there. He told her about his vegetables, a new and expensive and difficult project.

At a pause in the conversation he sat back, stood up, and paced a few times back and forth across the room, smiling to himself. "There, I even told you about my greenhouses."

She had become languid, sleepy. "You did, and I liked it. Usually men are so boring when they talk about business. I'd like to see your farm, you know. The only farms I've seen are the ones outside Lahore, where people give parties."

"Those don't count. The people who own those lose money by the handful, and they don't care. It's disrespectful, of the land and the people who work it."

"Don't be so serious." The call for prayer sounded from a nearby mosque.

Murad sat down again. "It's almost morning, I should go."

"No, stay. Should we smoke a joint or something?"

"I'm perfect the way I am. But I don't want your parents to see my car."

"They're in Lahore. It's only the watchman and my old servant Fakiru. They've both seen it all, and they know enough to keep quiet."

Looking into the fire for a long moment, he said, "I'm sleepy, but you're right, I don't want to leave."

"Why don't you carry me upstairs and put me to bed in that case?"

He picked up a lighter and spun it on the floor. "No, let's not do that now, let's save it. Bring a cover and a pillow and we'll sleep here by the fire."

They lay down by the fire and held each other and finally slept. At midday when they woke, instead of asking the servant for lunch they drove out to Kausar Market and bought food for a picnic, eating it in her garden lying on a carpet the whole afternoon, with wine and cheese and all the good things.

FOUR MONTHS LATER, to the amazement of all concerned, they were married. When Lily announced her decision to her parents, they took the news almost silently, her father immediately giving his blessing. The illness of Murad's father and the relatively recent death of his mother made it acceptable and even appropriate to have a small wedding, limited to family and just the essential friends. Her parents hadn't imagined the day would come when they would marry her off, and they immediately liked and accepted Murad. They knew Murad's family and were known to them, being of the same class.

Murad, on the other hand, had to pass through a raking broadside that his two formidable aunts delivered at tea one afternoon, poor Murad sitting alone on a sofa that at the moment seemed so large as to be a hallucination, and he the little boy sunk into it. His aunts, arrayed in wing chairs, one on each side, lobbed enormous, flaming, and unanswerable questions at him regarding his betrothed, quite openly stating that they believed her to be unstable and of poor reputation. They had been beauties, marrying well—and yet their lives had gone badly, just as his father's had. One had been on morphine for a time in the 1960s, until finally she was dispatched to a discreet sanatorium outside Lausanne.

Their words gained no traction in Murad's mind. He made a joke of the encounter, telling Lily the details. They both took strength from the perception that they were striking off into new territories, survivors, he from the wreck of his family, she from the superficialities of the life she had fallen into. His overwhelming mother, cut from the same pattern as his aunts, had destroyed his father by inches— that was one of their bywords, that they would achieve an infinitely better accord with each other. Another was that despite her past Lily at heart was a homebody, the efficient one, the one who took care of matters, of injuries. She had always been self-sufficient, as a girl kept a nurse's kit and doctored the household servants when they were sick, and as a grown-up she had always taken care of herself financially, tending the exclusive little atelier she had set up in the basement of her parents' house, with a single seamstress and an old tailor, making very expensive wedding clothes. That kept her grounded, and had always earned enough to keep her afloat, that and rent money from a few shops in Lahore that her grandfather had given her as a baby. She felt it important that she brought this to the relationship, not the money but the stance, and they both acknowledged an intention to join together protectively and go forth.

• • •

BEFORE THE ENGAGEMENT they had driven to Lahore to call on his father, through the Salt Range, off the Pothohar Plateau and down to the plains, across the rivers, the Jhelum, the Chenab, the Ravi. The father had entirely ceded his Islamabad house to Murad after his wife died, finding it too painful living in the bedroom where she had endured her last weeks and months, wracked by cancer. He moved to Lahore, to a huge run-down house that had fallen to his lot at the time of the partition with his siblings. The size of the house impressed Lily as much as its dilapidation shocked her, the front lawn bare of grass, with servants' children playing cricket in the center, quite at their ease.

The house had been built in the twenties, with many dark passages, musty fraying carpets, enormous ugly sofas and armchairs poked here and there, arranged quite irrationally, as if they had of their own volition waddled in from a furniture graveyard and huffed down and settled in for a long wait. Black dirt crusted the door, which scraped heavily against the floor, wheezing. The ancient valet greeted Murad with affection, one of the old school, corrupt, running the household for profit, taking a cut from the cook, the drivers, but nevertheless indulgently proud of his master's ordered purposeless day, the master's hand which had never turned to work, and his connections with the old Lahore aristocracy.

"He's been waiting for you since yesterday afternoon," confided the valet. "He comes alive again, sir, before your visits. He almost missed his nap this afternoon."

It's a little dying world, she reflected, this household, these servants, the old man at the center. She had seen this before among her own relatives, one of her great-aunts who lived on into her nineties, quarreling with her maidservants, absorbed in prayer, ill-tempered, reputedly with boxes full of cash and gold salted away, though none of it turned up after her death. She was known for being tremendously miserly, yet when Lily went to call on her, as she took her leave, the old woman would tell one of the serving women to bring her gargantuan handbag, and would pull from it a surprisingly large amount of cash, saying, "Now remember me when I'm gone, young lady."

MURAD'S FATHER MET them sitting up in bed, wearing a thick green tennis sweater, the sheets on the bed freshly starched—the valet must have changed them when Murad called from the motorway to say they were approaching the city. Murad kissed him affectionately, then introduced Lily, who felt suddenly that she had worn the wrong clothes, too fashionable, too bright—a costume halfway Western, the *shalvar* more like slacks, the *kurta* fitted. The poverty of the room spoke of hours spent with nothing to do, the cracked imitation-leather slippers, the ugly cream-colored thermos of water—and the profusion of medicines.

The father really was very weak, with a fringe of long white hair and a sweet expression like a child, eyes straining. A mild and correct gentleman, he had never made anything of himself, had been selling land all his life to keep up appearances, himself the son of a great landowner, and an almost complicit victim of his elder brother's machinations at the time of their inheritance. His wife had propped him up for as long as she could, the years wearing her down until her love shaded into contempt, difficult to hide, especially as the cancer cut away at her.

When they entered the room the father's eyes lit up and his face became animated. He spoke gallantly to Lily.

"My dear, you're prettier even than Murad told me. He's a lucky young man, you're both . . . very lucky . . ."

And then his voice trailed off and a set look came into his eyes, of resignation, of indifference—she found this fading in his manner disconcerting, expecting him instead to be distant and firm. Murad had not prepared her for this, the old man's helplessness. The father patted the bed next to his leg and told Murad to sit down. After asking Lily several questions about her family, her mother and father, quite evidently not listening to the answers, he asked Murad questions about the farm, mechanically, each question unrelated to the one that came before, as if a set number of inquiries must be made. Lily sat quite close to him, on a chair that had been placed for her before they came into the room, and as she sat she absorbed the odors and the presence of this man, the father of her beloved, earthy and rank, some sort of pomade that old people wore, talcum powder, clean heavy bedclothes, dusty curtains. She noticed that, in the midst of his indifference, the old man stroked his son's arm, tenderly, unconsciously.

"Excuse me, I just need to speak to the accountants," said Murad, as they had planned—he had begged her to spend a little time alone with his father.

When Murad had gone out, the father's expression became strained, the skin tight around his eyes. He appeared not to know where he should look. Just as she formulated an inconsequential question to break the silence, the old man looked up at her.

"He mostly resembles his mother, do you know."

She heard an apology in this, for the state in which she found him, lying in this bed.

Reaching beside him, the old man took a bell on a cord and rang it to call a servant. Then, turning to her, shrewd, he said, "The dance goes on, doesn't it, young lady. He'll be a good husband. And for you, I hope you'll keep the faith. Perhaps it doesn't matter either way. But I'm an old man, it would be better if you had waited till after I'm gone." He fell silent, the dentures in his mouth shifting and making a clicking sound.

In a photograph Murad had shown her of his father as a young man at Oxford many years ago, lanky, with Murad's long and delicate face, not quite smiling, wearing an overcoat, a scarf tied tightly around his neck—already he looked cautious, insulated, at a loss.

He yawned like a little boy, his eyes flat, as if unseeing, and she observed that his hair standing up from the impression of the pillow looked exactly like the tuft of a bird. She didn't comprehend his statement.

The valet came in and then Murad returned. As they left, returning to Islamabad, the old man pulled her close to him, kissed her on the cheek, and said, "Bless you, young lady."

If at first she didn't understand the old man's words, later she dated from this experience the first blow against her belief that marriage would allow her fundamentally to change herself. This old man, whose embrace of his formidable wife had been enough like final love that her death ruined him utterly, nevertheless took so limited a view of what marriage could offer his only son, what Lily could offer. Perhaps he knew of her past, probably he did—Murad would have told him something, to inoculate against later disclosures made by mean-spirited relatives, the aunts or others.

She knew the feeling to be irrational, but this half-welcome into the family, though issuing from the stream of a life that had lost its force, hurt her deeply and persistently.

RIGHT UNTIL THE last minute the old man insisted he would be at the wedding, held in Islamabad at the house of Lily's parents. It mattered a great deal to Murad, and she knew this, but they didn't speak of it. She thought of him as strong, going directly to his purpose—as he had in his pursuit of her, or as she had seen once when his managers came to Islamabad with the quarterly budget from the farm, the respectful and straightforward way in which they approached him,

the tough respect he accorded to them, and their businesslike appli-
cation to the work at hand.

Yet with regard to his father his strength failed, as if his father's
weakness infected him too, sapped him. Two days before the wedding Murad came to her and said in a broken voice, "He's not coming,
I knew he wouldn't."

"It doesn't matter, darling. He's sick, he wanted to be here."

"That's just it," he said angrily. "He never wants to be here. He sold the
best parts of the property for nothing, because he couldn't be bothered
to oversee the sales. He let my relatives take all the shops in the city, the
valuable city land. And then, after puttering around doing nothing for
most of his life, he took to his bed. I always felt unprotected, and I still
do. I always felt that he took the view, *Après moi, le déluge*. My mother
wouldn't forgive him, even when she was dying. I was the stolen prince
living in a stable, while the other branch of the family ate up whatever
they could reach. Now I've come back and taken some of what's mine,
but my father is still there, still refusing me."

Soothing him, touching his face, she thought of the blessing the
father had given her, almost malevolent. "I'm the same way, darling,
that's why we found each other. I'm cut off too. We'll do it together.
We'll have our own new separate life."

She didn't press him more than that, and soon the moment passed,
Murad covering his anger and grief by throwing himself into the last-
minute preparations.

A manager arrived the night before the wedding, bearing the
old family jewelry in a leather handbag that must have belonged to
Murad's mother, the *tikka* ornament for Lily's head wrapped in a
faintly scented handkerchief, a gold cloisonné choker set with pearls
and rough diamonds, and two long strands of emeralds, the largest of
them the size of toffees.

·   ·   ·

LILY INSISTED THAT the two main ceremonies, the *shadi* and the *valima*, be telescoped into one, that it be more or less merely a celebratory dinner, to the chagrin of both her family and his, cousins, uncles, old family friends, hangers-on, sponges, all inveterate marriage-goers—aunts and great-aunts, who hobbled around the party wearing flesh-colored socks and high heels under their brilliant but ancient Indian saris, complaining about the food; and sly second cousins, who thought this curtailed wedding the last and best stroke delivered against propriety by Lily, the perfectly aberrant coda to her career. On Murad's side several personages attended, out of consideration for his father—a governor of twenty years ago, several old hostesses, beauties and battleaxes from a generation back. Before the wedding Lily had dreaded it all, kept joking with Murad about eloping, then on the day of the ceremony worried that it would be a sad inadequate affair, had cried in her bathroom, piling on the misery by imagining herself as an orphan, as unloved. A tent had been set up in the garden, air-conditioned against the heat of the September night, and she had feared that the tables, decorated by Mino with calla lilies that he somehow procured from Karachi, would be empty. But the tables were full, her parents had acted exactly as they should, her closest friends had flown in. Girls she had known when she was little had crowded around her, and it was with them, surprisingly, that she had found the most joy in the occasion, as if she had been translated back to that time, to the person she was then.

Just before the guests arrived, Murad had whispered to her, "Come with me for a moment," and they had slipped away from her parents' house to the cottage. He wore a long formal coat, a *sherwani*, embroidered with gold thread, and she wore a green shot-silk gown designed by herself, heavily worked, and flowing pants, wearing his family *tikka* pendant on her forehead. Standing in front of the mirror in her bedroom, he said, "Look at us." There they were, the two of them in their wedding clothes. "We'll do it now," he said, "our own way." Very serious, looking into her eyes in the mirror, he swore, "I marry you, Lily, for richer, for poorer, in sickness and in health, in happiness and sorrow, till death do us part." She repeated the words, and that had been for her the real wedding, that is when tears had started into her eyes. From his pocket he took a ring that had belonged to his mother, an emerald intaglioed with a single iris just coming into bloom—he described it that way.

As he gave the ring to her, with a queer smile on his face he said, "I hope this isn't the wrong thing, coming from her—the poisoned chalice."

They had spoken of his troubles with his mother, his fear of being consumed by a woman. "We already agreed," she replied, soothing, dismissing. "That was in the past."

ONLY A SMALL crowd remained, it was late, her parents had gone to sleep, and the party had moved to Lily's cottage, where the bar had been set up in a screened verandah looking onto the garden. She went up to her bedroom, looking for Murad, who had disappeared somewhere, wanting a moment with him, to see him and believe it was real, that they were finally and entirely married, forever. Entering, she saw that he wasn't there, only the candles they had lit earlier flickering and guarding the room. Someone had strewn rose petals on the bed—this little pure gesture touched her. Her mother must have done it, a blessing, given as lightly as she was able. Opening a tall glass door, Lily walked out onto a balcony. The night, warm and sweet with the scent of jasmine, hung over the city, the music in the room below her expanding out into the darkness, the lights of the tent in the garden dimmed. Some men were standing in a dark corner of the driveway, smoking a joint. Not even listening, simply taking a moment of quiet under the night sky, she heard one of them say, very distinctly, "Don't worry, she'll peel the bark off him soon enough," and the others laughed, crude, delighted. It took a second for her to absorb it, and then she could only narrow her eyes and look up at the stars.

A bottle of champagne stood cooling in a bucket of ice next to the bed. She opened it and filled a glass, spilling, went downstairs, out through a side door so that she wouldn't meet anyone. There were people everywhere, and she wanted to be alone. It struck her that there would be no one in the tent. She entered the long carpeted space, grass showing at the edges. The tables had been cleared and the cloths removed, leaving ugly plywood tops with steel legs. A heavy odor of damp canvas filled the room, lit by two or three bare bulbs. In a moment she would find Murad and take him to bed.

From the corner of her eye she saw movement and turned to look. Where the canvas walls of the tent met the roof, a strip of clear plastic had been sewn. Hanging there at the far end, disembodied faces rippled behind the plastic, three, four, five of them, fixed on her, distorted, larger and then smaller as the breeze shook the tent. All evening they must have watched, sitting on the compound wall, invisible when the lights inside the tent were bright. These must be from the slum, the people who lived illegally on the banks of an open sewage channel that drained this millionaires' district. Why shouldn't they curse the rich lives of the bride and groom? She remembered the tale of a sorceress not invited to a celebration, the spell she laid.

It doesn't have to be that way, she told herself. *These men also ate from the wedding table.* The servants would have distributed the food left from the banquet to whoever appeared at the gate. They too could bless her, figures of propitiation, though they sat on the wall like crows. She absorbed the moment, the image, and then turned, not making any gesture toward them.

Part II: Jalpana

And so Lily and Murad were married, and soon afterward they went to live at his farm, known as Jalpana. This was Lily's idea, and one that he at first resisted. He had wanted to go on a honeymoon, somewhere romantic and traditional, the Loire or Venice, but she refused. "We'll do that when we need it, when we need to get away and when we have something to celebrate. I want to be at the farm. I'm going to be like an old-fashioned Punjabi wife, weighing out the flour and sugar every morning and counting the eggs. And everything locked up, a huge ring of keys on a chain around my waist."

She had softened, phoning Murad or sending him messages constantly if they were apart. As a child she had been plump, an inward little girl, absorbed in a private world, mostly brought up by her *ayah*. In her teens and twenties she would gorge on peanut butter, chocolate-covered maraschino cherries, Danish butter cookies, and then make herself throw up. Now she indulged herself, would eat a whole bag of salted cashews while sitting with him, or they would drive late at night to the bazaar and have food from the stalls, *haleem, dai bhalay, taka tak*. He liked to watch her eat.

They slept together for the first time only a few weeks before the wedding, tenderly, gravely—clumsily, both of them, after having resisted so long. She had bought new sheets, took down the bright embroideries hanging from the walls of her room and covering the furniture, instead decorating with white handwoven cotton, a new bedspread, new covers for the chairs, and in that setting she removed her clothes by candlelight, passing herself to him.

"There," she whispered to him, as they lay in bed afterward. "Now we know all the pieces fit together."

• • •

FROM BAHAWALPUR AIRPORT they raced to the farm through the twilight on bad roads, Lily falling asleep, waking in a bazaar, the jeep stopped in a tangle of traffic beside a stand piled with cigarettes, the owner staring at her through the window as if she were on display, until she covered herself with a head scarf.

A crowd of men stood along a drive half a kilometer long leading into the heart of the farm, saluting as the car passed, the chauffeur not slowing down, Murad responding with a wave. As they approached the farm he had become quiet—she sensed the weight of his responsibilities settling on him, and she too felt this weight. Their income derived from this place, and hundreds of men worked on the farm, all looking to Murad and now in some degree to her for their livelihood. People in Islamabad marveled that Murad could spend such long periods at the farm; how then would she do here, a city girl to the core. She would be dependent a great deal upon him, and even more upon herself, upon her resources, as Murad would put it.

A series of archways had been built of bamboo and tree branches, the final one illuminated with an electronic sign that signaled in flashing green and blue lights, HAPPY MARRAJ SIR WELL-COME MADAM.

"The poetry of arrival," joked Murad, breaking the silence, taking her hand and squeezing it.

They drove through an orchard, then through a heavy wooden gate that closed behind them, leaving the crowd outside. It was calm, the house servants offering garlands, men she had never before met, and who would now always be part of her life. The simplicity of the house at first surprised Lily, a plain wooden door leading from the car park, then only eight rooms, built in a U around a grassy courtyard. The lawn opening out from the top end of the courtyard, however, was truly immense, decorated with hundreds, no thousands of oil lamps in little clay dishes, burning along the walls, sparkling in the trees, making geometric designs along the edges of flower beds, disappearing in the far distance. The garden had been his mother's one contribution to the farm—*a legacy to a woman, to me,* thought Lily hopefully—six acres enclosed by a wall, with rose beds, groupings of jacaranda trees, flame-of-the-forest, thick banyans with their suckers planted like proliferating elephants' legs. A lily pond, the lily pads two feet across. His mother would come in the season and herself prune back the roses, hands which did no other work, as Murad had told her.

Two dogs of the local *bhagariya* breed, resembling wolves, capered around Murad, jumping up, licking at his hand, not quite daring to leap up on him, while he said, "Bad dogs, no, no!"—but playing with them, patting away their paws.

Her perceptions blurred from sleeping in the car, wishing she had a moment to reflect, to arrange herself, Lily knew how much her response to the house and the place mattered to Murad. Petting one of the dogs, which licked its lips with a shy tongue, its creamy yellow snout pricked with black whiskers, Lily felt the place resounding within her, strange sharp smells, servants wearing village clothes bustling past carrying the bags, so many people. The lamps arranged in the lawn blinked and flared as a breeze came up.

"This is our room," said Murad, opening a door. And in a shy tone, "I had it fixed for us, see. It was my father's bedroom."

It had been redone tastefully, the new-laid rosewood floor gleaming with fresh varnish, rosewood shutters, doors, windows—"The wood came from our own trees," he told her. A pale blue Persian carpet cooled the room and made it feminine, as did the modern white furniture, arranged too formally in front of the fireplace. He made her sit on the sofa, bounce on the new bed. "Do you know, I've never slept a single night in this room. I didn't want my father to come here and find that I'd stepped into his place. Until a month ago his farm clothes were still in the closets. I asked his permission. Now it's you and me, darling, now it's our turn."

• • •

THEY ATE DINNER in the bedroom, starting with the last bottle of excellent wedding champagne, which they had .brought from Islamabad—Mino had given them several cases as a present, unobtainable from the bootleggers in Islamabad, smuggled on a launch from Dubai into Karachi. Lily went to her suitcase, which a servant had carried in, and removed a packet of tea candles. She lit them all over the room, then turned off the lights and lay down on the sofa, feeling her muscles relaxing. In a moment she would unpack, finding places for all her things, shoes, shirts, her jewelry in a drawer, her toiletries in the bathroom, which also had been entirely redone, a parquet floor and an antique bathtub lacquered royal blue. She needed to make the room hers, to start with an ordered center and work her way out. Murad sat patiently watching her, didn't press her to go out and see the house and the garden, which Lily knew had absorbed so much of his love and imagination when living here alone.

The breeze had turned to wind, servants going around closing the shutters all over the house, making a clattering wooden sound.

"It's a dust storm," he said, when she had finished organizing her things. "Come on, I'll show you something that you've never seen before."

As she came out of the room, forcing open the door, climbing a circular staircase up to the roof, the wind struck her, bent her over, snatching away the words they shouted. The sand peeled over them, fine but hard, spattering, liquid in its movement. Before they went up Murad had wrapped cloths around their heads, leaving just a slit for the eyes, muffling them.

When they were up on the roof, above the treetops, he lit a powerful searchlight and placed it on the ground, then led her forward.

"Look," he shouted.

At first she didn't see anything, just the motes of sand streaming past in the light, like snow caught in the headlights of a car racing into a snowstorm. Then, in front of her, twenty meters tall, her shadow projected onto the dust flowing horizontally through the air. She waved her arms, the shadow mimicking her up in the sky, fuzzy, long-limbed. Running forward, right to the edge of the roof, balancing against the wind, she watched her shadow become tiny, diffuse, armless, headless. A line of eucalyptus trees close to the house waved and bent wildly, leaves being stripped away, leaves from distant trees in the garden swirling past, and she thought, in exultation, *This is life, this is real and actual. This is ours.*

Facing into the wind, she took the cloth from her head, held it fluttering like a pennant for a moment and then released it, letting it sail away, attenuated, white, flashing into the darkness.

"Be careful," shouted Murad in her ear, coming up and taking hold of her elbow. "Don't fall!"

"Dance with me," she said. She would always remember this sandstorm, this eerie yellow light. Taking his arm, putting it around her waist, she held him very close, her face buried in his neck, eyes closed, the wind singing and fading.

EVERYONE SPOILED HER, everyone smiled on the young pretty bride. A month passed, then six weeks. The servants studied her with wide-open eyes, wondering what role she would play in the household, cooked elaborate meals, quail *pilau*, veal in a thick brown curry, grilled lamb, carrot *halva*. The orchard manager sent the first guavas, pink-fleshed and sweet, another time an enormous honeycomb, still attached to the branch on which it had grown, carried to her on a broad plank, the comb sopping. Like the chicken at the farm, the eggs, she had never tasted such good honey, spiced sharp by the clover that the bees fed on. In those first weeks she slept as if making up for months and years, waking in the morning, kissing Murad as he went off to the fields, then falling asleep again. Her fibers loosened, her mind settled to the pace of the farm.

Murad and Lily always had their breakfast on the lawn, the air soft, birds calling, babblers, lorikeets, bulbuls, thrushes, hoopoes, the brain-fever bird, from the orchard the booming call of the coucal— Murad knew all the names, of the plants, the birds. Mongooses played in the road sometimes when they walked in the fields, through lanes of sugarcane, or in the orchard, being flooded now with water, so that the thick black soil newly turned by the plow glistened and gave up a ripe odor.

"Do you know why they sent you the honey?" he asked her at breakfast, as she devoured her second slice of crisp toast with quick little bites, finishing and licking her fingers.

"Because they think I'm too thin?"

"Because they think it helps you get pregnant."

He said this with a little moue, knowing that the subject irritated her. Perhaps it *would* be better, to leap into childbearing in this first surge of their marriage, to begin the new life with a new life beside her. She tried to imagine herself loving the child, but could think only of the pain, her body torn and stretched, the body that she cared so much about, which she had entirely lived for, its pleasures, wine and intoxication, clothing herself, pleased by herself in the mirror, undressing in front of men, silently expectant. And then, to be hostage to the child, fighting against it, finally with a sigh of relief becoming absorbed in applesauce and feeding, adoring its little feet and hands, buying it costumes printed with bunnies and ducks. Murad certainly wanted her to become a mother, to be mothering, even at the cost of losing interest in fashion and appearance, making baby talk, finding her joy in a child's first tooth and its first words.

Before the marriage they luxuriated in their plans, at parties ignoring the other guests, during long picnics, making lists of things to buy, apportioning responsibilities, making resolutions. She saw that now the plans must be renegotiated, reconceived. She had believed that her personality would be subsumed in their larger personality as a couple, living into each other, but already the strangeness of the initial engagement wore off and she went back to being—exactly—herself. A little crack opened up as if in the perimeter walls of the compound at Jalpana, through which a poisonous scent, like very strong attar, overpowering, overripe, musky, seeped into their life together—the pull of her old life, of other lives. Why did he have to speak so slowly, to explain in such detail the mechanics of the sprinklers in the greenhouses?

Already, just three months since they first slept together, she found herself pulling away when he began to touch her. He always did it the same way, on top, and became shy when she suggested, by her movements, not even in words, that they try other positions. The persistence of his shyness, which placed a limit on their physical intimacy, had disappointed her—when they first met she had thought him piratical and dominating, and had imagined that as they became closer and freer with each other that spirit would come to the fore, energy that would master her, but playfully. A friend had given her a bachelorette present of stockings and a garter belt brought from America. As a surprise, thinking to break up the routine of their love-making, one evening before Murad came home from walking the fields, she put them on, lying on the bed otherwise naked, candles lit. He said, "So that's how you wear those!" and then, instead of joining her in bed, he brought a clipper from the bathroom and trimmed a broken fingernail, sitting on the windowsill and speaking of a problem on the farm, a woman in the village whose husband beat her, and who had come to Lily asking for protection. Coloring, mortified, she had pulled the covers to hide herself, and when he left the room angrily threw the stockings in the fire. Accustomed to rush and passion, to first times, making love with Murad became a chore, something she wanted, but that required effort and planning.

• • •

THEY HAD BEEN too long on the farm, a month, then a month and a half, then two and a half, but neither had yet raised the question of returning to Islamabad. Neither could bear to leave the farm now while matters stood as they did—Lily knew this of herself, saw it in Murad. She would lie in bed and dream of food, of steak tartare at Ecotex, a restaurant in Islamabad run by a young Spaniard in his own house, or of foie gras and duck rillettes, which a shop in Paris sent to Mino. The two of them would wolf it down on buttered toast, to line their stomachs before going to a party. She missed Mino, missed the life of the city.

One evening Lily and Murad sat in the living room where they now usually had dinner, eating while reading or watching Lily's television shows—they joked about being like an old married couple. Restless, Lily kept piling more and more wood into the fireplace, poking and shifting the logs. Her colored pens were scattered on a table, she had been making impossible elaborate designs for dresses, fantasies. Now she sat down again and began doodling. They had been flirting all evening, Murad serious and busy, reading a book about greenhouse farming, Lily making excuses to disturb him. Idly wanting to startle him, oppressed by the hot room and his methodical studying, she wrote in large red letters on a sheet of paper, *Anal Sex at Noon Taxes Lana*, drew hearts all around the script, folded the paper into an airplane, and fired it at Murad.

"Let me guess," he said, reading it, putting his book down and smiling at her. "You're bored."

"It's a palindrome. Mino taught me. It's the same backwards and forwards, get it? Anal sex? Works both ways?"

"Very witty. You really profited from that boy's company."

She sat down next to him on the sofa, kicked off her little embroidered slippers so that they went flying, one into each corner of the room, and lay down with her head in his lap. "But I am bored, it's true," she said petulantly.

"You sound like you're eight years old. Why don't you read your book, my love?"

"Bo-ring! Don't tell me—you're going to say being bored means you have no inner resources."

He looked down at her face and stroked her hair. "I *was* going to say something along those lines. It happens to be true."

She sat up again, went over by the fire, and threw in another log, then took the tongs and stirred the burning chunks, sparks flying up and popping.

"Maybe I don't have inner resources then." She rummaged around some more in the fire. "Murad? I've been thinking. Let's have some people up this weekend. Won't that be fun? We'll have the gardeners light *diyas* all over the lawn when they arrive. It'll be a housewarming. That's the best way, instead of us going to Islamabad. They'll definitely come, those guys all love doing things at the last minute."

"I suppose you're right. It's difficult being alone together. You need refreshment—I'm used to this life, and I've got the farm."

She felt this as a reproach, his lugubrious tone, as if the guests were only for her.

"You make it sound like I'm a baby needing her bottle. We just got married, we're young. We should play."

Not waiting for his answer, she sat down at the table and began cutting a piece of colored paper. "Come on, Mr. Lone Wolf. I'll make a funny invitation and someone can go on the day bus to Islamabad tomorrow and deliver it."

Standing up and observing her for moment with his hands in the pockets of his khakis, he walked over and took her face in his hands, kissed her on the lips. "Well, I guess that's decided, right down to method of delivery! Actually I'm glad."

She wrote to Mino, inviting him to the farm that weekend—he had promised at the wedding to visit soon—and asking him to bring some amusing people. In the card she giddily called herself "the Châtelaine of Jalpana," and joked about battling scorpions the size of cocker spaniels, living with her husband and the camels for company. An illustration on the front of the card showed her, Murad, and a camel sprawled in planter chairs sipping martinis, all three wearing T-shirts that said, in purple letters, *The Home Team!*

THEY BLEW IN, Mino and the notorious Zora Fancy, one of the Bombay Fancys, who was visiting her family in Karachi after committing some enormity too grave for India to contain it. The security men at Bahawalpur airport, accustomed to seeing the same fat politicians and well-oiled businessmen pass through, didn't know what to make of this bright group, Mino's ear stud and Zora's tight black jeans, her brazen cigarette. The party also included a slender and mute and very handsome boy, a jewelry designer, sheltering under Mino's wing, a new protégé, introduced as such.

At the back of the group, soft-spoken, tall and slightly disheveled, came Shehryar Salauddin, known as Bumpy. He and Lily had a history together, though she had never granted him the ultimate favors, as Mino would put it. Lily realized that she had tipped her hand to Mino, that he saw through the tone of her invitation, guessed that all was not well at Jalpana, and brought Bumpy to provide a note of interrogation.

On the drive to the farm Bumpy sat next to Lily and almost too assiduously avoided touching his arm against hers when the jeep swayed. The little jewelry designer, sitting in the far back on a jump seat, looked gloomily out the window into the moonlit night. Murad drove, and Mino sprawled next to him, relishing this adventure, taking possession of the countryside, taking credit for the night air, the canals, the dust thrown up by passing tractor-trolleys piled with enormous loads of sugarcane going to the mill.

NEXT MORNING LILY wandered around the house, slightly intoxicated still on the fumes from the night before, preparing for the day, arranging flowers brought to her by a gardener, into the living room, where the servants had already cleaned up the glasses and bottles, the spills and cigarettes. Sunlight poured through the windows and through the French doors which led toward the swimming pool. She had told the gardeners to fill the pool despite the late-fall weather, thinking at some point they would be drunk enough to skinny-dip, in the depths of the night.

Calling the head servant, she told him to make several pitchers of fresh orange juice, to chill bottles of white wine for mimosas—Murad had sent a car to Islamabad for alcohol from his bootlegger, cases and cases of it.

"Let's do it right," Lily had said. "Full-blown. That way we'll get a name for hospitality. You need a river of booze if you're dragging people halfway out between Bahawalpur and nowhere. We'll have a Christmas party next and get people to stay through New Year."

Since last night Lily had experienced a kind of clarity about everyone, Mino, the others, her husband. She felt in tremendously high spirits, her perception wiped clean as when one is getting a fever—brittle and soul-sightful. All of them were types, all had their little motivations, the jewelry designer, unable to resist the force of Mino's personality, his liberties and expansive world, his money. Zora Fancy, a blunt strong-looking woman with a butch haircut and disconcerting green eyes, brusque to the point of rudeness, who had very evidently joined the excursion in order to add Bumpy to her list of lovers. Despite her plainness, people said about her, "Zora always gets her man."

As for Bumpy, Lily reflected that he and Mino were opposite sides of the same coin, but whereas Mino liked to watch, Bumpy liked to be the protagonist, what Mino would call "the brute," in the little dramas that took place around him. Belonging to a certain type, who are almost involuntarily successful with women and spoiled by women, Bumpy indulged himself, had a richer life than most, had a private life, spent months at a time in Paris, where he owned a garret apartment, and where he supposedly worked long days on the great Pakistani novel—though no one had ever been allowed to read it. Lily saw that both Mino and Bumpy understood her in a way that Murad did not. They were feminine in their perceptions, could follow her braided impulses and desires. Murad was wholly masculine, so that he experienced as a mystery Lily's indecision, her instinct when confronted with two choices to reach for both.

MURAD, WHO HAD kept up with Mino glass for glass right till they all staggered to bed, nevertheless had woken early and slipped out, leaving a note on the bedside table explaining that he had been called to Multan and would be gone all day. Scanning the note, Lily observed that he was jealous, and that he was removing himself from the scene to demonstrate his trust, perhaps not so much to her as to himself. The previous evening Lily had found herself caught up in a little conspiracy of flirtation with Bumpy. He was solicitous, but lightly, invisibly, and if she spoke he listened, responding, joining her perspective. If there had been any malice against the others Lily would have pulled back—out of loyalty to her husband, to Mino— but in the safehold of Bumpy's blithe nature she became the instigator, leading him apart, brushing against him, imbibing and sharing his droll or witty comments.

Murad of course had observed this flirtation. When they were alone the night before and undressing, he said to Lily, drunk but still keeping it together, "This Bumpy is pretty smooth," and she replied artlessly, "He's harmless. It's just a game, he can't help it."

BY THE TIME Murad returned from Multan they were all on a tear, the living room thick with smoke, Mino in top form. Murad came into the room as Mino finished a story.

"Oh my God, and there she was, the baby stuck to one hip, and making that same stew, stirring it with a huge spoon, with her boobs hanging down to her waist, completely drunk. She looked like some kind of depraved Mother Earth."

All of them erupted into meaty vodka-tonic laughter.

Standing up, Mino said, "Come on, Murad, if you're going to stay, you have to drink a few glasses by yourself. A forfeit."

He didn't say it particularly insistently, and Murad replied, "No, I'm going to bed. You people keep at it."

"We're leaving in the morning, we're on the ten o'clock flight. I hope you don't mind, I sent one of your managers to get tickets. Zora says she needs to get back."

"Well, if you must. You'll have to leave at six. Can you wake that early?"

"We'll stay up. But we haven't seen much of you, Mr. Talwan. It's too soon in the marriage for your wife to play the man of the house."

"Oh, I don't worry about that," replied Murad, disregarding him. "I'll see you in the morning. I keep farmer's hours." Saying a general goodbye to the others, he left.

"I'll be right back," said Lily after a few minutes.

"The devoted wife!" called Mino. "Don't forget the rest of us!"

In their room she found Murad writing in his journal, as he often did before going to sleep, a drink on the table next to him.

She felt shy, as if she had done something wrong. Standing behind him, she put her hand on his shoulder. "Is it okay? Why don't you come sit with us, if you're having a whiskey?"

He rubbed his cheek against her hand, but doing it consciously, as she observed, to show that he wasn't upset. "No, it's all right, it's fine. Your guests are there. It's not fun when everyone else is more drunk."

"Would you like me to stay with you?"

"If you want to, I'd like it, of course. You could have one drink with me."

"All right." She went to the bathroom, peed, feeling trapped with Murad sitting quietly by the fire, when the others were pounding hard. When it got late, she always kept up with the guys.

Coming out, she said indifferently, "It's just that it's a bit rude. It's their last night."

"That's true." Giving her dispensation, he stood up and kissed her. "You go. I'll be in bed in a minute anyway."

VERY LATE IN the evening, with Zora asleep on a sofa under a shawl, with Mino and the boy murmuring to each other by the dying fire, almost asleep himself, Bumpy said to Lily, "Come on, *someone* has to get in the pool before it's all over. Let's do it."

They walked across the lawn to the pool, stood at its edge, the water illuminated by underwater spotlights and very blue. One of the dogs came out of the darkness, wagging not just its tail but its whole rear end, sniffed at Bumpy's leg, and then went over to the steps in the shallow end and waded partway into the water, lapping at it, then standing and watching them. Bumpy's clothes fell cleanly from him, as if the buttons had been sliced off by an invisible hand. Lily pulled her blouse over her head, unzipped her jeans, placing a hand on Bumpy's bare shoulder to steady herself as she stepped out of them. In the cool November night she felt her skin tighten, shivered, anticipating the water and not wanting to get into it, and that shivering graded into her anticipation of what she knew would come next, her hand still on his shoulder. He became still, like a well-trained horse when the rider puts foot to stirrup, this stillness encouraging her. Not shy, Lily felt the shocking intimacy of their entire bodies touching, his face bending to hers. They lay down on a soft canvas-covered chaise longue. He didn't press her—if anything, she folded toward him. Hesitating just for a moment, she gave in. She even guided him inside her, the entry and movement satisfying, opening her eyes and looking up at the stars among the tree branches, until he finished, sooner than she wanted him to.

She held him inside her, legs around his waist, and then the emotion passed, desire crushed entirely. Pushing him off, annoyed with him, his weight on her, the cold, she whispered, "Come on, get up, we have to go back quickly."

They held hands walking up from the pool—she allowed it, as if the romantic gesture would mitigate the banality of their coupling— until they came around to the front of the house, and then without looking at him she pulled her hand away and walked toward her room. "Tell Mino and everyone goodbye. I'll see them in Islamabad. I have to go to sleep."

He whispered, "Hey, wait. Are you okay?"

"Forget it."

Going into the bathroom, past her sleeping husband, she cleaned herself as well as she could, in case he reached for her in the night. She sat on the toilet, trying to pee, as the horror of what she had done struck her. Married just three months, to a man who loved her, whom she loved, she had fucked a man she barely knew and cared nothing about. *I didn't know Murad when I married him*, she told herself. *He didn't know me. We're still learning.*

Why should it matter so much?

. . .

LILY KEPT FORCING herself back into sleep throughout the morning, till past noon, expecting Murad to come and ask if she was okay. Finally she called on the intercom and told the servants to bring her tea and fruit. When the servant knocked she asked where Murad had gone, learned that he was in Multan, would again be late. The vegetables were just being planted, the servant explained, and they were having trouble getting the right seed.

She remembered that he had been writing last night in his journal and against the weight of her apprehension and shame needed reassurance that all had been well, at least before he went to bed. When they first came to the farm he had shown her where he kept the journal. "You wouldn't, I know, but I'll say it. Don't read this. I need one place where I can put down whatever's on my mind, things that I don't even mean." And she had promised.

Now she went to the drawer, took out the black notebook and read the last entry, his precise handwriting perfectly legible. It spoke for a few lines about his worries over the farm, then turned to the visitors, noted their behavior with disparagement. Finally:

Worst of all, I feel as if this house is soiled, and Lily soiled, and our love soiled. Her shrieking laughter at Mino's vicious jokes and the affected way she holds her cigarette, drunk and sort of tapping it nervously, everything sped up—and I'm standing there like the dull host who has to be put up with—because it's his whiskey you're drinking. That's not the deal I made with her. I won't ever again be made to run away from my own house. We agreed to live decently and honorably and in peace. She says she wants all that, but I don't think she knows how—to live in peace. For her, chaos and willfulness are the same as independence, the way to a vivid life. And then—admit it!—there's too much genuflection in my attitude to her. Maybe I can't be any

other way, but by god and my strong right arm I will bloody
well try. I've got to fix this right now, at the beginning.

She replaced the diary back under some papers in the drawer, as
if by putting it quickly away she lessened the guilt of her spying.
A flash of anger overwhelmed her—so that's what he thought and
kept hidden—and then gave way to an awareness of her husband's
right intentions and his intelligence, cooler than hers. She thought of
the story he had told her early in their relationship, of seeing her for
the first time beside the swimming pool at the party in the mountains, finding her there, recognizing her. It pained her to acknowledge
how accurate he was in this appraisal, how correctly he identified
her desire for decency and honor and peace. She thought of Mino,
his world, a lakeside party with a beach made of sand brought in on
a convoy of trucks, washing away in the next storm, filtering down
to the depths of the lake. And what of her epiphany in the hospital
room in London, the forgiveness she received, with the snow falling
steadily all day? That at least was false, there was no moment of forgiveness, no renewal, just a series of negotiations, none of them final.

LILY WAS WAITING on the roof that evening, drinking her second
vodka tonic, when Murad came briskly up the stairs. She had been
sitting with her stomach in a knot, dreading his first words, which
would tell her the state of things. When he arrived she did not get up
from the chair on which she had been stretched out, wearing sweat-
pants and a baggy sweater.

"What a god-awful day. I finally ended up going to Sipahi's farm
and forcing his guys to load the seed in my jeep. I swear, it's impossible to get anything done in this country. We just sit around scratch-
ing our fleas and telling lies. The British should come back."

"I'm sorry, babe." Relieved, she went over and kissed him on the forehead, put her arm around him.

The sunset call to prayers, the *azaan*, had just finished reverberating from the twin minarets of the Jalpana mosque, which towered above the village a few hundred meters away, hidden by trees. Far away across the flat countryside other *maulvis* were in mid-cry—they began at different times in each of the surrounding villages, making a chorus, till the last one died away and the night fell.

Sitting down again, she took an unlit joint from the table next to her and tossed it to him. Lighting one herself, exhaling a cloud of smoke, she said in a bright voice, "There you are. That's my signature joint, the *Zeppelin*."

Neatly catching the joint, he put it on a side table.

"Not for me, my friend. I'm going at six tomorrow morning to meet old Mian Kachelu about that missing Dashti girl."

"At least have a drink then." Whenever he called her *my friend*, it signaled irritation or disapproval. "I'll have another one too."

"All right, just one."

Returning upstairs after ordering the drinks on the intercom in their bedroom, he began, "Darling, I know we've already been through this . . ."

"Let me guess." She deepened her voice, mimicking him. "We need to think about what we're going to do, about making a family. About work. About partying." She had decided to meet him straight on, she felt defiant. He knew nothing about Bumpy. This wasn't the time for confessions, and anyway she must clarify her own intentions first.

Above them crows gradually settled in the tall eucalyptus trees along the wall of the compound, squabbling, settling, then rising up in pairs, arranging themselves again.

He narrowed his eyes. "It's true. But honestly, this is serious. What are you on, third drink? Fourth? Let's take a couple of days off. It was fine when the guests were here."

"You can do what you want. I don't want to."

"Come on, Lily. What have you done since you got here? What happened to reading or running the house? Or setting up your collective with the village women? Remember that? I'm on your side. But you'll go crazy like this, you've got to engage."

"You like me when I'm tied up with a pink bow around my neck like a kitten. I'm not the type to be dutiful. I'm messy and willful and self-destructive. You knew that before you married me. That's the way I lived my life, you knew that."

He spoke coldly. "Yes I did."

"How dare you! Either get over it or tell me you can't."

"I meant your dresses, your shop. Your friends." And then, "Remember, we promised never to say unforgivable things when we fight."

They sat in silence for an uncomfortably long time, Lily fighting down the anger that washed through her, bitterness in her mouth, the vodka.

Finally, he looked up at her, with a gentle smile on his face. She couldn't for months forget his look, earnest, serious, severe, loving, penetrating.

"Do you know the saying? At the beginning of a love affair, and at the end, the lovers can't bear to be alone together."

It hit her with a crack, so that her response came out in a gasp. "And you warn *me* about saying unforgivable things?"

"I was joking, darling. Leave it. This is a marriage, not a love affair, it's different. Marriage is process. Love gets knocked around."

"No, I won't leave it. I can't live like this." She felt injured by him for adding to her troubles now—perversely, knowing the blame lay with her. Breaking into tears, she stood up and went quickly downstairs. Taking both drinks from the tray carried by the startled servant, who shrank back in alarm as she stormed past, she drained both glasses one after the other, then went into the living room and took a bottle of whiskey from the cupboard. Crossing the small back lawn, she found her way outside the compound, leaving through a door that led directly into the fields.

SHE HAD NEVER been outside the perimeter walls after dark, never been outside alone, now was in the mango orchard that surrounded the house, each tree aligned with the next, the full moon casting thick shadows. A watercourse ran past her in a concrete channel, making little gulping sounds, the orchard fading into blackness at the limits of her vision. No other sounds, no footsteps, no pursuit. Murad must think that she had simply gone to their bedroom. She wanted him to chase her, yet knew that he would be sitting calmly on the roof, indulging her in his thoughts. He always expected that she would come around to his view of things; and in fact, she usually did, because it was to his life as much as to him that she had attached herself.

Behind her stretched open fields—there she might be seen and would easily be found—but ahead lay the orchard, hundreds of acres. She feared walking in the alfalfa under the mango trees. Murad had warned her about the snakes, kraits, vipers, especially cobras, which will attack instead of retreating as other snakes do. A few days after they arrived at Jalpana a gardener killed a cobra at the far end of the garden and brought it to show Murad, claiming a reward, the snake a dull black, smaller than she expected, its hood folded in death, a little dab of blood as red as nail polish smeared around its mouth.

Nevertheless, she withdrew among the mangoes. Away near the canal that flowed into the property she heard voices, one man calling to another, and then murmuring as they walked along. She approached one of the trees, bowed her head, and climbed under the canopy. Scrambling onto a thick branch running parallel to the ground, she settled comfortably, leaned against the trunk, took several pulls of the whiskey, and then exhaled hard, fighting back the nausea. Holding the bottle between her thighs, looking up into the dark branches, her mind wandered, thinking of the sounds around her, a tractor working in a field—it must be one of her husband's—the workers were hurrying to plant the wheat, as he had told her, explaining why he came home so late one night. The land stretched away around her, the villages, the fields of wheat and trees in lines along the boundaries of fields, the tractors bumping along the roads, water running through channels all night. None of it had reference to her, she controlled nothing here.

That afternoon she had gazed in the mirror for a long time, searching, and known how pretty she looked, her skin glowing now because of their healthy life, early nights, not too much alcohol, regular food. No one saw her, and soon she would be old, her hair turning gray, having experienced so little. The world was happening elsewhere. She felt ungrateful, knew that she wronged Murad—that she had wronged him terribly by sleeping with Bumpy—and yet the tension of her past and her sense of being unworthy had disappeared. His constant little attentions exasperated her, his attendance on her. She had complained about the tea at the farm, and he sent someone all the way to Islamabad, to buy Earl Grey at Esajee's, the expensive grocery used by diplomats' wives. *I can't do it, I won't, I just won't,* she said to herself, and knew it was much too late for that. She had proven nothing the other night, had not established her independence, if anything she had deepened her obligation to Murad. Where could she go, except to him?

Swinging her legs, about to step down, she heard a sound, movement in the dry leaves under the tree. A little crackling, then more, a weight moving very lightly, brushing through the brown dry leaves, heavy but silent. Going away. She sat perfectly still, listening, her skin prickling. The whole time it had been there. She imagined a black figure bounding up out of the shadow, not a snake but a man, with hair on his face, upon her and at her throat. The sound moved out to where the leaves of a branch touched the ground, and there just for a moment she thought that she glimpsed something black creeping forward in the grass. In a flash it came to her, a whispering voice. *Reach for it.* She slipped nimbly from her perch to the place where she had seen movement, expecting to be struck instantly, expecting a blow, like a knotted cloth swung hard against her leg. She waited, eyes closed, ready to sink down, melt—but entirely resolute. Nothing happened. Ten and then twenty heartbeats. Exhaling, she heard the night resume, spreading like spilled ink, first near her, around her head, breeze in the leaves, then sounds further away, dogs barking from distant villages, carrying over the flat landscape.

Steady, she opened her eyes and looked at the patch of ground boxed in by trees, moonlight silvering their outmost branches. What a small innocent place, a stage. *That's it?* she asked. Taking another swig of whiskey and flinging away the bottle, she responded—*That's the point. You take chances and then nothing really changes.* She considered the tone in which Murad had told the aphorism about the beginning and the ending of love—exposed, hardened, ironic—a tone that couples settle into when they are broken and at odds forever, but bound; and countering that, his diary, his willingness to force a change.

Among the possible futures, Lily now recognized the likely one, the one she must avoid. Murad would be rich and powerful, she knew that, having seen him at work here on the farm. He would be shrewd, trusted by men, sometimes warm to her in comradeship, but finally cold, irreproachable. And in the very act of drowning she would be left to bear the blame, to injure him, blindly or by neglect, becoming one of those thin sharp women from the cities who can hold their liquor but are desiccated by it, who are well dressed without taking pleasure in it, living much in London, bored—and ultimately, she hoped, she would depend on this, becoming old and wise, old and self-forgiving.

A Spoiled Man

There he stood at the stone gateway of the Harounis' weekend home above Islamabad, a small bowlegged man with a lopsided battered face. When the American wife's car drove up, turning off the Murree road, Rezak saluted, eyes straight ahead, not looking at her. She sat in the back and smiled at him from the milky darkness of the car's interior. What a funny little man! Once he had happened to be walking past as she was driven through the gate, and she had waved. In the few weeks since, he had waited hours to receive this recognition from her, Friday when the family came, Sunday when they left. He had plenty of time.

The car continued up the winding flagstone drive and disappeared among the rows of jacaranda trees, blooming purple now in late April. Below lay the roadside town of Kalapani, the bazaar pierced by the horns of buses collecting passengers; above stood these walls, which enclosed ten acres of steep land, planted with apples, pine, jasmine, roses, and lilies that the wife had brought from America. The wind blew with a rushing sound through the pine branches and combed the fresh green grass sprouting all over the hillside after the winter rains.

He made himself useful. In May pickup trucks full of summer flowers were brought up from the nurseries that surrounded the city on the plains below. When the first truck arrived he stood at the gate, watching the gardeners unload the pots, handing them down to each other and then carrying them up to the house—the loaded vehicle couldn't make it up the steep drive. Without asking he passed through the gate, which he had never done before, took one of the clay pots in his arms, and walked up with it, rolling slightly on his down-at-heels shoes.

"Hey, old man, you better leave that before you hurt yourself," called a gardener standing in the bed of the pickup.

"I'm from the mountains, brother," Rezak said. "I can carry you up on my back, and one of these in each hand."

The pickup driver, who stood to one side smoking a cigarette, grinned.

The old majordomo, Ghulam Rasool, had strolled down to watch the show, a potbellied figure with a tall lambskin hat resting at a slight angle on a fringe of white hair. He sent one of the gardeners up to get his hookah and, comfortably settling himself in the watchman's chair by the gate, looked out over the valley below. At midday he said to Rezak, "Come on then and break bread with us."

Rezak looked down at his feet. "I'd need to put stones in my gizzard like a chicken to digest the rich food that you good people eat."

The majordomo tried to convince him, and the gardeners also pressed, but Rezak remained stubborn. "You didn't ask for help, you don't owe me anything."

"Suit yourself then," Ghulam Rasool said finally. The gardeners walked up the drive, talking, and Rezak stood watching them, wishing he had accepted. He was alone now. In the distance he could see a swimming pool, with curving sides, overhung by chinar trees and willows. Melancholy invaded him, and also peace, borne by the whirring of cicadas nestled among the rocks that punctuated the grounds of the estate. He took a bag from his pocket, undid the elastic band, and tucked a quid of tobacco in his cheek, chopped green *naswar*.

IN THE KALAPANI bazaar he ate at his usual teahouse, day-old bread soaked in milk, prescribed by a quack homeopath against a fistula that had tormented him for many years. The waiter brought the sopping bread and, when the crowd subsided, he came over to have a few words, about the flow of tourists up to Murree, more each year, this season begun so early. Lonely as he was, Rezak relied upon his welcome in the teahouse, his connection with it. When the older chickens at the poultry sheds where he worked were culled, Rezak would bring down one of the healthier birds, asking the teahouse to cook it, as a holiday from his bread diet. He shared with whoever was there, insistent, forcing his friend the waiter to eat.

"There, look, I've taken some," the waiter would say, pulling off a wing. Even he, hardened by a diet of stale leftovers from the kitchen, was dubious about eating this time-expired bird.

"No, you have to really eat." Rezak even became angry about it once, leaving abruptly, the chicken still on the table.

After finishing his lunch Rezak walked through a government pine forest to the poultry sheds. The owner had bribed the wardens to allow construction extending into the forest, and each summer his men set fires at the base of pines planted by the British a hundred years earlier, in order to kill the trees and open up more space. Rezak came to his home, not the workers' quarters attached to the sheds, but a hut that he had built for himself, a little wooden cubicle, faced with tin and mounted on thick legs. Several decades before, in his early twenties, he had fallen out with his stepbrothers over shared property up in the mountains, a few acres of land on which they grew wheat and potatoes, bordered by apricot trees. Outmaneuvered, dispossessed, he had come down to the plains, vowing never to see his family again. This box had become his home and consolation. Each place he worked he set it up, and then, when he quarreled with the other workers or the boss, as he invariably did, he would take it apart and cart it away—always he kept a store of money, untouched no matter what, enough to pay for trucking this little house, this nest, to whatever place his heart had set on next. This was his guarantee of independence.

Opening the heavy padlock, he lifted the door hatch and climbed in, tucking his shoes into a wooden box nailed below the cramped hatch. Run off an electrical connection drawn from the poultry sheds, tiny red lights strung all over the ceiling warmed the chamber. He could sit but not stand inside, and had covered the floor with a cotton mattress, which gave off a ripe animal odor, deeply comforting to him. A funnel and pipe served as a handy spittoon, a mirror and shelf allowed him to shave without getting out of bed, an electric fan cooled him. Photographs of actresses plastered the walls and ceiling, giving him company. Fickle and choosy, he shuffled and moved them, discarding one, stripping the photo from the wall with a cold expression. For several months he had been favoring a Pathan actress known as "the Atomic Bum"—who had wagged her way through a string of hit movies in the past year.

A FEW DAYS later, loitering around the gates of the Harouni estate again, Rezak decided to go in, stepping through a narrow entry set into the wall. The owners would be in Islamabad for the week, and earlier he had seen the watchman down in the bazaar. By climbing the slope of the mountain opposite, he had observed the household routine, marked the servants' quarters, watched the owners sitting on a terrace, brightly clothed. Close up the house seemed to him ugly, made of large rough-hewn stones, with a vast wall of glass all across the front, looking out over the valley and down to Islamabad, forty kilometers below. Nothing to it—no metalwork, no paint, no decorative lights, plain, only size to recommend it. The house blended into the landscape, as if it were one of the boulders littering the mountain slope.

He found the majordomo sitting in a chair under a tree, reading a newspaper.

"Ah, the volunteer," he said amiably. "Come on then, have a pull on the hookah."

Rezak sat down on the edge of a *charpoy*, dangling his short legs. "I'm killing myself with this poison instead." He spat and then dipped green coarse tobacco under his gum.

"You work up in Ayub's sheds, don't you?"

"When Ayub needs me I work. He pays me in dying chickens and loose change." He tried to make a joke of it.

"That's what I hear—Ayub shaves both sides and then trims out the middle piece."

Rezak laughed mirthlessly. "The way I'm going soon I'll be eating grass." He paused. "I've been thinking, I can do woodwork, I know about trees. I'll carry things, work in the garden. Feed me and I'll work here and do whatever you want. You don't even have to give me a room, I've got a portable cubicle that I live in, you can stick me in some corner."

THE OWNER OF the estate, Sohail Harouni, son of a man who made a fortune in cement and other industries, had while at university in the United States married an American woman named Sonya. "No, I really love it here," she would say defensively when asked at a party. "It's strange, it's like a drug. I think I miss the States so much—and

I do—and then after a month there I'm completely bored. Pakistan makes everything else seem washed out. This is my place, now. I don't do enough, but I feel as if here I can at least do something for the good." She did fit in more than most foreign women, she studied Urdu, to the point where she could communicate quite effectively, made an effort to meet Pakistanis outside the circuit in Islamabad. Even her husband's catty aunts admitted that she was one of the few foreigners who wore Pakistani clothes without looking like either an Amazon or a Christmas tree.

And yet, though she insisted that she loved Pakistan, sometimes it all became too much. "I hate it, everyone's a crook, nothing works here!" she would sob, fighting with her husband. Then she would storm out to her car and retreat to the Kalapani house, forty minutes away, arriving unannounced, withdrawing darkly into the master bedroom, while the servants scrambled to prepare her meal. In the evening she would wander the large stone house, slowly becoming calm, speaking with her friends on the telephone. Her husband would drive up to spend the night with her, bringing their little son as a pledge of their love, and they would make peace.

It happened that, soon after Rezak made his plea to Ghulam Rasool, Sonya had a huge row with her husband and ran away to Kalapani. The next morning, she sat drinking coffee on the sunny terrace, which had a view out over the government forest, now heavily logged by poachers, and then down to Islamabad and Rawalpindi. The strain of the fight had shaded into a desire for simplicity and order, an almost pleasant tearfulness.

Ghulam Rasool came up from the garden, coughing so that she would not be startled. Of all the servants he was the one she most trusted with her son. She herself felt comfortable with him, with his gentle, stoic manner, with his prayers and his superstitions.

Her blond hair held back by a black velvet band, she wore a simple white blouse, white slacks, and lay on a divan, immaculate, reading a slender volume of poetry—she had been an English major, and turned to a handful of familiar books as a restorative, Yeats or Rilke, Keats, to be taken as needed.

"Excuse me, Begum Sahib. I wanted to ask, it's time to think about the roses."

She knew that he wanted to soften her attitude toward her husband. In any case, she liked him to come and talk with her, and they used as a pretext his supervision of the garden, although he had always been a valet and knew very little about flowers or trees. She put down her book and they considered the roses and the placement of the annuals.

"Begging your pardon, the local people drive their goats into the Ali Khan orchard, and they're destroying the saplings that you brought from America. There's an old man, he can't do hard labor, but he's a reliable person. His family abandoned him. He even has his own portable hut—he'll take it there and live as a guard. You don't have to give him a salary. Just food and a few rupees for pocket money."

But she wanted to give the old man the same as all the others. It made her happy to think of spoiling him in his old age.

Newly hired, Rezak moved to the Ali Khan lands, a walled parcel of four or five acres just up the road from the main house. Like the other servants and gardeners, he received a salary of nine thousand rupees a month, more than he had ever made in his life. The gardeners from the big house transported his cubicle in pieces, then helped him reassemble it next to a hut that was already standing there, a single stone-built room, with an open hearth, which Rezak could use as a storeroom and kitchen. The land had no electric connection, so he bought oil lamps, which glowed soothingly at night as he went about his last chores, his routine of dinner and bedtime.

. . .

THE SEASON TURNED hot just as Rezak moved to his new home, coloring the green fruit on the apple and peach and pear trees imported from America. He devoted all his grateful heart to the little orchard, watering the trees with a bucket from the stream that ran through the property, working manure into the soil with a spade. Taking a bus to Islamabad, with his own money he bought three grape vines, carried them back wrapped in straw, and trained them up the legs of his little tin-clad cubicle. He planted radishes, corn, cauliflower, onions, peas, more than he alone could eat, so that as they ripened he could take baskets of produce up to the big house. With his second paycheck he bought a goat for milk—before, in his previous jobs, it would have cost many months' savings.

One day the master and his wife took some guests to the Ali Khan land for a picnic lunch. In the morning servants brought carpets and divans, tubs full of ice for the wine, grills for the meat, firewood in case the party lasted into the night. Rezak spent hours ferrying boxes and chairs and rugs down from the main road to the picnic spot, taking the biggest loads, pushing himself forward, claiming precedence on his plot of land.

The guests arrived, Pakistanis and foreigners, a dozen or so of them, and were soon sprawled on the carpets, drinking wine, resolved into several groups. Walking briskly down the steep path, sure-footed, holding a floppy yellow sun hat with a trailing ribbon in her hand, Sonya had said to Rezak as she passed, "*Salaam*, Baba." His heart, his soul melted, as if a queen had spoken to a foot soldier. She had given him charge of the garden, of the trees that she brought from her homeland, and now she was seeing the results of his husbandry for the first time.

All the other servants knew what to do—Ghulam Rasool poured the wine and passed the hors d'oeuvres, a cook readied the fire and skewered kebabs on metal rods, the gardeners spread out as a kind of picket, to prevent anyone from looking over the walls. Rezak's shyness and diffidence contested with a desire to take part, to show off all the work he had done in the orchard. He squatted under an apple tree, trying not to look at the sahibs, pulling up sprigs of grass, tying them into figures and knots, hoping to be summoned. Restless, he knelt down by the cook and took over the job of tending the fire, pushing aside the weedy boy who acted as the cook's helper.

Sohail Harouni was a handsome cheerful man with never a care in his life, who enjoyed giving parties more than anything else. After a few glasses of wine he called a young valet and told him to bring the stereo from the main house and hook it up. A driver raced to Murree, ten kilometers up the mountain, and bought a roll of heavy wire. Glasses in hand, the guests and even the host enthusiastically helped string the wire down through the trees from a roadside shop.

When the party had come far along, when Harouni and the guests were standing in a circle, drinks in hand, gesturing expansively, speaking loudly, Sonya walked away from the group. Looking along the length of the valley, she caught sight of Rezak's cabin, several terraces below the picnic spot. Finding the pathway, she picked her way toward it, and Rezak, who had been watching her, quickly followed, leaping down a steep bank so that he could receive her at his little hut, saluting.

"It's *wonderful!*" exclaimed Sonya, circling around the cubicle, Rezak at her heels. "Hey everyone," she called to her guests, going over to where she could be heard. "Come see."

Short bowlegged Rezak bustled around, showing off the appliances and refinements—the pipe that drained the inside spittoon, the cupboards and drawers set into the outside walls for his tools and clothes and kit, windows that could be propped open or removed entirely, a skylight made of red glass, thick rush matting on the roof to keep the inside cold or hot, with a rubber bladder fixed to the wall that shot water up through a pipe when he squeezed it, wetting the rushes—evaporative cooling. Sonya poked her head inside the stuffy, lurid chamber, considered the photographs of movie starlets plastered on the walls. The guests peered about, inspecting this nest, its door and windows ajar, like a car on a dealer's lot with hood and trunk propped open.

"If there's electricity, then it's really something," Rezak said, eager, grinning with all his teeth, surrounded by the sahibs and the memsahibs. "I used to have colored lights inside. There's work to be done, that's true. It's all broken from carrying it up and down and all over." In his exuberance he pulled at a cupboard door that wouldn't open till it tore off in his hand. Even this didn't dampen him. "See, that's one way to take it apart!"

"That's the man's whole life in a nutshell, isn't it?" the Australian Ambassador, a tall man with a correspondingly tall forehead and ginger hair, remarked.

As they were returning to the picnic, Sonya said to her husband, "The poor man should have electricity for a radio and for lighting. He lives all alone here, imagine how bored he is."

"Are you kidding?" Harouni said. "These guys don't get bored."

But after the party, the wire that had been laid temporarily so that there would be music remained in place—for the next party. Rezak strung lights on the outside of the cubicle, like wedding decorations, and hung a lightbulb in the stone hut where he cooked. He bought a radio, and finally bought a cheap television, something he had never even thought of wanting. He would lie in his cocoon, soft red lights glowing, the television volume turned up, and drink cup after cup of tea kept hot in a vacuum thermos, a refinement that made him smack his lips with appreciation.

SITTING IN THE Kalapani teahouse one morning, Rezak met a young man who lived near his childhood home high in the mountains.

"The government pushed the road up to Koti," the man told him. "The bus runs from Kowar. That changed things, you can bet."

Hearing of the places he had known all his life made Rezak restless. He had left home determined never to go back. Now he wondered what his stepbrothers had told the neighbors about his disappearance. He wanted his family to know of his success.

"You and I grew up drinking from the same streams, breathing the same air. You have to accept my hospitality now that we've met. I beg you. Come for a cup of tea, and then I'll walk you back down here." He took the man by the arm and almost dragged him out of the tea stall.

He hurriedly carried a *charpoy* onto the terrace in front of the stone cooking hut, put a pillow on it, ran inside and lit a fire in the hearth, then brought out a table, wiping it with a rag. Luckily he had a packet of biscuits and he arranged these on a plate and carried them out with the tea.

The man knew of Rezak's family, but had little news of them. Forgetting his bitterness and the wrong they had done him, Rezak began speaking of his stepbrothers and nephews, of their fertile land, of the well near their fields.

"God has been good to me, more than I deserve. I have only one wish, that He had given me sons of my own, as my brothers have." He ran his hands over his face.

Rezak had not been able to resist boasting of his salary.

The man considered for a moment, his eyes alighting on a locked trunk inside the cooking hut that must be full of clothes and who knows what else. He looked at the neat vegetable patch and at the two goats—Rezak had bought another when fodder ran low in the forest and they were cheap. The man had been shown the weird little cubicle, furnished with a radio, a television even.

"Look, my cousin has a daughter. Something went wrong when she was born, and she's a bit simple. But she can cook and sew and take your goats out to graze. She's quite pretty even. She's young enough to bear you a son. Her father can barely take care of his other children. Why don't you let me arrange a marriage?"

"You're making fun of an old man," replied Rezak. But hope and desire pierced his heart when he thought of it. A woman in his house, even one who was not right in the head! And she could bear him a son, and that would be worth anything at all. Now that Rezak had money, the boy would go to school, he would learn to read and write, become—Rezak could not even imagine what. The son of an old servant at the main house had become a doctor and now continually begged his father to retire and come live with him. Rezak would die happy after that.

They spoke back and forth all afternoon. In the end they agreed not only that the girl would be without a dowry, but even that Rezak would pay a quite substantial amount of money for her, which the family would take in installments.

A few days later the father delivered the feebleminded girl. The girl's family had not come, and the two men did not celebrate the marriage, but brought the *maulvi* quietly to perform the *nikah*. When the father left, the girl followed him and cried, until finally they were forced to lock her in the hut.

After seeing the father onto the bus, Rezak wandered down through the bazaar, stopping to talk for a minute with the man who sold *samosas*, saying nothing of his marriage, but saving it for himself. He felt more equal now among these people, the shopkeepers, passersby, families. Someone waited for him also, the house he returned to would not be empty.

The poor girl must be frightened, he thought, and turned homeward, stopping to buy a three-kilo box of sweets, fat yellow *ludhoos*, *ghulab jaman*, *barfi*, *shahi tukrah*.

He rattled the chain as he opened the lock, so that she wouldn't be startled. She wore makeup, lipstick that had smudged, rouge that made her cheeks almost pink, new clothes made of shiny white cloth—at least that much had been done to celebrate their wedding day. It pleased him that she reached and covered her head with her *dupatta*—shy before him, her husband.

He sat across from her. She kept her eyes cast down.

He opened the box of sweets, carefully unknotting the string, took out a *ludhoo*, and held it out to her on his palm, whispering, "Take this, it's okay, don't be afraid." He held it there. "Go on." And after a moment, without looking up, she reached out and took it.

Gradually, she became accustomed to living with him. He let her roam as she wanted, once he saw that she would not run away. The girl, a tiny thing of nineteen or twenty, had an impediment and spoke not in sentences but rather in strings of sound, cooing or repeating words—her condition was really worse than Rezak had expected—but when she settled in he found that she could more or less cook.

He let her sleep in the stone hut, until one night, as he was watching television in his cubicle, she cautiously lifted the door flap, stood absorbing the lit red chamber for a moment, and then nimbly leaped in, eyes fixed on the television. After that, she always slept with him.

As an adolescent boy Rezak had been married, so long ago that he couldn't remember what his bride had looked like. She had died in childbirth less than a year after the marriage, and the child too had died. Now, after so many years, Rezak again had a companion in his home. Life and hope, the flames of individuality that had burned out to nothing, to smoke, again flickered within him. Returning at night from the bazaar with a treat of late-season mangoes or a bit of meat, or stopping work in the orchard at noon to have his midday meal, which the girl warmed and served to him with hot *chapattis*, he looked forward to her chattering. She had a pretty, almost animal way of watching him while he ate, perched beside him, and after he finished she brought him a glass of water from the clay pot. In the evening before he came in she made tea, and when he groaned because of the aching in his legs she massaged him. Gradually he found himself able to communicate with her, and more important, she communicated with him, showed happiness when he returned at night, cared for him when he felt ill or sad. She did not, however, bear him a child.

NOW THAT HIS wife cooked for him and pastured the goats, Rezak had less to do, especially after the trees lost their leaves and work in the orchard ceased. His wife sat in the dark smoky hut, cooing to herself. He would often go down to the teahouse in Kalapani bazaar and sit for several hours, watching buses fill and lumber off up the mountain to Murree or to Kashmir, or race with brakes squealing at the curves down to the cities, honking their horns to call the passengers. He strolled idly through the bazaar, wearing a new woolen vest and carrying a walking stick; or he went to the big house and sat smoking a hookah with Ghulam Rasool.

Returning to his hut at dusk after one of these excursions, he found that the fire had burned out in the hearth and his wife was gone. The goats too were missing, although she should have brought them in by this time. Sitting in the cold room, he stared at the calendar nailed up on the wall, which showed an elaborate Chinese pagoda. He rubbed his hands together, trying to control his anger. Twice before, when she had disappeared at nightfall, he'd found her far down in the valley, cowering behind some rocks. When he approached her she grew frightened and covered her face with her hands.

At dark she still had not returned. Rezak took the lantern, lit the tiny flame, and went out, the two goats scrambling in, bleating, when he opened the wooden gate that led down into the valley.

One of the neighbors called, "Hey, Rezak, can't it wait till morning?"

"What can I tell you. My poor old lady's disappeared again."

The neighbor sent a little boy to help with the search.

Rezak walked all over and called and called. He went home, hoping that she would be there waiting for him, but he saw no glimmer of light in the cooking hut. As he sat in the cold, the sound of twigs breaking as he laid the fire seemed particularly loud. The fire caught, crackling, slowly warming the room. Mechanically he threw a handful of tea in the kettle, boiled the water, mechanically poured it into the cup. He didn't have it in him to be angry now. Without eating dinner, without turning on the television, as he did every night, he lay alone in the dark cabin, wondering what could have become of her. What if she was lying hurt somewhere in the forest?

In the morning he woke before first light, hurriedly dressed, and went out. He didn't know where to look, which direction to turn. Living alone for years, he had learned not to ask for help. Neighbors would do whatever they could once or twice or five times, but ultimately, they would grow cold and resentful. He walked along the paths that she might have taken, then deep into the woods to the places where she cut grass. Once he saw a cloth that he thought might be her shawl, but coming close he saw that it had been rained on and must have been lying there for days.

FINALLY HE WENT to ask the Harouni retainers for help. Going into the servants' common room, he found Ghulam Rasool lying peacefully on a *charpoy*, his unlit hookah beside him. The fireplace chimney had backed up, as it always did, filling the low-ceilinged room with layers of acrid pine smoke.

As Rezak walked into this familiar room, he broke down for the first time. His arms hung loosely as he shuffled up to the bed and stood with his face contorted.

"My wife disappeared," he blurted out, before he had even said *salaam.* "I can't find her anywhere. She's gone." Flat tears slipped out of his gummy eyes and disappeared into the wrinkles of his face. Remembering himself, he reached down and shook Ghulam Rasool's hand respectfully.

"What do you mean, 'disappeared'?" asked Ghulam Rasool, startled. Squeezing Rezak's arm to make him sit on the *charpoy,* he called out through the door, "Hey, one of you boys come here."

Four gardeners answered the summons, and, after asking a few questions, ignored Rezak. They huddled together and made their plan, eager as a pack of hounds, then headed out, their wooden staffs tapping quickly as they walked off on separate paths.

Late at night they straggled back, one by one, having found no trace of the woman. In the morning early they went out again, determined to find her. They searched the mountains, the furthest terraced fields, went to the nearby villages. The next day again they searched from dawn to dusk, and then the next, but with less and less determination. One of them asked at every bus stop from Murree down to Rawalpindi. Another went all the way to the girl's family home up the mountains almost in Kashmir, but they had seen nothing of her—in any case, she couldn't possibly have made the long journey alone.

Finally, only Rezak kept searching. He forgot even where he had already been, returning to the same places, as if this time he might find her there.

One morning, getting ready to go out and continue the search, he sat down again, took off his coat, and lay down on the bed. Imbecile, chattering—but she was gone, dead or stolen, taken to the brothels of 'Pindi or Karachi. He prepared himself to bear the loneliness again.

. . .

EVERY YEAR AT Christmas the Harounis gave a big party at Kala-pani, with roast goose, a twenty-foot tree in the entrance hall of the house, and a ho-hoing Santa Claus for the children. Trucks brought logs for a bonfire from the Harounis' farm down on the plains, so that late at night the servants could grill spicy, greasy kebabs on the coals for the heavy drinkers and mull cauldrons of spiced punch for the rest. The guests came up from Islamabad singly or in long chains of cars, blowing in through the door with wrapped presents and bot-tles of wine and champagne, which Ghulam Rasool placed on a long table standing in the hall.

Before dinner, the mistress came into the kitchen. The cook stood rubbing his hands on his apron, sidelined in his own domain, as she took a big bowl under her arm and poked with a spatula at the mashed potatoes, which the cook had already beaten to a creamy smoothness.

Ghulam Rasool had been following her impassively as she per-formed her inspection.

"Excuse me, Begum Sahib, may I trouble you with a small request?"

"Of course," she said, touching him lightly on the shoulder. He had become accustomed to this, although at first it had disturbed him.

Briefly, he explained about the disappearance of Rezak's wife.

"But Ghulam Rasool, you should have told me right away. What can I do?"

Ghulam Rasool had an encyclopedic knowledge of his master's friends, their power, their wealth, and he took great pride in these connections. When he saw Omar Bukhari, the son of the inspector general of police, arrive at the party, he had sent a gardener to fetch Rezak and told him to wait in the kitchen.

"If Bukhari Sahib would speak to the police in Murree . . ."

She went into the living room and found Bukhari looming over a French girl, who had come with someone else, insisting that she must let him arrange a trip into the tribal areas of the Frontier, which were off-limits to foreigners.

"Really, Delphine—you should go, it's amazing, and you'll never have the chance otherwise," said the hostess. "Omar, can I pull you away for a moment?"

Bukhari followed her to the candlelit dining room. "So, Ghulam Rasool Sahib, what's going on?" The Harounis' friends all knew Ghulam Rasool and joked that he had more power than many federal ministers.

Ghulam Rasool explained, emphasizing the girl's attractiveness to make it seem like an abduction by one of the gangs who kidnap or buy women for prostitution—a scenario in which the police could help, since these things generally happened under their protection and they received a cut of the take.

"We'll break the bastards' legs when we catch them," said Bukhari, who had been drinking quite heavily. "Go fetch the husband."

Rezak came in, trembling, and couldn't explain himself, but stood with a grief-stricken face, expectant, as if his wife might there and then materialize through the power of this important sahib.

Bukhari had dealt with many cases of missing women, and knew that the family was almost always involved. He fixed Rezak with a hard gaze. "Who took her? The father? Did the family take her back?"

"Only God above in His mercy knows, sir—I came home one night and she had gone, I couldn't find her, sir. I'm an old man, I'm nothing."

Recalling the presence of his hostess, Bukhari relented. Flipping open his tiny cell phone, he punched a number.

"Get me the D.S.P. Murree." After a moment, a voice came on the line. "Hello, Qazmi, how are you? This is Omar Bukhari. Yes, everything's fine. I'm in Kalapani, at the house of Mr. Sohail Harouni. The wife of one of his servants has been abducted. I want her back by tomorrow night . . . yes . . . no, come to the house in the morning and take down the details. I want you personally to handle this." Without saying goodbye he snapped shut the phone.

He smiled at Sonya. "Done."

Rezak, who understood none of the conversation, which had been conducted in English, crouched and touched Bukhari's knee with both hands, began to speak and then fell silent, bowing his head. Ghulam Rasool raised him up by the arm and led him away.

IN THE MORNING the deputy superintendent of police himself showed up at the house, in his official jeep, flying a police flag, and accompanied by a pickup full of policemen carrying beat-up rifles. Unfortunately, the Harounis and all the guests had already left for Islamabad. The D.S.P. sat on a chair placed in the middle of the hall, with the quivering staff lined up in front of him.

"Where's the husband?"

Ghulam Rasool, the only one not perturbed by this policeman with stars on his shoulders, explained that Rezak lived at another property, down the road.

"Get him."

Rezak came in, breathless, led by a policeman.

"So, old man," the D.S.P. stated, "they tell me your wife has run away." He began asking questions, in a low voice. Though at first he spoke gently, his tone soon became irritated.

"What you're saying is, her parents sold her to you. Where did you get that much money?"

Ghulam Rasool stepped forward. "Sir, she's not well in the head, this man took her from kindness as much as anything. And then, our sahib is very good to us, he gives us everything we need and more."

"Women don't just fly away on their own. Either this man knows something about it or she's in Karachi by now. The best thing is for him to be quiet."

The D.S.P. looked intently at Rezak for a moment, clasping his hands on his stomach, then stood up.

"Please give my regards to Harouni Sahib," he said to Ghulam Rasool, speaking politely and almost formally. "I am always at his service." He begged off taking a cup of tea, claiming that he had an appointment.

Watching the policeman and his escort drive off, Ghulam Rasool said to Rezak, "Better stay out of the bazaar for a couple of days. He seemed like a pretty rude character."

JUST AFTER DUSK, four policemen in an unmarked car picked up Rezak from his orchard and took him to the police post at Tret, twenty kilometers down the road.

"Did you find her?" he had asked, when they came to his cubicle.

The youngest policeman, the only one in uniform, said, "Yes, yes, don't worry."

But he grabbed Rezak by the shoulder, took his arms, and handcuffed him. Rezak said nothing more, and allowed them to do as they liked.

Only when they put him in the back of the car did Rezak ask, "But what have I done? Where are you taking me?"

"Shut up, Baba," said the policeman, who up till then had been quite gentle.

They walked him into a windowless room in the police station and hung him up on a hook by the manacles around his wrists, so that his feet touched the ground only when he stood on his toes.

He hung on the wall all evening, long past the time when it seemed possible that the excruciating pain in his shoulders and back could be borne. In the next room policemen came and went but he was no longer aware of them.

At one point a policeman who had just come in from outside asked, "Who's he?"

"No idea. The D.S.P.'s guys sent him in. Strip, polish, and paint, I suppose."

"Ah," said the newcomer. He went out, singing, "The night is made for lovers . . ."

AFTER MIDNIGHT A large man wearing civilian clothes came into the room. Two uniformed policemen came behind him and shut the door.

"All right, let's see," said the big man. "So, what's your name, old man?"

"Mohammed Rezak, sir." He began weeping and blubbering. "I beg you, I've done nothing, I'm innocent, and now you've hung me up here. I beg you, remember, there's a God above who judges everything . . ."

The large man became suddenly angry. "I see," he said menacingly, gritting his teeth. "I'm the one who's being judged? It's my fault, is it, I'm the one who's guilty?" He slapped Rezak with all his strength. "Where's your wife, you bastard? I know all about it. Nobody took her—you sold her down the road, you pimp, and now you'll tell me who to and when and for how much." He walked to the opposite wall and back, then came up and looked closely into Rezak's face. "Or perhaps you killed her? She didn't have children? You bought a lemon? Ready for a new one, moneybags?"

He slapped Rezak again, cutting his lip. "You listen to me, I can make you fuck your own daughter if I want to, you'll hump her all night, like a dog fucking a bitch."

"For God's sake, for God's mercy, I don't have a daughter, sir . . ."

"You're really trying to piss me off, aren't you?" And then, to one of the men, "Take him down."

The two uniformed policemen lifted Rezak off the hook and threw him to the ground. Rubbing his hands together, the big man looked down at Rezak appraisingly, as if considering his next move.

"Stretch him out and bring me the strap."

They pulled down his *shalvar*, carried him to a bench, and stretched him on it, one pulling his arms and one pulling his feet. They had removed his *kurta* when they hung him up on the wall.

The big man brandished what looked like the sole of an enormous shoe, with writing on one side in thick black script. "See what this says? It says, 'Sweetheart, where did you sleep last night?' Understand?"

Without warning, he swung.

Rezak shrieked, a startled high-pitched sound. He never had felt pain like this, which spread flickering all through his body.

Another policeman came into the room when Rezak screamed and stood by the door, watching, with a grin on his face.

"Come here," said the big man. "You do it, since you're so interested. You need the practice, anyway."

Of course he could tell them nothing. "I don't know," he sobbed. "She's gone, I don't know anything." After a few strokes he fell into a rhythm, shrieking when they hit him, then when they stopped groaning, "O my God, O my God, O my God . . ."

After beating Rezak for five or six minutes, they threw him into a storeroom.

THE D.S.P. STOPPED at the Tret post on his way down to Islamabad from Murree. The big man stood up and casually saluted when the officer walked in. They shook hands.

"What's going on? Anything new?"

"Call from Awaz Khan Sahib. He keeps asking why we haven't picked up those two clowns from Mariani."

They discussed this, something to do with a road contractor, villagers blocking the line of a new road—they needed to be shown the stick.

As he started to leave, the D.S.P. asked, "What about that missing girl?"

"Someone driving by must have seen her and snatched her. The Chandias say they didn't do it."

Only the Chandias, the most powerful of the gangster clans in the area, would have presumed to abduct a woman without cutting in the police.

"And we pulled in the husband and worked on him. He's clean."

The D.S.P. made a face. "You didn't! This is some American woman's pet servant. Tell me you didn't do anything severe."

"He's fine, he's fine. Do you want to see him?"

"No. You're positive, right?"

"I'm definitely positive."

"No marks?"

"Well, sir, no visible marks. I have to work somewhere."

The D.S.P. laughed. "I suppose you do."

After thinking for a moment, he said, "I'll have to go see Bukhari Sahib and explain that she's disappeared off the face of the earth. It's a good idea to put in an appearance there anyway."

"What about the old man?"

"Dump him at home and tell him he better keep his mouth shut."

SHORTLY BEFORE DAWN, almost tenderly now, they bundled Rezak into the same unmarked car and sneaked him back into his hut.

"You've tasted it once. Don't make us dose you again. Not a word to anyone—do you understand?"

Rezak stared at his feet. Finally, he nodded his head.

He lay all that day without sleeping, into the dusk, then the dark. His buttocks had swollen up, puffy and white like bread dough, so that he had to lie on his stomach. His mind whirled—without touching on any one thing for more than a moment, the wife he married when almost still a boy, who died so many years ago, then his second wife, the little mentally disturbed girl. His stepbrothers, who took his land, the fruit trees in the garden there in Kashmir and the fruit trees here, brought from America. His things, his television, the day he went to the store and bought the bright red plastic television.

"Why should I complain? The policemen did as they always do. The fault is mine, who married in old age, with one foot in the grave. God gave me so much more than I deserved, when I expected nothing at all."

He made sure to be perfectly silent about what had happened.

AFTER HE RECOVERED, he was left with one last wish. In Rezak's mind good fortune and grace were wound together, so that the Harouni family's connections and wealth established not simply the power of the household but also its virtue. Ghulam Rasool had served the Harounis for more than fifty years, some of the other retainers had served almost as long. He could never equal that service. But nevertheless the family took him in when otherwise he might have begged in the streets. They gave him the money to live beyond his station, they made him hope—for too much. And when he lost the girl, their instruments punished him for having dared to reach so high, for owning something that would excite envy, that placed him in the way of beatings and the police. Now he belonged to the Harounis. This was how he understood justice.

He said to Ghulam Rasool, "I beg you, ask our master to bury me here on this land, in one corner, whichever one he likes."

This became his dream and his consolation. He lived on for another year, then six months more, collecting his salary, never spending a rupee more than was sufficient to keep his body warm. He sold the television, sold the goats. At the end of eighteen months, he went up to Murree, to the stonecutter, and said that he wanted the very best gravestone in the shop, and carved marble to sheathe the rest of the grave.

After his night in the police station Rezak walked gingerly and made grunting noises under his breath—everyone remarked on how he had changed after his wife disappeared. The stonecutter, seeing his bent trembling figure, thought, *This old bird doesn't know what good marble costs.*

But Rezak took out a roll of bills, tied in a greasy handkerchief that he pulled from under his shirt. Blue notes, thousands.

"Well, that's different," said the stonecutter, taking Rezak's hand and leading him into the back room. "Look at this piece, now. Look at the color, the grain. Look at the size of that. I swear to God, I've been saving it for my own mother."

NO ONE HAD seen the old man for several days, and the gardener sent to inquire rattled and knocked and then found him dead in the little cubicle. Ghulam Rasool had the gardeners dig a grave along the wall of the property, and that evening they buried him, just a few people attending the *janaza*, the servants from the big house, a few men from the bazaar and from houses on the hillside next to the Ali Khan lands. A poor man from nearby had been paid to wash the body, the *maulvi* from the mosque in the bazaar said the prayer.

The next Friday, Sonya came up from Islamabad at nightfall, bringing just her young son and his *ayah*. Ghulam Rasool, dropping a pill of sweetener into a cup of tea, said, "I beg your pardon, madam. The old man Rezak, whom you so kindly put in charge at the Ali Khan lands, has passed away."

The electricity had failed, as it often did up on the mountain. At dusk, by candlelight, the tall rooms of the stone-built house were solemn and chilled, like an empty church or a school when the children are gone.

"Poor poor thing. All alone, and his wife disappeared."

At moments, as now, she felt closer to Ghulam Rasool than to anyone else in Pakistan, his large dark compassionate face, heavy body, his shrewd and yet ponderous manner, his orthodox unshakable beliefs.

He was silent for a moment, then continued, "Please forgive me, but I took the liberty of having him buried in the Ali Khan orchard. He had asked me to speak with you."

Still not touching her tea, looking up at him as he stood with his hands crossed on his belly, she said gently, "I'm so glad you did, Ghulam Rasool. Of course Mian Sahib and I would want that."

The old servant had come far by knowing the ways of his masters. Saying no more nor less than this, he withdrew quietly, leaving Sonya musing by the fire on having done the right thing for a lonely old man, having done a little bit for the good.

THE NEXT MORNING, slipping out of the house, Sonya took Ghulam Rasool and a single gardener and walked up to the Ali Khan lands. The smallness of the grave surprised her, the mound decorated with tinsel in advance of her visit, the marble stones he had bought stacked beside it. Ghulam Rasool and the gardener said the *fatiyah*, holding their upturned palms in front of them and silently reciting a prayer, and Sonya stood also with her hands upturned and eyes closed, thinking first of the old man, a life drawn to a close with so little fanfare, and then of her own dead, her father and mother lying under the snow in a Wisconsin graveyard.

When they had finished, she walked around the garden, looking at the fruit trees, the leaves colored and falling as the autumn season advanced.

"What would you have us do with this?" asked Ghulam Rasool, leading her to the cabin, which sprouted a television antenna and bouquets of crude plastic flowers, their petals thick as tongues, bought by Rezak soon after his marriage, nailed up along the roof one day, to please his wife's innocent heart. "The old man didn't want his family to have anything from him."

It seemed to her vividly alive, a motionless hirsute presence, the antenna, the flowers, the four massive legs, the pipe that drained the inside spittoon trailing into the grass as if drawing nourishment.

She told them to bring it up to the big estate and park it in a shaded corner somewhere not too visible, as a memorial. Her husband, a raconteur, could show it to his guests and tell them about Rezak, the old man who entered service bringing his own house.

At first the cabin sat inviolate below the swimming pool, locked, Rezak's things still in the cupboards and drawers. Sonya went once to look at it, then not again, her attention fading. Gradually, like falling leaves, the locks were broken off, one person taking the thermos, another the wood tools—files and a hammer, a plane, a level. The clothes disappeared, the last cupboard emptied, even the filthy mattress pulled out and put to use, taken by the sweeper who cleaned the toilets in the big house. The door of the little cabin hung open, the wind and blown rain scoured it clean.

IN OTHER ROOMS, OTHER WONDERS

Daniyal Mueenuddin

DANIYAL MUEENUDDIN ON WRITING
IN OTHER ROOMS, OTHER WONDERS

For many years I have run a farm in Pakistan's southern Punjab. Most of the stories in this book have their origins in my experiences there, and many were written there. Half Pakistani and half American, I have spent equal amounts of time in each country, and so, knowing both cultures well and belonging to both, I equally belong to neither, look at both with an outsider's eye. These stories are written from that place in between, written to help both me and my reader bridge the gap.

My father was a graduate of Oxford, a member of first the Indian and then, after Partition, the Pakistani civil service, and—most fundamentally—a landowner of the old Punjabi feudal class. My American mother, a reporter with the *Washington Post*, met my father in Washington, where he was negotiating a treaty. She was twenty-seven years younger than him. They married and soon after, in 1960, moved back to Pakistan.

We lived in Lahore, where I attended the Lahore American School until I was thirteen, my classmates the children of westernized Pakistanis or the few foreigners pursuing their oblique lives in this marginal place. My family spent most vacations on the farm that I now manage, where I ran free day and night with the children of the village, was in and out of their houses, ate with them, explored with them, swam with them. In Lahore I was closer to the old servant who brought me up than to anyone else—thirty years after his death I still wear the bracelet he gave me when I went off to school in America. Because I was a child, the servants and the villagers were not guarded against me, unaware that I was watching, and therefore I learned the rhythms and details of their lives in a way that I never could as a grown-up. I heard the women in the village calling to each other over their common walls, walked out with the boys when they took their buffaloes to be watered at the canal. These people, their gestures and intonations as I observed them in my childhood, appear throughout the stories in *In Other Rooms, Other Wonders*.

At thirteen I was packed off to boarding school in Massachusetts, and by the time I arrived at Dartmouth College five years later, I more or less passed as an American. In college I wrote, protested against apartheid, sweated it out in the library stacks, and popped out after four years with a degree in English literature. My aging father had been sending increasingly pressing letters, telling me that I must return to Pakistan and take care of the family property, and so, after reflection, I complied.

My father, just turned eighty, was ill. For years, he had been losing control of his lands to the managers, who sent less and less money to Lahore each quarter, as they became increasingly confident that he could no longer visit the farm. In his calm and perfectly rational manner, my father explained to me soon after I returned that, if I wanted the land, I would have to go fight for it—that otherwise it would be lost.

On arrival at the farm I went through the books with the accountants, walked the lands, met with revenue officials, trying to get some sense of what we owned, what we produced, what we spent. The place was a total disaster. There were no maps, no deeds, no titles. The accountants had wound the books into an impenetrable ball. The managers were all from the same extended family and were unified against me. I returned to Lahore five weeks later shell-shocked and hungry for company, but hardened, sunburned, and at least now aware of the scale of the problem. I decided to stay and fight it out.

For the next seven years I lived more or less uninterruptedly at the farm. It was a tense and yet intensely happy time, long days walking across the lands or sitting in hot rooms poring over ledgers—and then, against that, the early mornings, when I wrote poetry, looking out from the window of my study to the garden my mother had planted. In the evenings I wrote letters and read endlessly, ordering crates of books from Blackwell's in Oxford, who had supplied my mother's books in the 1960s.

My father died soon after my return from college, and I lost his backing, the influence he still had wielded—but I stayed afloat. Gradually I learned about the crops, about selling and buying, about fertilizer, diesel engines, the qualities of soil, the depths and shallows of the local politics, the depravity of the police. I learned to be a hard negotiator, to manage the farm rigorously, to form alliances, to deflect threats. These were very different lessons than the ones I learned as a child, much harder lessons, and equally valuable to the stories that I would be writing.

By the sixth year, I felt I had to get away and spend time in the West again. I applied to law school, got in to Yale, and spent three lively years there, my concerns far removed from Pakistan. After graduation I took a job at one of the large New York law firms.

Sitting in my office on the forty-second floor of a black skyscraper in Manhattan, I gradually developed confidence in the stories I had lived through during those years on the farm. I realized that I was in a unique position to write these stories for a Western audience—stories about the farm and the old feudal ways, the dissolving feudal order and the new way coming, the sleek businessmen from the cities. I resigned from the law firm, returned to Pakistan, and began writing the stories that make up this book.

DISCUSSION QUESTIONS

1. The figure of the wealthy landowner K. K. Harouni is the recurring thread that connects the lives of the disparate characters in Daniyal Mueenuddin's *In Other Rooms, Other Wonders*. Describe the nature of the feudal system as defined by this figure sitting atop the pyramid and all his subordinates, acquaintances, and relations.

2. Even as Mueenuddin reveals that his stories are set in the present day, the reader is struck by the timelessness of the stories, as if they were fables. How is this effect achieved, and to what end?

3. Many of Mueenuddin's characters fall into predicaments beyond their control, and these predicaments define the conflicts at the heart of their stories. Women and the poor, in particular, are powerless and suffer because of it. At the same time, the characters reinforce their disadvantages by the choices they make, and so to a degree are agents of their own misfortune. Describe the interplay of these two factors in the fates of his tragic characters. Are the characters responsible for the tragedies that befall them? In the context of these stories, how are responsibility and blame defined and apportioned?

4. The Pakistani society that Mueenuddin describes contains a striking blend of spirituality and materialism. Spirituality is generally thought to be undermined by materialism. Is this true in the world that Mueenuddin describes? What form does spirituality take in these stories?

5. The feudal world is sometimes described as being dependent upon a complex system of responsibility and privilege among the different classes. What are the responsibilities and privileges of the lower and higher classes in these stories? Is the system stable? Why or why not?

6. What is revealed about the possibilities of social mobility in contemporary Pakistan in stories such as "Provide, Provide," "In Other Rooms, Other Wonders," and "Lily"?

7. "About a Burning Girl" is the only story narrated in first person. How does this set it apart from the others in the collection? Why do you think the author chose to tell this story in first person? Are the stories generally uniform in tone or perspective?

8. Some critics and readers have dwelled on the darkness of this book. How does humor enter into Mueenuddin's stories?

9. "Our Lady of Paris" and "A Spoiled Man" feature prominent Western characters. How does the inclusion of these characters, as well as of Pakistani characters who have returned home from abroad, serve to broaden the scope of the collection's depiction of Pakistan?

10. How sustaining is sexuality as a form of power for the women in these stories?

11. How do the stories "Lily" and "A Spoiled Man" reveal the idealization of rural life by the wealthy? Why do their characters retreat to the countryside? Do the lives of the poor characters in Mueenuddin's collection support any of their fantasies?

12. Might these stories be called morality tales?